For my mother, who keeps me from harm.

THE PEARL STARTS ITS LIFE AS A SPLINTER—something unwanted like a piece of shell or shard of dirt that accidentally lodges itself in an oyster's body. To ease the splinter, the oyster takes defensive action, secreting a smooth, hard, lucid substance around the irritant to protect itself. That substance is called "nacre." So long as the splinter remains within its body, the oyster will continue to coat it in nacre, layer upon beautiful layer. I always thought it was remarkable that the oyster coats its enemy not only in something beautiful, but a part of itself. And while diamonds are embraced with warm excitement, regarded to be of highest, deepest value, the pearl is somewhat overlooked. Its humble beginnings are that of a parasite, growing in something that is alive, draining its host of beauty. It's clever—the plight of the splinter. A sort of rags to riches story.

age 13

THERE IS A HOUSE IN THE BONE, with a broken window. A sheet of newspaper covers the hole, secured around the edges with thick pieces of duct tape. The siding on the house sags like old flesh, holding up a roof that looks as if it's bearing the world's burdens.

I live in this house with my mother. Under the rain, under the oppression, in the room with the broken window. I call it the eating house. Because, if you let it, this house will devour you, like it did my mother. Like it tries to devour me.

"Margo, bring me the washcloth."

My name followed by a command.

I do. You can barely call it a washcloth. It's just an old rag, smoothed over by too many uses and discolored by the dirty things it has scrubbed. She takes it from my hand without looking at me. Her fingers are elegant, nails painted black and chipped along the edges. She moves the washcloth between her legs and cleans herself roughly. I flinch and look away, offering her minuscule privacy. That's all the privacy you get in this house—the aversion of eyes. There are always people—men mostly—lurking around the doors and hallways. They leer, and, if you give them the chance, they reach for you. *If* you give them the chance. I don't.

My mother steps out of the bath and takes the towel from my hand. The house smells like mold and rot, but for an hour after she takes a bath, it smells of her bath salts.

"Margo, hand me my robe."

My name followed by a command.

She hates taking baths alone. She told me her mother tried to drown her in the bathtub when she was a child. It still scares her. Sometimes, at night, I hear her whimpering in her sleep, *No mama, no.* I didn't know her mother. After the drowning incident, my mother was put into foster care. *A nightmare*, she calls it. By the time she'd matriculated from the system, my grandmother had died of a massive heart attack and left her only daughter the house—the eating house.

She looks at herself in the mirror as I unfold her robe—a red thing, filmy to the touch. It is my job to launder it twice a week. I do so with care, as it is her most prized possession. My mother is beautiful in the same way that a storm is beautiful. She is wild and destructive, and in the middle of her fury you feel her God given right to destroy. We both admire her reflection for a few more minutes as she runs the pads of her fingers over her face, checking for flaws. This is her mid-afternoon ritual before things get going. She takes out the little tubs of creams that I bring her from the pharmacy, and lines them along the chipped sink. One at a time, she dabs them around her eyes and mouth.

"Margo," she says. I wait for the command, breath bated. This time she is looking at my reflection, slightly behind hers. "You're not a pretty girl. You could at least lose the weight. What you don't have in the face, you can have in the body."

So I can sell it like you do?

"I'll try, Mama."

Submission. That's my job.

"Margo, you can go now," she says. "Stay in your room."

My name followed by a double command. *What a special treat!*

I walk backwards out of the bathroom. It's what I've learned to do to avoid being struck in the head with something. My mother is dangerous when she doesn't take her pills. And you never know when she's off. Sometimes I sneak in her room to count them, so I know how many safe days I have left.

4

"Margo," she calls when I am almost to my door.

"Yes, Mama?" I say. My voice is almost a whisper.

"You can skip dinner tonight."

She offers it like it's something good, but what she's really saying is, "I won't be allowing you to eat tonight." That's all right. I have my own stash, and there's nothing in the cupboards anyway.

I go to my room, and she locks the door behind me, pocketing the key. The lock on my door is the only working lock in the house, besides the one on the front door. My mother had it installed a few years ago. I though it was to keep me safe, until I figured out that my mother was stashing her money under a loose floorboard in my room. Her money is all there under my feet. She doesn't spend it on clothes, or cars, or food. She hoards it. I skim money off the top to buy food. She probably knows, since I'm still alive and also fat.

I sit on my floor and slide a box out from under my bed. I choose wisely in case she's listening at the door: a banana and two slices of bread. No noise, no crunching, no wrappers. The banana is black and sticky, and the bread is stale, but it still tastes good. I pull off pieces of the bread and squash it between my fingers before putting it in my mouth. I like to pretend I'm taking Holy Communion. My friend, Destiny, took her first communion. She said the priest put a flat piece of bread on your tongue, and while it was sitting on your tongue it turned into the body of the Lord Jesus. You had to wait for the Lord Jesus's body to melt before you swallowed it, because you couldn't very well bite the Lord Jesus's body, and then you had to drink his blood. I don't know anything about the Lord Jesus or why you have to eat his body or drink his blood to be Catholic, but I'd rather pretend to eat God's body than stale, old bread.

When I'm done with my dinner I can hear muffled thuds and the floorboards groaning under the weight of feet. Whose feet? The tall man? The man with the gray, curly chest hair? Or perhaps it's the man who coughs so hard he makes my mother's bed rattle.

"The croup," I say to my limp banana skin. I read about the croup in one of my books. A library book I keep checking out because I don't want to give it back. I slide it out from my school bag as I eat a Honey Bun, and look at the pictures while licking the sticky off my fingers. When I hear Mama's headboard creaking against the wall I eat another. I'm going to be fat for as long as I live in the eating house. For as long as the house eats me.

age 14

I DON'T KNOW WHERE THE MEN COME FROM. How they know to drive to 49 Wessex Street and park their cars in the shadow of the eating house. I don't know how they know to walk the three cracked steps to the front door and stand under the bulb that never stops flickering. Or how they know to take the rusted brass knob in their hands and let themselves in. They were, perhaps, men who my mother knew in her former life. The life in which she wore pleated skirts and pantyhose, and caught the bus to work every day.

She briefly went to church in those days, lifting her hands during the music like she was catching God's blessings in her palms and letting them swim there. Smiling teary-eyed when the pastor told the congregation that God would not forsake us in our darkest hour. And when our darkest hour came, and she lost her job, I'd come home from school to find her speaking in tongues at the kitchen sink, buried to her elbows in soapy water, her eyes shut tight during her onslaught of prayer. When she'd seen me standing in the kitchen doorway, my book bag slung over my shoulder, she'd smiled through her tears and beckoned me toward her. "We are under a spiritual attack," she'd said, grasping my hands. "We need to pray against Satan and his demons."

I'd latch on to her cold hands, squeezing my eyes shut like the quality of my prayer depended on how tightly I closed them, and prayed with her, our voices filling the eating house in a cacophony of urgent appeal. My voice had been aimless, blasting up, up, upward without any belief to keep it there. I preferred Destiny's muted Catholicism where they ate body parts like decent, faith-driven zombies to this loud, demanding behavior my mother had adopted. *God, give me! Give me! I'm your child and thus you must give me!*

She doesn't believe in God anymore; she left him somewhere between losing her job and the first man she invited into her bed. I always thought her faith was flimsy—like paper—useful until you get it wet. I've heard her talking about religion with one of the men who comes—the one who laughs so boisterously my mother, who hates loud noises, is constantly shushing him. "If there is a God," she'd said, "then I believe he's more insulted by religion than he is by atheism."

I do not believe in God either; I never have, not even when I'd squeezed my eyes shut and prayed with her in the kitchen, the soap from her hands running down my elbows. My mother doesn't know that we share this similarity. She would know if she asked, but she never does. I believe in loneliness so deep and profound it has a physical presence. I believe in choices—hard ones that people in charge seldom seem to get right. I believe that everyone needs something: a woman's touch, companionship, money, forgiveness. And to acquire those things a person will accumulate as much sin as they need to. I often look at my classmates and wonder what it is they'll grow up to want, and what they'll give up to have it

The men come two a night. It's all a perfectly planned dance with never a moment of overlap. I don't know if they know about each other, or if they believe themselves to be my mother's only companion. She meets them at the door, her voice lilting and friendly, her red silk robe rippling around her like blood water. It is a fake her, not the blank-faced woman who stares for hours at the scratched, wooden floorboards, tilting bottles of pills down her throat. She asks how they are, then leads them up the stairs. They speak to her with familiarity, old friends, who call her Wendy and laugh at the things she says. I match their cars with their voices: the cornflower blue Volvo with a dent in the front bumper, a yellow

Corvette with the disco ball hanging from the mirror, and the most frequent visitor, an old Mustang—not a beat up clunker either, but the restored kind, with bright, cherry red paint and custom plates that read LWMN. I never see his face—the Mustang guy, he's always looking at the ground. Once I caught a glimpse of the back of his head as he was leaving my mother's bedroom. He was bald, shoulders broad and curving forward. He left cigar smoke and the smell of cedar wood lingering in the hallways. On one occasion he left his watch behind on my mother's dresser. A heavy thing with the symbol of a crown behind the glass face. I snuck into her room to look at it when she was asleep. Wondering how someone could stand to have something so heavy hanging from their wrist. *Like a ball and chain.* Where did I hear that? Must have been at Destiny's house. The next night, when I went to look for the watch, it was gone.

I tell Destiny.

"The Mustang man probably came to get it while you was at school," she tells me. "You know what that was right?" She has her hand on her hip, and her head is tilted to the side while she wears her signature you-don't-know-shit face.

When I don't answer her she continues.

"It was a Ro-lex," she says. "Probably real. My uncle wears a fake one. You could have stolen that and pawned it for a bike or something. People will pay at least a hundred dollars for sumpin' like that."

"I don't want a bike," I say. What I want is my mother.

Destiny rolls her eyes, and then her hips as she turns away and walks to her dresser.

"I have to go," I say, standing up. I feel anxious … devious for telling Destiny about the man and the watch.

"I thought we was gonna watch a movie."

I sit back down. I can never say no to a movie. And there is always popcorn at her house. Her mother buys the value pack because she knows we like it. Destiny tells me that the popcorn in the movie theater tastes a million times better than the stuff she makes in her microwave. "And your fingers get all greasy from the butter…" she says.

There isn't a movie theater in the Bone. You have to catch the bus two towns over. Destiny's dad takes her and her brothers all the time. I don't even have a TV at the eating house, so watching movies while sitting on Destiny's red-and-white striped couch is enough for me. We start to watch *Pretty Woman*, but halfway through I tell Destiny I have a stomachache. Julia Roberts's character is too much like my mom—the toothy smile, the vulnerability.

I walk home in the rain, wishing I'd taken some popcorn. By the time I reach my front door, my white T-shirt is soaked through. I pull it over my head as soon as I get inside, failing to notice the car in the driveway. I walk toward the kitchen and stop short. A man is standing on the stairs looking at me. I gasp. *Stupid, stupid, stupid.* I clutch the shirt to my chest, but it's twisted, and I can't straighten it out to cover myself. I hear my mother's voice.

"Robert...?" she says. I catch a glimpse of her red robe as I run for the kitchen. I find the laundry basket that I keep next to the washer and grab a clean shirt. As I'm struggling to get it over my head, she walks in.

"What the hell were you thinking?"

This is more than she's said to me in six months.

"I-I didn't see the car. I was wet..." I dip my head and swallow my shame.

"You embarrassed me," she says between her teeth. "Walking through my house showing yourself like that." She speaks of my body like it's a thing of disgust. Something to be hidden and never shown.

I say nothing. My chest heaves. I hate myself. She swoops out as quickly as she swooped in—in a flurry of red silk and condemnation. I can smell her vanilla perfume as I begin to cry.

I want her back. I want to know what changed her so that I have somewhere to lay my blame. If there was a cause, I could stop blaming myself. I trace my memories, over and over, searching for the root—the moment, or month, or day she vanished.

From my mattress, I stare at the ceiling. Deep brown watermarks stain what was once cream paint. In those marks, I study our years in the eating house. The gradual recession of happiness. Your life can be nicked away so slowly that you don't even notice it.

Her laughter went first, then her smiles, which were so deep they showed more gum than tooth. The last thing to go was her eyes—her brilliantly expressive eyes. They stopped looking and gazed right through. They stared at walls, and cabinets, and floors.

They stared at everything except me. In the early days I'd tried everything to get her to look at me: drop a bowl of cereal and milk on the floor, right in front of her so that her toes were flecked with milk, or scribble all over my arms and legs with marker until I was as deeply blue as a Smurf. With grim determination, I lied to her face, broke her trinkets, swore loudly, and sang songs she hated at the top of my lungs. Hateful attempts met with milky-eyed ambivalence. She's slowly dying, and I'm not sure she knows it.

age 15

FOLD YOUR HANDS IN YOUR LAP. Smile. Don't smile. Don't look anyone in the eye. Pretend you don't care. Study your shoes. Don't smile ... don't ever smile. God.

I am fidgety and awkward. I never know what to do and when to do it. A boy smiled at me once; he was cute. He'd already passed by the time I smiled back. Too little too late. I couldn't make my face move in time. School is a reprieve from home; home is a reprieve from school. I don't belong anywhere, so I travel from place to place hoping no one notices me—but if they do, I hope they won't be overly cruel. I think about the past. Days long gone.

Everything different, everything so strangely the same. People become different, I realize. It's the landscape that never changes: the highway signs marred with graffiti, the pink and orange blended sunsets that kiss the top of the evergreens, even the line of cars waiting to turn into the Wal-Mart parking lot. That's what jars me the most: same sky, same Bone, same house, different mother.

So I remember the old mother, tracing the past, recoloring the memories. The weight of bad memories blossoms and expands under the good memories. I try to think only of those—the good things that carve me into my childhood, not the ones that carve me out of it.

I think of the way my mother always had a leaf between her fingers. That's what I remember most. She'd pull one from a bush or a tree and hold it between her fingers, compulsively rubbing little circles until the leaf was rubbed clean of its veins and membranes and her fingers were stained green. I liked when her fingers were green; it reminded me of the finger paints we used at school. It made her seem strange and fun, organically different from the other mothers who were always sour-faced and stiff. When we were outside, I'd study the way she'd examine the plants, mimicking her movements, wanting to be close to her, wanting to be her. And it was difficult because my mother carried her grace around her shoulders, a regal class that was almost impossible to imitate.

That was when I was real little and things were almost right. Before she lost her job at Markobs and Jacob, before she started smoking, before the men. Nowadays, my mother's fingers are stained with nicotine. The smell rolls off her skin when she moves across a room—stale smoke and tobacco rot. Her shoulders hang from her neck like an old housecoat. When she stopped leaving the house a few years ago, she would send me out to buy cigarettes, the ones with the Indian chief on the carton, because they were healthier for you. Somewhere in between her smelling like the outdoors, and her smelling like an ashtray, I stopped wanting to be her. And during that same time, while she was shrugging off the mantle of parenting and becoming a stranger, she stopped saying my name.

At first I didn't notice it. It wasn't until a teacher said my name at school, calling me to the front of the class to solve an equation, that I realized I hadn't heard it in some time. My mother still delivered commands, but at some point skimmed my name from the top of them. *Margo.* It took me a minute to recognize that it was me Mrs. Lerson was calling. The other students laughed as I made my way through the line of desks to stand in front of the blackboard. *Margo,* I thought. *That's me.* And then, as I walked home from the bus, I tried to remember the last time I heard her say it, and I couldn't.

My mother, a Perry Mason fan, named me after Margo Albert, an actress she once saw on his show, *The Case of the Sad Sicilian*. In Margo's final role, before she died of brain cancer, she played a murderess named Serafina. My mother, stricken by her doleful eyes, vowed to name her first daughter Margo. It feels like a cruel joke to be named after a woman who was cast in tragic roles, and even more so to have the meaning of one's name be something so beautiful and delicate when you yourself are anything but.

In the eating house, I remain nameless. White blonde hair, forgettable eyes, ugly, tattered clothes.

"Hey Margo!"

I spin around. The school bus is retracting its STOP sign, doors closing. Destiny comes barreling down the sidewalk toward me, slinging her backpack over her shoulder. I eye the cut of her jeans, and the way her shirt hangs fashionably off her shoulder. She's even wearing the type of shoes the other girls are wearing: sparkly flats. She stopped speaking to me sometime around seventh grade, after the kids at school started calling me "the whore's daughter." I don't know if it was by her parents' command or self-preservation, but she just left me.

"You forgot this on the bus," she says, handing me the paperback novel I'd been reading. I take it from her without meeting her eyes.

"Thank you."

Her house is in the opposite direction, but she hesitates before leaving like she wants to say something. In the end, though, she just shrugs and walks away. I don't watch her go. I know if I do, I will cry.

The eating house is still when I get home. It naps during the day while I am at school: a night house. I go straight to my room, because that's what she likes me to do. It's later in the afternoon that she emerges from her bedroom to begin her ritual for her night: the washing and applying of creams and makeup. In recent years, she hasn't wanted me around, not even for her bath. And I don't care. I hated watching her wrinkle in the chipped, rose-colored bath, pieces of paint peeling off and floating in the water around her. I pull out my box, choosing a candy bar and a warm can of Mountain Dew, and begin my homework as the eating house wakes up and creaks around me.

When the first of her visitors come, I pack up my notebooks and pencils and crawl to the wall that separates my bedroom from hers. This is the way I know her. She has not gone completely silent. I hear her speaking to them. I am so desperate for the sound of her voice; I spend nights pressing my ear between our walls. They tell her things—things about their lives, and their wives, and their jobs. They punch up their sentences with words like fiscal year, college tuition, and parole violations. She only speaks when they need her to. She's perfected the art of the pause and response. A word here, a word there. Her voice never changes from an agreeable purr. They find it sexy, her willingness to listen and her reluctance to speak. A beautiful woman who does, and does not disagree. I am learning so much about men, the way they want and what they want. They pace her bedroom, their heavy steps a dull thud on the chipped and marred wood of the eating house. Once I hear her give advice: *Sell the house, downgrade. You don't need all of that space now that the kids are gone.*

Where is my advice? I wonder. *Where are my words? Whose kid am I?*

16

age 18

WESSEX, a street cobbled with crack, crack whores, dealers, drunks, girls who had barely dried the milk from their own chins before giving suckle to their little undernourished babies. It is pitiful, this thing we call life. I know that, but I'm not sure they do. One grows accustomed to suffering, especially in a place like Bone Harbor. You take your first steps, everyone claps, and then you cease to be remarkable. Nearly surrounded by water, it used to be a harbor before they moved it farther south to be closer to Seattle. But that was before my grandmother was born. The people around here call the area the Bone. A kind of joke that developed after all the business dried up. I kind of like that they call it that. No use calling yellow, blue. And that's what we are, rubbed down to the bone.

Six days a week I take the bus to work. To get to the bus, I have to walk up Wessex and down Carnation. Carnation is only slightly better than Wessex. The windows aren't broken, and a couple people mow their grass. The people who live on Carnation

Street call us trash. I suppose in a world such as this, unbroken windows and mowed grass make all the difference.

God is not in the houses that stand side-by-side down Wessex. I wonder if God lifted Himself from this place and put us behind a veil to suffer alone. It's a nightmare street. The people in the outside world don't know we exist. They don't want to know. But our houses stand, almost collapsing under the weight of the sin they contain. Before the eating house comes the crack house. Before the crack house comes Mother Mary's house. Mother Mary can see the future, but not any future. She can only tell you how you'll die, and she'll charge you forty dollars to do it. Which brings us to the bad people house. I only call it that because it's where the ex-cons hole up after they're released from prison. I don't know what they get up to in there, but once a week there's an ambulance outside and someone is hauled out on a stretcher.

There is only one house I like on Wessex Street. It's the very first house on the block, and it belongs to Delaney Grant. Delaney grows pot in her garage. She doesn't even sell it. She just smokes it all herself. Everyone calls her greedy. Sometimes, when there's a pot shortage at the crack house, you can see people knocking on Delaney's door. But she chases them away with a shotgun she calls Horace.

The reason I like Delaney's house is because her son, Judah, lives there. Part of the time. The times he's not with Delaney, he's with his dad. We've never actually spoken, but he sits out in the yard a lot, and he always waves when I walk by. When you look at him you forget that he's in a wheelchair. He's handsome, and he'd be tall if he stood up. Six feet at least. He never went to school with the rest of us. A bus came to pick him up every morning. It could fit his wheelchair, and it drove all the way from the city. Delaney pissed her own life to shit, but when it came to Judah, she made sure the world saw him. You had to kind of like her for that. Especially when you had a mother like mine.

The bus is late. I tap my foot impatiently and crane my neck to peer down the street. If the 712 gets here in the next five minutes, I can still make it to the Rag O Rama in time for my shift.

"Good times," I whisper as I see it bouncing around the corner. There are three of us who climb onto the 712: myself, Cuoco, one of the neighborhood heroin addicts, and little Nevaeh

Anthony who catches the bus to her grandmother's house every afternoon while her mother works.

"Hi Margo," she says.

"Hi, little girl. You going to Granny's house?"

She nods.

"Good. Walk fast once you get off the bus. You know how it is after dark." Nevaeh nods. She knows. We all know. Splintered in between the normal things like school, grocery shopping, and work are the things that belong to the Bone. A fear that wanders like a mist through the streets. We live with it chained to our ankles. It's so tangible that there are rarely visitors, and when they come, whether to visit a family member or to pass through, they hurry out, usually cutting their trips short.

"Let me fix your hair," I say, and Nevaeh scoots closer to me on the bench. "Have to look pretty for Granny," I tell her. She nods in agreement. My fingers work deftly as rain pounds against the windows. I finish her braids as the bus stops and right as she finishes telling me about her good report card, counting out the ten dollars her granny gave her as a reward. I watch her pull out a marker and draw a heart on each one. We climb off together, pulling our hoods up over our hair. She waves to me as we head in opposite directions, her fingers spread like starfish. I watch for a minute as she bounces down the street, her Hello Kitty backpack slung over her shoulder, bright colors cast against a gloomy day. I look at Destiny's old house as I walk by. It's green now, with white flower boxes on the windows. Her family moved to Oregon a few years ago. After she moved, she wrote me a letter, and then I never heard from her again. I wrote twenty before they started to come back with RETURN TO SENDER stamped on the envelope. Oh well. Letter writing is a luxury anyway.

The Rag O Rama smells like shit. Literally. The sewage plant is right across the river. Sandy, the manager, has those room deodorizers all over the shop, stuck in corners and up on shelves, but all it does is make the Rag smell like shit covered in apple blossom.

Because I'm thirty minutes late, Sandy makes me sort through inventory in the back room. I eye the black garbage bags lined against the wall, stuffed so full that half of them have split open, pant legs and shirtsleeves spilling out like intestines. There are only seven to sort through today. Sandy makes us save the bags that aren't damaged. "Money don't grow on no trees," she says. "This is a thrift shop. We reuse everything." Which leaves me plucking at the knots, swearing under my breath as sweat runs down my back and between my breasts. I untie the first one and spread the bag open. The musty smell has become familiar to me; it is the smell of un-wash, of people's homes, mothballs, and occasionally—if we get a bag from an Indian family—tumeric and cumin. I separate the things inside: clothes in one pile, toys in another, household items in the third. It's funny how one person's crap can be so valuable to someone else. Employees get half off anything on the sale rack. It's the things people don't want times two. I finish off a bag and start to fold it when I feel something I missed at the bottom. I pull out a large canvas bag—the kind rich people take to the store to avoid using plastic. "Groceries & Shit" is stenciled on the front. I laugh. Its last owner drew stars around the words in purple sharpie.

"Groceries and shit," I say out loud. Sandy walks in carrying an armful of hangers. "You can keep that," she says. "It's your summer bonus."

I roll my eyes, but I am secretly pleased. It's not often you get something for free in this life. I fold my new bag into a square and tuck it into the back of my pants so one of the other girls doesn't take it.

Sandy's boyfriend, Luis, hits her. She tries to hide the bruises, but there are a lot of them, and she wears makeup that's about three shades too light for her skin. On the days he doesn't hit her, she brings us stale doughnuts from the place where he works. I saw the empty box in the trash when I got to work. It's a good day for her.

When Sandy feels like I've been punished enough, she sends me up front to work the register. It's mostly a boring day until a woman tries to steal a pair of shoes. Sandy catches her before she can walk out with them stuffed under her jacket. The woman can barely stand she's so drunk. Sandy grabs her by the forearm and shoves her into a chair in the office. She tells me to call the police.

"Maybe we shouldn't," I say. "Look at her, Sandy." The woman is rocking back and forth, clutching her chest and mumbling something that sounds like Zeek.

Sandy doesn't look at her. She looks at me. "I thought you wanted this job."

I do. I really do. If I didn't have this job I'd have to be home. And if I were home...

I call the police.

The police arrive forty minutes later with grease stains on their pants, looking bored as hell. They load the woman into the back of their cruiser and drive away. I carry the shoes back to their rack on the children's side of the store. They're a beat up pair of Jordan's. The price tag says six dollars. She didn't even have six dollars. I wonder if she spent the six dollars getting drunk. The shoes were probably for her kid. That's the way of things here. Your thoughts go to yourself first, and if there are a few thoughts left, your children might get them. But from my experience, the only things children get in this neighborhood are drunk parents and partially full stomachs. *You're alive, you'll survive.* That's what my mother used to tell me.

Before my shift ends, I pay for the shoes and shove them in my new Groceries & Shit bag. I walk the two blocks to the bus stop with my head down. It's raining—warm rain—not the cold kind that makes your bones ache. I wish I had money for a coffee, but I spent what I had on the shoes, and I need the rest for bus fare. I decide to walk the five blocks instead. I stop at a food truck and hand them my bus fare. In exchange, I get a paper cup of coffee with a dash of cream and three sugars. It's delicious.

The police station on Bone Harbor Hill is always busy. I walk into the lobby and a dirty-faced toddler crashes into my legs. A baby cries, a woman curses, a man who barely speaks English is arguing with a clerk. "A meeestake! A meestake!" he cries. I look around, trying to decide if this is worth it, when I see one of the cops who came to the Rag O Rama to arrest the woman. He has a gym bag slung over one shoulder, and the look of a man who just ended his shift.

"S'cuse me," I say. He is reluctant to stop. "Excuse me," I say louder. He is wearing sunglasses despite the lateness of the day. I stare at my own reflection and say, "The woman you picked up earlier from the Rag O Rama. Is she still here?"

He sticks his thumbs in his belt loops like he's some kind of boss, and looks at me like he's trying to place my face. He won't be able to.

"Yeah, why?"

I shove the shoes at him. "She left these there," I say. And then I turn and leave without looking back. My own shoes, the ones on my feet, are the only shoes I own. Torn up sneakers from the Wal-Mart clearance rack. You can do without a lot of things in this life, but shoes are a necessity. If you're stealing shoes, it's a desperate necessity. And I will not stand in the way of people trying hard to survive.

I'M WALKING TO THE CORNER STORE for healthy cigarettes, watching the way the fat of my knees bulge with each step, when I see him. He's reading a book, his head leaning on his upturned palm. There is a glass of water beside him, untouched and filled to the brim, sweating. The fact that he looks so at ease with himself is what abruptly redirects my feet from the cracked sidewalk to the pathway that leads to his gate. I smile. I don't smile. I wring my hands. I fold them behind my back. No one really knows if it was a car accident, or a tumor, or something like Multiple Sclerosis that made Judah Grant a cripple. We knew him when he walked on his legs, then one day he couldn't. As I watch him, I have a thought that startles me in its clarity. *He wears his wheelchair. His wheelchair never wears him.* I've never had this thought before. As a general rule, I try not to look at Judah. Staring at someone in a wheelchair doesn't seem polite—even if he is beautiful.

There is a fence surrounding his yard. It was once pretty; you can still see the remnants of eggshell blue paint in some places where the rust hasn't eaten through it. I remember being little and thinking the fence looked like Easter. The gate groans loudly as I push it open with my fingertips. Judah's head comes up, but not at once. He's so casual as he sets his book aside and watches me walk up the ramp that Delaney had built for his chair.

"What are you doing?" I ask him. I glance down at the book he is reading. It's a biography.

He holds up the thin joint between his fingers. It smells hella strong. Like weed smoking weed.

"Can I have some?" I ask.

His eyes lightly graze me. "I've never seen you smoke," he says, and makes no move to pass me the joint. His voice is clear and deep.

"You never *see* me," I say.

"Sure I do." He puts the joint between his lips, sucks in a little. He exhales before he says, "You walk past here every day to go to work."

I tuck my chin in, surprised. "How do you know I'm going to work?"

"Dunno," he replies. "Maybe because you look miserable."

He's right, of course.

"Okay," I say. "So you see me walking to work once a day and you suddenly know me?"

He smiles a little and shrugs, extending the joint toward me like he doesn't care whether I hit it or not.

"No thanks," I say. "I don't smoke."

His laugh is a slow build up. It pools in his chest and bursts forward. He laughs like he's been laughing his whole life, and he knows how.

"I like your bag," he says, extending a pinky finger and pointing to it. The remnants of his smile are still lingering around the corners of his mouth. "Groceries and shit. Is that literally what you put in there?"

"Literally?" I ask. "You want to know if I literally put my groceries, and my shit, in this bag?"

His teeth slide over his lower lip as he studies me. I can tell it's a habit by the narrowing of his eyes, the side-to-side bobbing of his head.

Finally, he says, "I was testing you. I don't like people who misuse the word 'literally.' Now we can be friends."

"Literally?"

He sets his joint in a little ashtray at his feet and holds out his hand.

"I'm Judah," he says. "And you're Margo."

"How do you know my name?" His hand holds on to mine a beat longer than what is considered normal. If I weren't so ugly, I'd think he was into me.

"This is Wessex Street; we're all parasites on the same vein in Washington." He reaches his arms back and cradles his head in his hands while he waits for my reaction. *Look at him, sitting in his wheelchair all cool.*

"I'm not a parasite," I say calmly. "I'm not on welfare. I have a job." I feel bad right away. That might not even be what he meant. *You don't always have to be so defensive,* I tell myself.

"Don't look so guilty," he says. "I wasn't accusing you of mooching off the government. I have a job."

"I'm not guilty. You don't know what I'm thinking," I say defensively. *Oops.*

Judah picks up his joint. "Yeah, I do. You've got the kind of face that speaks." He makes jazz hands when he says the last part. I don't smile. I want to though.

I scrunch my whole, entire face together because I don't know what he means. Then I know.

"Oh," I say.

I look down at him. What kind of job could he have? Maybe something at his school.

"I know what you're thinking," he says. "What kind of job could I possibly have?"

"Ew! Stop reading my mind … and my face!"

We both laugh.

"So what do you do?"

He takes a hit of his joint. "Are you kidding?" he says. "I'm in a wheelchair. I don't have a job."

"Oh my God." I shake my head at him and look up at the sky. It's about to rain. "You can't just steal my shit like that." I need to get her cigarettes before it pours. "Gotta go," I say. I head back down the path, my Groceries & Shit bag swinging on my arm.

"Bye Margo. Come see me again, you hear?" he calls after me.

When I get home an hour later, it's already dark. I can hear voices from my mother's room. I wonder if I have enough time to use the bathroom before he comes out. Whoever *he* is. I have to be back at the Rag first thing tomorrow, and I need a bath. I wish we had a shower like normal people, but the eating house was built before people washed themselves standing up. I grab a towel from my room and fill the bath. I'm halfway through washing myself when there's pounding on the door.

"Margo," my mother's sharp voice calls out. "What are you doing in there?"

I know better than to answer her. What she wants is for me to vacate the bathroom. I do a quick rinse and jump out, being careful not to get water on the floor. She hates that. The next twenty seconds is me frantically pulling on my clothes. It's not fast enough. I know that. I was stupid to think I had enough time, and now there will be consequences.

When I open the door she's standing there in her red, silk robe with a cigarette dangling between her fingers. It makes a trail of smoke toward the gray ceiling. She glares at me, making silent promises for later. There's a man standing behind her, looking as pleased as a newly fed baby. He leers at me as I squeeze past my mother and run barefoot to my bedroom. I didn't even get to wash my hair. You can't be ugly in this life and have dirty hair. For some reason I think of Judah Grant—the opposite of ugly, and the reason I wanted to wash my hair.

Judah Grant isn't sitting in his yard when I walk to the bus stop the next morning. Delaney is digging around in her garden with a big straw hat on her head. She looks like one of those women you see on the cover of a gardening magazine. She waves at me when I walk by. Sometimes she gives me money and tells me to bring her things from the Rag. "I need a new pair of shorts," she'll say. "Size two." Delaney's whole entire body is the size of my thigh. I get things for her in the teen section of the Rag. "Hey Margo," she calls. I stop. "Judah needs some shirts. Fancy ones. Something a man should wear to work."

The liar! I'm tempted to ask where he works, but she's busy pulling money from her bra, and I'm distracted.

She hands me a ten and a twenty. They're both damp. I hold them between my thumb and my forefinger.

"What size is he?" I ask dumbly. I wonder why Delaney can't go to the Rag herself and choose his shirts. I wonder why Judah is such an effing liar.

"Get him a couple nice ones with collars," she says. I want to ask her where he's working, but we've never talked other than me taking her clothes orders.

"All right," I say. "Something nice."

I'm going to get him some really ugly shit just for lying to me. Besides, a person who looks like him doesn't need to be well-dressed, working legs or not. You have to leave some room in the world for the rest of us.

I buy Judah four shirts: pink paisley, purple with tiny white hearts, and a white shirt with red stripes so he can look like a candy cane. Christmas is all about lies anyway. The fourth shirt is nicer because I found a little mercy in my heart. It's just plain blue. Delaney acts like I'm America's Next Top Model when I hand them to her.

"They're perfect," she says. "You should work in fashion."

I can't wait to see him in the candy cane shirt, but I doubt he'll even wear it. Tough luck for him, the Rag has a very strict NO RETURNS policy. But, he can donate it back if he likes. I'll make sure Delaney re-buys it for his birthday.

When I get home, my mother's door is closed. She's left a note taped to my door, though. *Pick up my medicine*

Sure. Why not? I'm my mother's unpaid errand girl. I crumple up the note and throw it at her door. It's unfortunate that she chooses that very moment to exit her room. The note hits her left breast and bounces to the floor. She watches it fall to her feet, and then brings her eyes back up to my face. My mother doesn't have to say anything to punish me. She's not verbally abusive. She turns back around and shuts her door. The message is clear. I disgust her. She wouldn't even keep me around, except she won't leave the house anymore, and I get shit for her. I head back outside and walk to the crack house for Wendy's medicine. At least she didn't send me to the bad people house.

"Yo, Margo!"

"Yo," I say.

Judah is wheeling himself back and forth on the driveway. He's wearing a thin white t-shirt and all of his muscles are popping out.

"Ew, gross. You have muscles."

"Yeah, I'm a stud," he says.

"Why are you doing that?" I ask. He's wheeling himself left, then right, around and around, as fast as he can go.

"Workin' out."

"Cool, I don't do that." *Like it's not evident in the fat pockets around your knees,* I think.

I keep walking, but he follows me out onto the sidewalk. I can hear his wheels squeaking behind me. I grin.

"You don't smoke or work out. What do you do?"

I don't know what I do; I'm kind of a loser.

"I talk to you once ... now you think we're friends?"

"You're kind of mean looking," he says. "I was scared of you. Once you got things rolling..."

He's full of shit. He can't even say it and keep a straight face.

I fall back into step, and he has no problem keeping up with me.

"I read," I say. I look at him out of the corner of my eye to see if he's judging me.

"I do too," he says. I remember the book he was holding, the day I walked up his pathway. "Mostly biographies."

"Ew," I say. And then, "I get enough of real life in the Bone. I want to go somewhere good when I read, not into someone else's crappy life."

"Good lives aren't worth reading about," he argues. "I read about the struggle. Other people's growing pains."

"I like happy endings," I say. "Real life never has a happy ending."

"God, you're depressing. I don't know why we're friends."

I turn into the crack house's cracked driveway. "We're not," I call. "Now wait for me out here, and if you hear gunshots, call the police. They won't come, but call them anyway."

"I've got guns," he says, flexing his arms. "I can protect you."

I laugh. I didn't know I had a laugh in me.

I stop laughing when Mo opens the door. I'm hit in the face with the smell of weed and cooking steak. He shoves his eight-month-old son at me. "Hold him," he grunts. I take Mo Jr. and sit down on front step with him. I have to brush aside a bunch of cigarette butts. Mo Jr. smells like a week-old diaper. He looks up at me like I'm the most boring creature alive, before staring off into the bushes to the left of the house.

"Mo," I say. "Little Mo." He won't break his gaze with the bushes. I start whistling. I'm a fairly accomplished whistler; Judah looks up from where he's doing wheelies on the sidewalk. Little Mo turns his face to me.

"Finally," I say. "It hurts my feelings when you don't pay attention to me."

I whistle him a song I've heard on the radio at work. He smiles a little. When Big Mo comes back to the door, he reaches down to take the baby and slips a couple baggies in my lap. I stand up and dust off my pants. Mo leans against the doorframe. "Your mom okay?"

"Yeah," I say. "Same as always."

"She used to babysit me, when I was real little."

I keep my face blank, but I'm more than surprised. She never told me. Not that she tells me shit.

I leave the wad of twenties on the stairs.

"Bye Little Mo," I say. But the door's already shut. I put the baggies into my Groceries & Shit bag.

When I reach the street, Judah looks at my bag.

"Those for you?"

"Nah, my mom's a prescription pill druggie."

He looks relieved. "Even if they were, you'd have no right to judge, pot head."

"Marijuana is different," he says. He pronounces it mari-jew-wana.

"No. It's all an addiction. Emotional, physical. You do it because you need it. It doesn't matter if your body craves it or not. Your mind does."

"I like you," he says.

I'm surprised.

He walks me home. He wheels me home. Which is better, because anyone can walk you home. I don't let him get right to the house. Everyone knows what my mom is, but you still don't want anyone to see it first hand.

"What are you addicted to?" he asks me before I can say goodnight.

"Isn't it obvious?" I ask him.

He nods his head knowingly. "Sarcasm," he says.

I shift my Groceries & Shit bag from one arm to the other.

"Food," I say. "Namely Honey Buns. But, if it's processed, I'll take it."

No use keeping secrets in a place where everyone airs their sins. Mine is gluttony.

"I'm fat," I tell him. And then I add, "Because I eat Honey Buns for dinner."

"You're not fat," he says. I don't stay to hear what he says next. I beeline for the front door.

A FEW DAYS AFTER I CONFESSED to Judah Grant about my Honey
Bun addiction, there is a knock on the front door.

Pra pa pa pa pa

I am trying to glue the sole of my sneaker back on when I hear
the knock. I'm so startled I drop the shoe and the tub of gorilla
glue. I stand frozen, not sure what to do, watching the amber stuff
leak onto the linoleum. No one comes to the eating house at this
time of day, not even the Jehovah's Witnesses. I glance up the
stairs to my mother's bedroom with my heart still raging. She won't
wake up for another few hours. My mother has severe
agoraphobia, not to mention the paranoia and the prescription pill
addiction. If she were awake right now, she'd be tossing little white
pills in her mouth and sweating bullets. Nights she left the door
open for her men, just so she wouldn't have to hear them knock.

Ra pa pa pa. Louder this time.

I pad, barefoot, to the door, and peer through the eyehole. A
cluster of humans is crowded in front of the eating house. They are
all different sizes and ethnicities, packed together under the slight
overhang to remove themselves from the rain. I latch the security
chain before I unlock the door. Then I peer through the gap at
their hodgepodge group.

"Yes?"

A man, near the front of the group, steps forward and shoves a piece of paper at my face. He's grizzly looking, with a gray beard and a brown head of hair. I look from him to the paper. There is a little girl's face in the center; she has pigtails and two missing front teeth. HAVE YOU SEEN ME? is written in bold, black letters along the bottom. A chill creeps up my spine.

"We are part of a search team for Nevaeh Anthony," he tells me. "Have you seen this little girl?"

I slam the door shut and unlatch it. When I throw it open, everyone, including me, looks surprised. *Seen her? Seen her?* I see her every day. I saw her what...? Two days ago? Three? I take the paper from him.

"Wh-when?" I ask him. I press my palm against my forehead. I feel funny. Clammy and sick.

"Mother says she hasn't seen her since Thursday. Got on a bus to see her gramma and never came back?"

Thursday ... Thursday was the day I braided her hair.

"I saw her on Thursday," I say. I step out of the house and pull the door shut behind me. "I'm coming with you."

He nods at me real slow. "You have to go down to the po-lice station. Let them know what you seen," he says. "When they done with you, we'll be canvassing this whole area. From Wessex to Cerdic. You come find us, hear?"

I nod. I'm running down Wessex, barefoot, my fat jiggling around my body like jello, when I hear Judah call my name.

I stop, breathing hard.

"You seen her?" he calls. His brow is furrowed, and he's pushing himself up out of his chair by his arms so he can see me.

"On Thursday," I yell back. He nods. "Where are your shoes?"

"They broke." I shrug.

"Go! Go!" he says. I run—fast and barefoot.

I wait for Detective Wyche at his desk while he gets himself a cup of coffee. When I walked in, the first thing he did was ask where my shoes were. "I need to speak to the detectives in charge of the Nevaeh Anthony case," I said, ignoring his question. He looks startled for a minute, then he leads me to his desk, announcing that he needs a cup of joe. He has bobble heads of the last ten presidents lined up around his computer. I examine my filthy feet and wonder how a person's shoes can fail them on a day like this. I'm bleeding in a couple places where the sidewalk nicked me. *Even the sidewalk in the Bone is broken*, I think.

Detective Wyche comes back with his partner—a much fatter, older man with sweat stains around his armpits. He grunts loudly when he sits down next to me. He smells of Old Spice and desperation. They question me for two hours while I bounce my knees up and down and wish I could have a cup of coffee, too. I don't ask for one, because I've been taught to believe it's wrong to ask for things. You suffer quietly so no one has the right to call you a pussy. Detective Old Spice takes the lead. He wants to know when I last saw Nevaeh.

On the seventeen bus; she was going to her grandma's, I was going to work. I don't know exactly where her grandma lives.

What was she wearing?

Red tights and a T-shirt with a smiley face emoji that said: *Don't text your ex.* When I say that, Detective Wyche raises his eyebrows. *Oh shut up*, I want to say. *Nobody has money for clothes.*

Did she say anything unusual?

No, she was happy. Normal.

Did she have any bruises on her arms and legs? Not that I could see.

Did she ever mention anything about abuse? No. She spoke a lot about her grandma. She loved to be with her.

Do I know Nevaeh's mother, Lyndee Anthony? Just in passing.

We've never spoken? And on and on it goes. When I finally think it's over, they ask me all of the same questions in a different way.

I walk home in the rain, my feet throbbing, and grab my raincoat. It's getting dark. I wonder how long the search party will look for her in this weather. It's too late to find them now.

I am walking down Wessex with a pile of the posters I took from the detectives when Judah wheels himself in my path. I stare at him blankly before he hands me a pair of rain boots.

"They're my mom's," he says. "She doesn't use them."

I take the boots. They are green with red cherries. I pull them on my bare feet without saying a word.

"Give me some." He holds out his hand, and I slide a thick stack of posters between his fingers. We decide to hand out the flyers at Wal-Mart. Neither of us speaks. I'm not entirely sure

Judah knows Nevaeh; he never had reason to run into her, but his face is drawn and pale. That's how it is in the Bone. You are scared for yourself, mostly, but sometimes you are scared for someone else. As for me, I know what it is like to be a kid, and to be alone. When we run out of posters, we go home.

"We had to shove them at people," I say. "It's like no one wanted to look."

"You have to understand something about the Bone," Judah says. "Every bad thing that happens here reminds people of what they're trying to forget. When you're rich and you see stuff like this on TV, you hug your children and feel grateful it's not you. When you're from the Bone, you hug your children and pray you're not next."

I'm quiet for a long time, thinking about this. I've been sitting alone in a dark room with a box of Honey Buns for so long that it's nice to talk.

"Why don't they do something? Why don't we do something? We could all leave here—every last one of us—and go look for something better."

"It's not that easy," Judah says. "The Bone is in our marrow. It's complacency and fear handed down from generation to generation."

Judah stops at a food truck and studies the menu. I wait for him under the stubby metal awning of the bus top, trying to stay warm. The guys behind the window seem to know him. They step out of the truck to bring him his bag of food, which he sets on his lap when he wheels over to me.

"Dinner," he says.

I sit awkwardly as he doles out tacos and chips onto napkins he puts on our laps. There are little cups of bright red salsa to go with everything, and a large fizzing cup of Coke. It's the first time someone's bought me dinner.

The rain is a fine mist tonight, but it's not overly cold. If Nevaeh is outside—hurt or something—she won't freeze. I hate that I'm thinking that.

"Where could she be?" I ask, gingerly picking up a chip. "This is a small town. Hardly any strangers even come through here."

"Maybe she ran away," Judah says. His mouth is full of taco. I can smell the cilantro and meat. "You know how little kids are around here. I used to want to run away once a week when I was her age. I probably would have if I had the legs to do it."

I shake my head. "No, she's not like that."

"I know," he says. "I'm just trying to make myself feel better."

I nibble on the chip I'm holding, crunching it between my two front teeth like a gopher.

"Did you know her?"

He hesitates. "Yeah…" He licks the sour cream from the corner of his mouth and continues eating.

I try to think of all the ways he could have come in contact with Nevaeh and come up empty. Nevaeh didn't live on Wessex; she lived on Thames Street, two down, one over. She went to school, she caught the bus to her grandma's, she played on her street, but never wandered farther than the end of the block. How does a crippled, college-aged man know a second grade girl?

"Why aren't you eating?" he asks.

Because I don't want you to think I'm fat.

"Not that hungry, I guess." *I am so hungry.*

He sets his taco down and stares at me. Pieces of lettuce tumble off his lap and onto the ground. "If you don't eat, I'm not eating. And then you'll be responsible for starving a cripple."

I unwrap my taco, smiling a little.

"Where do you work?" I ask. We are finished eating, wrappers disposed, hands dusted on our pants. I step down from the curb and then turn back to help him over a patch of bad street—cracked and rippled. I know he takes classes in Seattle because three times a week his school sends a white van to pick him up. Though I don't know what he's studying.

"At my job," he replies.

"Okay, smartass, what are you studying?"

"Elementary education."

I am surprised by his quick answer, when he's been dodging the other for so long. Though something about him being a teacher fits. It's glove-like, appropriate.

"Is that how you knew her? *Know* her…" I correct myself.

"Yes," he says. And that's all he says. And even though he bought me dinner, I have the urge to reach out and smack the back of his head. I'm a hypocrite, I realize. I don't like intrusive questions either.

I feel as if I've known him for a very long time.

I SKIM TEN DOLLARS from the floorboards to buy myself a new
pair of shoes from the Rag. I have seven work checks, made out in
my name, and no bank account in which to deposit them. I need
picture identification to open a bank account, and so far I haven't
even been able to find my birth certificate. I asked her for it once,
and her eyes got bleary before she walked away without saying
a word. I have a social security card, Margo Moon and a nine-digit
number that tells the world I'm a valid American. Since I don't
have a photo ID, Sandy had to take my word for it when she
hired me.

All seven of my checks sit inside my worn copy of *Little
Women*. I wear Delaney's rain boots to work in the meantime. Judah
says his mom won't even know they're missing, but I'm not in the
habit of stealing rain boots then parading them around their owner.

Sandy looks me up and down when I walk in. "It ain't even
raining," she says. "And those are happy boots. You ain't happy." I
shrug. Sandy just got braces. It's hard to take an adult with braces
seriously.

Before the store opens, I find a pair of red Converse with
minimal wear in the teenybopper section. I switch them out with
the rain boots and put my seven dollars in the register. I've never

had a pair of Converse before. Just sneakers from Wal-Mart. I feel like a million bucks—or seven, depending on the way you look at it. When Sandy sees my new shoes, she gives me a thumbs-up. I do a moonwalk across the Rag's floor. I don't know why I'm so good at moonwalking. Sandy tells me that I'm a white girl with a gift, as she eats a bluffin from the gas station and bops her head to "Billie Jean." I stay late at work, helping Sandy sort a late delivery, and I almost miss the last bus of the night. The driver frowns at me when I pound on the doors just as he's pulling away, but he lets me on and I give him my biggest smile. By the time I climb off at my stop, I'm so exhausted I can barely keep my eyes open. I carry the rain boots to Judah's house and prop them against the front door. Most of the neighborhood is sleeping already—even the crack house. I am creeping away when he calls out to me. I can't see him. He must be sitting in the dark at the window that faces the street.

I walk quickly toward his voice and crouch down, trying to see him through the screen.

"Hey," I say.

"Hey." His voice is different.

"I brought back your mom's boots," I say cautiously. Then, "Why are you sitting in the dark?"

There is a long pause. I can hear his breath moving in and out of his lungs.

"I was waiting for you to walk by."

I look over my shoulder, at the dead night, the dead street. Not even the frogs are singing tonight. I make a decision.

"Can I come in?" I whisper.

His head moves up and down, but just barely. I go to the door and open it slowly. No creak escapes from the hinges, and for that I am relieved. The last thing I want is Delaney coming out of her room to find the prostitute's daughter creeping around her living room. The house is dark except for a candle that is burning in the far corner of the room. It smells of cinnamon.

Judah's chair is pulled right up to the window. I wonder how often he sits there watching the world from his chair. His shoulders are curled inward, his head drooping from his neck. *The chair is wearing him tonight,* I think. I go to him, kneel down, and put my hands on his knees. I've never touched him before. Never dared. His knees are frail, thin. Not like the rest of him. Judah was born to be big, and tall, and powerful, and life stole that from him. How heavy is that burden? His head comes up a little, just so we can exchange looks. He seems ... tired.

"Judah," I whisper. "Why were you waiting for me?"

He blinks slowly, like he's in some kind of trance, then he looks back out the window.

"I always have." There is such utter dejection in his voice, I draw back.

He lifts his arm and points across the street. "There, where the blackberries grow in summer..."

I look to where he's pointing. There is a thicket of bushes across the street. No one ever trims them back so they grow wild around an empty lot.

"I saw you there for the first time, picking berries with your mother. I mean, you'd lived here your whole life, and so had I, but that was the first time I looked. You were real little—missing teeth, scraped knees little. Your hair was ratty and so blonde it looked white in the sun."

I search for this memory. Blackberry picking with my mother. Yes. She used to make pies. We'd take bowls and fill them up, staining our lips with the purple juice as we ate and picked. She would tell me stories about how she used to do the same thing with her mother. Before she tried to drown her, that is.

"Your skin gets real tan in the summer," he continues. "In the winter you're like the snow, but when summer comes you look like a Native American with spun gold hair." I look down at my arms. It's too dark to see the color of my skin, but I know he's telling the truth. I don't know where he's going with this. He's not himself.

"You know what I thought when I saw you? She's going to fight. You'd reach into those thorns to get the best berries for your mom; it didn't matter if you got all scratched up. You saw the one you wanted, and you did what you needed to do to get it."

"Judah...?" I shake my head, but he shushes me. Puts two fingers right over my lips and presses softly. It's the closest I've ever come to a kiss.

"I was already in my chair by that time. I couldn't do that. Not even if I wanted to. It's funny," he says, "it took the wheelchair for me to see you ... to see a lot of things actually."

The candle is dancing, swinging light gently around the room. I study his face, wanting to hurry his words and savor them at the same time.

"I'm half a person," he says softly. "I'll always have limits, and I'll never have legs. Sometimes it makes me want to ... quit."

I swallow his "quit" because I too wanted to "quit," on many occasions. Namely when I am paralyzed by the thought that there might not be any more to this life than the Bone. A deep hollowness overtakes me, and I have to tell myself that I'm too young to know for sure. *Give it a few more years before you quit, Margo.* Right now, the thought of Judah quitting makes me panic.

"So what?" I say.

He looks at me. Waiting. I'm waiting too. I don't want to tangle my words—say something flippant. I'll never be good enough for Judah Grant, so I want my words to be what he's thirsty for. Meeting a need makes you feel more rooted. How do I know this? *Because I buy my mother cigarettes? Bring her tampons and saltines from the drugstore?*

"I have legs, Judah, and I don't know how to use them. Your life walks, and you're going to walk out of the Bone and be something. The rest of us, and our working legs, are going to live and die in the Bone."

"Margo..." his voice cracks. His chin dips to his chest, and I'm not sure if he's crying until I hear the sniff. He grabs me, before I can grab him, and he holds me tight.

"Margo," he says into my hair. "I'll save you, if you save me."

I nod, the words caught in my throat, sticky with emotion. That's the best deal life has ever offered me.

"Don't you feel like we need to do something?" I say to Judah a few days later. "Like really just jump up and *do* something." He is sprinkling green leaves onto a sheet of thin, white paper. I watch, transfixed, at the nimbleness of his fingers as he licks, then rolls.

"Like what?" he asks. "Start our own investigation?"

"Maybe," I snap. He finishes one joint and sets about rolling another.

"Let me try," I say, pushing his hands aside. He leans away from the table, an amused expression on his face. My knees press against the wheels of his chair. My fat, bulging knees. I hope he doesn't look down and notice. The wind picks up, and I can smell the tang of his skin—sweat and cologne.

"It's not as easy as it looks," I say. I don't like the way Judah's smell makes my body react.

"No, it isn't."

He's watching me closely. It makes me self-conscious. My hair is shaggy, and my skin is stained red from the sun exposure. My fingers fumble, and I spill flecks of green across the table.

"Easy there, Slim." Judah picks up a few pieces and drops them back onto the paper. I glance at him briefly to see if he's angry, but he's not even looking at me anymore. He's watching the trees across the street.

This morning, I got up early and met with one of the search groups scouring the woods on the east side of the Boubaton River. They gave us doughnuts and coffee and neon yellow vests to wear over our clothes as a safety precaution. Some of the police officers brought their dogs—great big German Shepherds wearing vests that said POLICE in bright yellow lettering down the side. We walked a straight line through the woods, looking for anything that might be out of place—a piece of ripped clothing, blood, hair. I grew more breathless with each step I took. Wondering if I would be the one to find Nevaeh.

Children went missing every day, with one percent of those cases making it into national news. People hurting kids. When it's a kid you know, one who rides the bus with you, and walks down the same shitty streets you've been walking down your whole life, it feels black. Evil was allowed to pick us off one by one, starting with the weakest.

"My joint sucks," I say, holding the fail between my fingertips. It's baggy. Some of the grass falls out one end and blows off the table when the breeze kicks up. He plucks it from my fingers and begins again.

"You are helping," he says. "You're searching the goddamn woods. What more could you do right now?"

"Find her," I say. "She's somewhere, right?"

It's the look on his face that sets me off. He tries to cover it with what I want to see: hope or something equally as pathetic. That's what I am, I guess—a pathetically hopeful human who wants to believe that a little girl is still alive. And even if she were, what condition would she be in after all this time? I shake my head, and my voice quivers a little when I say, "You don't have to look at me like that. Like I'm stupid or something."

"That's the last thing I think you are, Margo. The last. She's been missing for two months..." Has it really been two months? I think back to the last time I saw her. It was June; the sun had started to consistently shine. School had just let out, and all the children in the Bone had a wild excitement on their faces. Nevaeh had told me that her granny had given her two dollars for every 'A' she'd earned on her report card.

Ten dollars! She'd boasted proudly. *I'm going to save it and buy something really good.*

She never got to spend her money, I'm fairly certain of that. It was probably still in that little Hello Kitty wallet in her book bag, stuffed behind packets of Gushers and the purple teddy bear she kept hidden at the bottom. She'd called it Bambi.

I can't just leave her at home, she'd said, her little voice ringing sweet and vulnerable. *She goes where I go.*

I walk off, suddenly sore with grief, and leave Judah to smoke his blunt. Let him use his grass to curve the sharp edges. I would rather take them—feel the pain—because that was more real. What a hypocrite I am; I spend my whole life reading books that allude to happiness, when I refuse to experience it.

Sadness is an emotion you can trust. It is stronger than all of the other emotions. It makes happiness look fickle and untrustworthy. It pervades, lasts longer, and replaces the good feelings with such an eloquent ease you don't even feel the shift until you are suddenly wrapped in its chains. How hard we strive for happiness, and once we finally have the elusive feeling in our grasp, we hold it briefly, like water as it trickles through our fingers. I don't want to hold water. I want to hold something heavy and solid. Something I can understand. I understand sadness, and so I trust it. We are meant to feel sadness, if only to protect us from the brief spiels of happiness. Darkness is all I'll ever know; maybe the key is to make poetry out of it.

I find myself in the woods, touching the knotty bark of the trees and rubbing a leaf between my fingers. I think about Lyndee Anthony, Nevaeh's mother. I've seen her a few times standing on her porch, looking out at the street, her eyes darting to and fro, mimicking the movement of her brain. She is a thin woman, her dark hair cropped close to her scalp. She'd look almost childlike, except her features are sensual and full. Sometimes, when I used to see them together in town, I'd think that Nevaeh looked more like the adult than her mother. Nevaeh, with her all-seeing, soulful eyes. The steady movements of her body. Lyndee's eyes were hollow and bored. They reminded me of puppy eyes.

Ever since Nevaeh went missing, Lyndee's face has been on the front page of the *Harbor Bone*, drawn and sad. I started collecting the articles, the varying shades of Lyndee's sadness spread out on the covers with headlines such as: *'Mother pleads for information about her missing daughter;' 'Mother gives police new leads about missing girl.'* Nevaeh's father never showed during the first weeks of the search. It was rumored that when Lyndee called to tell him what had happened to their daughter, he asked for a paternity test. When the local news stations picked up the story, he changed his tune and began doing a series of teary-eyed interviews, claiming that Lyndee never let him see his daughter, and that would change as soon as they found her. I never for a second bought into his damp-eyed pandering for attention. And when the case died down a few months later, so did his act.

I walk out of the woods and approach the eating house from behind. The weeds tickle my calves as I trudge through the overgrowth of the yard. The line my mother once hung our wet clothes on has snapped free of its pole. I pick up the loose end and examine it. I look up to see my mother's drapes parted, her face staring down at me. We catch eyes for a moment before I look away first. When I look down at my hand I realize I've rubbed a hole in my leaf.

AUGUST IN THE BONE is summer's hot breath, mixed with the cinnamon sweet smell of the nootka roses. The claustrophobia gets to you. It makes you feel like you can't breathe, and then you do something loony like Velda Baumgard over on Thames Street, who skinned the family dog and fed it to her family because she was tired of his barking.

I cross the street and walk under the cover of the trees, which are bright shades of lime green and deep hunter. Weeds press themselves through cracks in the street and sidewalks, flowers bloom where they shouldn't—a cluster of daffodils from the side of the Bone Harbor Bank, begonias hanging from the overpass on Twelfth and Laurel almost touching the roofs of the cars. There is even a small field of lilacs next to Wal-Mart, where you can often see people standing, admiring the wildness of it. In the summer, everything is lush and plump with life—even the people. They stop complaining about how Harpersfield, a town ten miles away, has a Safeway and a QFC and a little shopping area with cobbled streets where you can drink designer lattes and see a movie at the Eight.

They forget, and they grill hot dogs and graying beef patties in their yards, inviting their friends over to drink lukewarm beer and gossip. In the summer, they forget that their jobs pay minimum wage, and that their cars need new brakes, and that the rain will soon come to wash away their smiles. In summer, the people of the Bone hum and laugh and let the sun melt their worries. But Nevaeh has ruined the summer this year. People are searching the woods instead of grilling. Looking around wearily instead of turning their faces toward the sun. We all feel it.

I forgo the bus and walk the five miles to work most days. It's not so bad. I eat a granola bar as I walk, a ritual I've come to enjoy—my hard steps and the oats and raisins rolling around in my mouth. It feels very organic to be walking through the Bone in the summer, eating granola. Evenings, when I leave the Rag, I grab a coffee from the food truck and walk my way back to the eating house. Within a few weeks, my normally pasty skin has acquired that deep tan that Judah once mentioned, and my pants hang around my hips like loose skin. My hope is renewed by the brief, three-month respite from the rain. But there is a dampness to it as well, a rotting guilt. A little girl is missing, her mother is suffering, her grandmother so distraught she no longer leaves her little house on Cambridge Ave. I want to go to her, offer my services in some way—anything to ease her suffering. But, in the end, I am just a stranger, and the most I do is whisper a prayer when I walk past her house. My words blow away as quickly as they leave my lips. There is no comfort for the broken.

Nevaeh was the younger version of me, except she had a grandmother who loved her. That one difference could have centered everything in her life. When I was Nevaeh's age, I spent hours fantasizing about a father who never knew I existed, but would want me as soon as he knew I did. He'd take me from the eating house, from the Bone, and he'd demand to know me. He'd spend hours accumulating information about my person with the rapt attention of a man in love. I imagine that being wanted is the greatest feeling. A feeling that solidifies your stay in this life, justifies it.

When Judah Grant offers his friendship in the form of his porch, talking about books and listening to music, I take it. I feel dizzy at first, confused about why. But, then I fall into the routine of it, and forget to overthink. On the days I don't go into the Rag, we make a day of living. We trade dog-eared paperbacks, reading them in the sun while Delaney carries out Bagel Bites and mini carrots on her chipped china.

"She loves this," Judah says to me one day. "She's always wanted me to bring my friends home, but my real friends are too sick to come, and the people here are too sick to be invited."

"Sick from what?" I ask, thinking they might have the stomach virus that has been going around.

"From life, Margorita. Walk into any school or aftercare program here and you'll find a bunch of sticky-faced kids wearing clothes that are either too small for them, or so rough from the wear that their knees and elbows are falling out of the holes. But, if you go to their parents' house, you'll find them well stocked with their coping mechanisms: weed, alcohol, drugs…"

"So what's your point?" I ask, thinking about my own raggedy wardrobe, the holes in the elbows of my favorite sweater. My mother's medicine cabinet stocked with Seroquel, Opana, and jumbo bottles of Ambien, which she's hoarded.

"It's not about the clothes," he says. "It's the principle. The excuses and the selfishness. People want a different life, but they get pulled down by the same life their parents lived; same town, same poverty, same struggles. They have their own kids and remember the promise they made to themselves to get the hell outta Dodge. But, they don't get out of Dodge, because it's not that easy. So they take it out on themselves, their kids, their neighbors. It's an excuse, sure. There are plenty of opportunities, scholarships, grants. All you have to do is be brave and jump. It helps if you're smart, and well spoken, and well dressed. Because no one is going to hire someone who uses too many double negatives, or speaks through their rotten teeth, or is wearing a dress they bought at Wal-Mart. Not if you want the job that can change your life. "

"You smoke pot," I point out.

"Yeah, I do. My mother grows it." He shrugs. "She never took from me to feed herself. She wanted marijuana, so she grew it instead of shortchanging her kid."

I don't believe him right away. The people from the Bone were stepped on; the younger ones, not yet bitter from the world, have a steely determination in their eyes to live a better existence than the ones their parents lived. They are trying to be better.

"Listen to their conversations," he says. "They want something more, but they don't have the courage to try it out. Plus, I'm going to have to stop soon; I got into the teaching program at UW."

I make a squealing noise and throw my arms around his neck.

On my way home I think about what Judah said. The problem of clothing your kids is an epidemic in the Bone. Most of the families are on government assistance. My mother refused the little blue card with her name on it, and made me fend for myself instead. I faked ADD through most of middle and high school, so I could sell the Adderall they prescribed me to the upper classmen. I needed lunch money. When I found my mother's hidey-hole in the eating house, I was miraculously cured.

I remember the woman who tried to steal the six dollar Jordan's, so filled with liquor she could barely form a coherent sentence, yet she was determined to put shoes on the feet of Zeek, even if she had to steal them. And that was her choice, not Zeek's. Judah was right.

A week later I hear two women talking in the Rag. One is complaining about her boss refusing to give her the raise she deserves. Her companion clicks her tongue in disgust, assuring her that she's been with the company long enough to deserve one.

Their conversation suddenly turns when the first woman tells her friend: *He did say that if I moved to the branch in Seattle, I would get one. But I can't leave Meemaw, and all of my friends are here...*

No, no, her friend assures her. *Leaving would be stupid. How could you afford to live in Seattle? Those people have money to begin with.*

I want to scream out and tell her to take the risk. Go!

I feel a stirring of hatred for what we are forced to become here in the Bone, and what we are too weak to escape. *I'll get out,* I tell myself. *As soon as I can.*

And so will Judah, who is too tall for this place, even in his wheelchair.

JUDAH AND I outgrow the rest of the Bone and cleave to one another. Nothing is better than the discovery of another living, breathing human, who fights the same as you do, loves the same as you do, and understands you with such clarity that it feels erotic. A friendship between the fat, ugly girl and the crippled, handsome boy. It is a friendship that we both had waited for. One we both needed.

We unite our strengths and make plans to leave the Bone. We have inside jokes, and movie quotes, and foods that neither of us like. And isn't that the best thing—to not like something together? Our days are revelations, filled with talk about studio apartments and going to Pike Place Market on weekends to buy fruit that actually tastes like fruit, and to walk along the Sound and watch the ferries. Judah has been to Seattle many times, his school just a short drive away. I question him about the sights and the sounds, the people with their tattoos and multi-colored hair. The people in Seattle are accepting and liberal. They don't judge you—he tells me. A crippled man is just another human with valuable ideas. I wonder if an ugly girl will be valued. If I can make something of myself without using my looks or body to do it.

"It's stupid to talk about these things," I tell him.

He shakes his head. "No, it's never stupid to dream. Dreams are plans; they get your heart moving, and once your heart gets moving, your brain will follow."

I don't know if I believe him, but I pretend I do, for my brain's sake.

"What kind of movies do you like?" he asks me one day. We'd spent most of the day exchanging theories about Nevaeh, our conversation eventually ebbing into a thick silence.

I didn't know. With Destiny, I'd watch movies like *The Notebook*, *The Wedding Date* and *Ever After*. When we got bored with the modern romantic comedies we'd dip into the eighties, watching things like *When Harry Met Sally* and *Moonstruck*, at first laughing at the high hair and neon-colored clothes and then becoming serious and drugged at the heady dosage of love that Hollywood delivered. My favorite movie from my time spent on Destiny's red and black striped couch had always been *Splash*, though Destiny made fun of me for it.

"Of all the lovey movies out there, you like the one about a damn mermaid," she'd said. "The most unrealistic of them all…"

What I didn't tell Destiny was that I thought love was unrealistic in general. The pretentious chance meeting, the swift slide into love, and then the ability of the men to always say the right words to win back the heart of the heroine. *Splash* may be outlandish, but love is, too. It is nice to watch, and foolish to believe in. Perhaps I don't like romantic comedies as much as I thought.

"I don't know," I say to Judah. "I've always watched the type of movies that make you believe in love even when you have no reason to. It's silly and babyish. I guess I just want someone to convince me."

"Do you have cable?" he asks.

"Cable? I don't even have a television," I tell him. For a moment I am a space alien to Judah Grant. I touch my face to make sure nothing's changed or become deformed in the last few minutes as he gapes at me.

"What?!" I snap. "Why are you looking at me like that?"

His mouth is open, and his eyes are spacey.

"I'm just thinking about all the movies I want you to watch. I'm making a list … shh."

I sit quietly while Judah scribbles things down on the back of a receipt. He doesn't judge me or call me a freak. All he's concerned about is showing me what I don't know, not calling attention to that fact that I don't know it. When he's done, he looks at me expectantly.

"Let's go," he says.

"Where to?"

"Where do you think? he asks. "The movie store! And you should probably go home to get pajamas; this is going to be an all-night sleepover binge."

Judah wheels himself out of the house and onto the sidewalk with gusto. I follow dumbly behind, wondering if he was serious about the sleepover. I've only been in his home a few times, and never past the kitchen—except for the night he called my name from the window.

We are making our way along the sidewalk when, from two houses down, Mother Mary calls my name.

Mother Mary, namer of your death, so wrinkled that she looks more mummified than real. I make my way over to her house, careful not to let the fear show on my face, careful not to step on the cracks in the sidewalk. I heard she docked a year off your life for every crack you stepped on.

I stand at the bottom of the three stairs that lead to her front door. Judah is behind me, waiting at the border of the swampy grass that is the start of Mother Mary's property.

She stands on the top step, her tiny frame looming over me. Is it my imagination, or are her eyes blue? Blue eyes amidst the dark, coppery skin. I've never been close enough to see her eyes. She extends a hand and beckons me up the stairs. I follow the tiny, purple buds of her fingernails to a rocking chair, where she has me sit. An invitation by Mother Mary can only mean one thing. Judah is spinning his chair in circles on the sidewalk. He wants to go to the movie store.

I laugh out loud as I watch him. Mother Mary lowers herself into the rocker next to me and watches my face.

"You look over there with such love?" she says. Her voice is strong and smooth, not at all what I expected.

"No," I say. "It's not like that … he's my friend." I'm alarmed that my feelings for Judah are so obvious.

Mother Mary rocks back and forth while eyeing Judah.

I wonder how she knows my name.

"He," she says. "Gives you hope?"

"Yes," I say.

"Then keep him," she says with so much finality, I glance up at her face to see if she's kidding. After that, the silence stretches so long I begin to squirm in my seat.

I open my mouth to offer an excuse to leave, when Mother Mary cuts me off.

"Your mother," she says.

"Yes..." I urge her.

Judah does a wheelie and spins around on his back tires.

"She's between worlds, can't decide where she wants to be. You are much the same—you and her."

I want to tell her that my mother decided long ago where she wanted to be—safely locked up in the eating house, locked up even tighter in herself. And then it occurs to me what she's saying about my cold, hard-eyed mother. Could she be entertaining thoughts of her own death? To escape what? The box she put herself in?

I look over at the elderly woman, too frail to be frightening. Why have I always feared Mother Mary?

"Haven't you heard?" I say softly. "Only the good die young."

"You can change that," she says.

I stand up then and begin to descend the stairs, my legs heavier than they were a few minutes ago, before she called to me.

"Margo..."

She's standing, and both of her arms are extended toward me, as if she wants to enfold me into them.

I take the short, two steps back up the stairs, where Mother Mary wraps me in a hug. I am surprised by her strength, the fierceness with which she holds me. She smells of cinnamon and hair relaxer—a smell I grew accustomed to at Destiny's house, where her mother did hair in their small, third bedroom.

"You must not let hatred destroy you. You will lose your soul," she says.

I don't look at her as I walk back to the boy who she says gives me hope. I want to tell her that she need not worry about my soul. This boy will save it.

SANDY COMES OUT OF THE OFFICE and tells us that they found the little girl's body—the one who went missing. It's all over the news. They found her in a field near the old harbor, burned to blackness.

I think of Nevaeh, the bright, innocent beauty of her all burned to blackness, and I run to the bathroom to vomit. I ask Sandy for a break, and she says no; we're too busy today. I have to go back to the register.

I ring people up in a trance and wonder if it was one of them who killed Nevaeh. My hands are shaking, and one of the customers leans in conspiratorially and asks if I need a fix. A fix? I want to laugh. How do you fix evil?

By the time my shift is done, I'm angry. I stand on the bus, bouncing on my heels until my stop. Then I jog to Judah's house. When I knock on the door, Delaney answers holding Horace and reeking of weed. She looks surprised to see me. Judah is right behind her in the kitchen, and when he hears my voice, he calls out to her to let me in.

"Did you hear?" I ask. He nods. I'm breathless from my running. Delaney props Horace against the wall and has me sit down at the kitchen table. She brings me a glass of something sweet and red. I hold the glass between my hands, but I can't drink it. I still feel like I'm going to be sick.

"I hate everything."

Judah runs his finger along the outline of his lips. He looks like he's thinking deeply about something.

"It's all over the news," Delaney says.

I look at Judah. "What are you thinking?"

"What if it was someone from here, in this neighborhood, that did that to her. One of us."

"It could have been someone coming through the Bone. Doesn't mean they're from here."

He nods, but he's not committed to that nod. I stand up. "I have to go," I say.

"Where?" Judah asks.

"Are you sure you're okay?" Delaney says.

"Dunno. I need to think."

I walk the Bone in the drizzling rain. Up and down the streets, counting the scattered, balled up candy wrappers, until I am so cold my whole body is shaking. I walk past Nevaeh's house. I want her to come running down the stairs like she always did when she saw me, her shoelaces flying around like a scraped knee waiting to happen. I want to steal her away before someone can steal her life away, and show her something other than the Bone. I want to show myself something other than the Bone. I don't even know if that's possible. Judah says that where we're from is in us—in our marrow. You can put us anywhere else in the world, but we carry our origin with us everywhere we go. If he's right, I'll never fucking get away.

My new Converse are soaked through when I reach the end of the Bone. The highway that runs through our town is 83. It's non-committal, winding this way then veering off like it can't decide if it wants to be with us or not. If I keep walking, I'll end up in the Cascades. I pass a hand over my face to wipe the rain out of my eyes. I should do it. Keep walking. Die trying. Anything to get out of here.

Ugh! I kick at a puddle. *Kick, kick all you want. You're too shit scared to leave.*

I turn back, overcome. Shame drags my head down. I watch my cowardly feet plod through the puddles, water flowing down my neck, until I spot a blur of red in a pool of water. Bright red. I bend at the knees to retrieve it, my hand plunging into the little puddle without thought. I pull up a pair of sunglasses with red, plastic heart frames. Without hesitation I put them on.

Like the emotional defeatist I am, I stop at the Quickie Corner when I get back to town. I eye the rack of my usual choices: Honey Buns, Pecan Wheels, Oatmeal Crème Pies, Cosmic Brownies, Ding Dongs, Twinkies, and powdered doughnuts. They're all on sale, but I can't eat that shit today. Or maybe ever again. I don't want to kill myself *that* way. I walk over to the refrigerators at the back of the store and choose an orange juice. I grab a super-sized box of raisins and a box of matches that has a teddy bear on them, which reminds me of Nevaeh. I feel around in my pockets for my money.

"What's that for ... you don't smoke?"

Joe. We call him Knick Knack because he collects porcelain figurines of the Virgin Mary and hides them all over the store. Sometimes you'd pull a loaf of bread off a shelf, and the Holy Virgin would be right there, staring straight at you

"I'm going to commit arson," I say, pushing it toward him. "I'll need a gallon of gas, too."

Knick Knack Joe reaches below the register and puts an empty gas can on the counter. It's red with a spout, and someone's written *I'm Gassy* on the side in sharpie. "You'll need this, too," he says, grinning. "Who you burning?"

I roll my eyes. "Everyone," I say. I leave a crumpled ten on the counter and start to walk out. "You forgot your can!" he calls back.

"What?" I say, turning to look at him.

He pushes it toward me. "It's a gift," he says. "For your project."

I don't know why, but I take it.

I don't take the normal way home, on the sidewalk, past the houses. I walk along the grass next to the highway, wearing my glasses, carrying my gas can. *Winner, winner, chicken dinner*, I think.

"Hey Gassy." A rusted, brown pick up slows down next to me. Two men sit in shadow in the cab of the vehicle. An arm covered in red flannel hangs limply out the window, a single finger tapping the side of the door in time with the music on the radio. I can see the outline of a baseball cap on the driver. "Want a ride?"

I poke up my middle finger, letting them know how much I want a ride.

"Don't be like that, baby. A girl like you has to take what she can get."

Their laughter is like fingernails on a chalkboard, the keys of a piano being pounded on by a toddler. I am the joke. The hapless fat girl who needs two strangers to give her a ride and feel her up in the smelly cab of a truck. Fuck them. I throw my bottle of orange juice at their car. Fuck the whole world for making me feel like a loser when my life has barely begun. One of them throws a can out the window—beer. It hits the ground near my feet and sprays my legs. There is a kench of laughter as they speed off, kicking up gravel a few feet ahead of me, before swerving back onto the road. The back of the truck fishtails for several seconds, then the tires cling to the tar and propel them forward. I can see two heads through the back window. Two drunken idiots polluting the planet. I wish I had the power to flip their truck before they flipped someone else's. Life is all about allowing people choices to be who they want. But the majority of people choose to be worthless. Not me, uh uh.

I've never been to the ocean, never heard the waves lick the sand in that quiet shushing you read about in books. I've never been to the zoo, smelled the elephant piss, and heard the cries of the monkeys. I've never had frozen yogurt from one of those places where you pull on the handle and fill your own cup with whatever you like. I've never eaten dinner at a restaurant with napkins that you set on your lap and silverware that isn't plastic. I've never painted my nails like the other girls at school, in bright neons and decadent reds. I've never been more than ten miles from home. Ten miles. It's like I live in the forever ago, not where buses rumble and trains have tracks. I've never had a birthday cake, though I've wanted one very much. I've never owned a bra that is new, and had to cut the tags off with the scissors from the kitchen drawer. I've never been loved in a way that makes me feel as if I was supposed to be born, if only to feel loved. I've never, I've never, I've never. And it's my own fault. The things that we never do because someone makes us fearful of them, or makes us believe we don't deserve them. I want to do all my nevers—alone or with someone who matters. I don't care. I just want to live. Nevaeh never had any of those things either—and now she never will.

I can't stay the way I am. I don't remember what it's like to be free. To be wide open without fear. I need something to break me.

Just enough so that I have new pieces to work with—make them into something else. I don't want to give anyone the right to treat me like a loser. I don't want to be fat, I don't want to live in the Bone, I don't want to be without knowledge. I won't be the girl who people laugh at. Not anymore. Good thing I memorized their license plate. Just in case.

A WEEK LATER, a rusted brown pickup truck sits in the parking lot of Wal-Mart. I am supposed to be buying more granola, and shampoo for my mother, but all I can do is stand on the curb and stare. The license plate matches the one in my memory. I stare into the window; it's filthy—trash and mud everywhere, a waterlogged copy of a nudey magazine lies on the floorboards, a piece of blue gum stuck over the model's exposed breasts.

The door is unlocked. I climb into the driver's seat and place my hands on the wheel. It stinks of manure and stale beer. I breathe through my mouth and try to picture what goes on in a jackass's head. Probably everything that's littering the floors of his truck: sex, food, and beer. I bend to retrieve the magazine, paging though the pictures, flinching past spread legs, and hard, round, baseball tits. Glossy lips, parted to remind men of all the places a woman's body can accommodate them. I tear off one page, then another. I keep tearing until the magazine is a ripped pile of tits and ass and feathered hairdos, then I scatter them across the cab of the truck. There is a hammer in a toolbox on the seat next to me. *A fix it man!* I pick it up, weigh it in my hand, then I swing it at the windshield.

Crack!

The glass splinters straight across. I like the way it looks, so I hit it again to make sure he won't be able to see when he drives. As an afterthought I look around to see if anyone is watching me. There is a mother a few cars away, wrestling her screaming twins into her car, but she is too distracted to notice me. I dig around the toolbox until I find a box cutter. Climbing out of the truck, I lower myself to my haunches, flipping the switch to draw out the blade. An old station wagon is to my back, and beyond that the field of lilacs. If the driver of the truck leaves Wal-Mart now, I won't be able to see him coming. I should feel something, fear or anxiety, but I don't. I don't feel anything. On the side of the truck I carve the words: I DRINK AND DRIVE, AND I HAVE A SMALL DICK. When I'm finished I toss the box cutter into the back of the truck. Dusting my hands on my pants, I head into Wal-Mart to do my shopping. Until the windshield cracked, I hadn't realized I'd been holding such a grudge. The minute the hammer hit the glass it was as if everything surged out of me all at once. Anger, so much of it. I decide that there must be more grudges hiding in me. I wonder what it would feel like to exact revenge on people.

My mother has left me a note to get cigarettes. I sit at the kitchen table and tap it with my forefinger as I stare out the window and watch a jay until it takes to the sky. *Cigarettes*, it says. No smiley face to soften the command hidden in those neat, curlicue letters; no lopsided heart. Just *Cigarettes*.

She is floating around the kitchen in her red gown—right in front of my face—but she left me a note rather than tell me herself. I've long stopped asking *why?* Why, as it turns out, is the most self-indulgent waste of time. There is no real reason for her to be in the kitchen. We are out of the crackers she likes, and I stopped buying coffee to piss her off. I'm comatose, watching the linoleum like it's *Fargo*. I saw that movie once at Destiny's house. We were supposed to watch *When Harry Met Sally*, but someone had already checked it out at the video store. So we watched *Fargo* instead. All that snow and those weird accents. It was just a different kind of ghetto from the one where I live—full of hopeless, worried humans. I've never met anyone from Minnesota, and I don't want to. That's what I'm thinking as my mother floats around the kitchen demanding cigarettes. I think about Jean Lundegaard. Running around the house covered in the shower curtain until she falls down the stairs.

She was stupid, and she wore ugly sweaters, but she didn't deserve that.

She wants her cigarettes, and I just want to sit here and think about *Fargo*. I wish I had a better movie to think about. All that snow...

If she asked, I would tell her about Nevaeh. How I'm grieving for a little girl I saw around the neighborhood. Children shouldn't have to suffer. To be alone. To feel unloved.

I get up and walk out of the kitchen. Out the front door. I'll go get the cigarettes.

When I walk past Judah's house, he's sitting outside in his chair, slapping at the bugs landing on his arms.

"Hey Margo!" he calls. "Where you going?"

"To say goodbye to Nevaeh." *And also to buy cigarettes.*

"Take me with you." I don't question him. I just walk up the pathway to his house and push his chair toward the street. He's wearing one of the shirts I bought for him from the Rag—the one with the little hearts. It looks good on him, which makes me sour. I can't even take him down when I try. He's quiet as the wheels of his chair squeak across the pavement. One of his hands is up and under his chin as he looks off to the side. His eyelashes are black and thick. They remind me of broom bristles, and then I feel ashamed that I'm comparing a man's eyelashes to broom bristles. He must have gotten those from his dad since Delaney is as fair as I am.

"Do you have your groceries and shit bag?" he asks me suddenly.

"Yeah." I move my body so he can see it hanging at my waist.

"Good," he says. "There is a memorial for Nevaeh, over at her mom's house."

I'm quiet for a moment. I wonder if he wants to go. I walk past the corner store where I usually buy my mother's cigarettes and turn toward the main road. "Let's go get her some flowers," Judah says. There's a Wal-Mart a few blocks up. I tell him that's where I'm going. He points out a secondary pathway that's not quite as bumpy as the one we're on, and I wheel him over. As we walk, people call out to him.

"Hey Judah."

"What's up, Judah."

"What's up, man. You look good."

"Wanna come hang out tonight? We gonna play poker, and Billy is bringing over his shit."

Judah declines multiple invitations to "hang out" and tells them he's going to Nevaeh's memorial.

"Who?" they ask.

"The little girl they found by the harbor. Man, where the hell is your head?"

Their eyes darken at that point. *Yeah man, that's some shit,* they say. *Fucked up, that's what it is. That shit happening to a little kid.*

Judah tells them to come to the memorial. He tells them she was one of us, and we have to go remember her.

Everyone knows him. They give me strange looks, like I'm the one in the wheelchair. It's because they don't see his chair. Judah is Judah. How large does a person's humanity have to be to look past their big, clunky wheelchair? I wonder how large I can make myself so that no one will see my fat, or my mother, or my ugly face? Then they'll call out.

"Hey Margo."

"What's up, Margo."

"Looking good, Margo."

I give the back of Judah's head a dirty look.

We go straight to the toy aisle in Wal-Mart. I choose a stuffed unicorn, because I'd like to believe Nevaeh is somewhere better—magical. Judah wants to get flowers. He asks me to grab a bunch of rainbow carnations that he can't reach. I hand them to him, and for a little moment our hands are wrapped around the same bunch of flowers. He squeezes my fingers like he knows I'm hurting.

"Can you hand me the roses too?" he asks.

He holds the flowers and the unicorn while I wheel his chair to checkout lane. After we pay, he hands me the roses.

"These are for you," he says. A woman walks by, her arms loaded with blue and white bags, and looks at us strangely.

I must look dumbfounded, because he presses them into my hands and says, "I'm sorry about Nevaeh."

I clutch the roses, my eyes brimming with tears. No one has ever bought me flowers. I try to be normal as I wheel him out the door and back into the street. I won't let go of the roses even when he offers to hold them for me. I don't let my tears spill, or my heart spill. Tonight is about Nevaeh, and I won't be selfish.

Since the local news picked up Nevaeh's story, there is a bigger turnout than I expected. There is a large crowd gathered outside the squat, blue house she shared with her mother and eight other people. I see her grandmother standing in the swamp of humans, crying into her hands. People have stuck letters and pictures into the chain link fence around the house. Nevaeh's school picture is there in the middle of the chaos. I stare at it long and hard so I won't ever forget her face. There are piles of teddy bears, and bouquets, and toys that her classmates have left for her—some with letters scrawled in little kid handwriting. I push Judah's wheelchair to the front of the crowd so he can give her his flowers. He lays them down gently, in front of a note that says, *We love you, Nevaeh. You're safe in God's arms now.*

It's my turn next. I kneel in front of the fence and bow my head so no one can see my tears. It's just a stupid unicorn from Wal-Mart, but I want Nevaeh to see it and know that I love her. Loved her. Love her still.

"This isn't right," I say. Judah looks at me earnestly.

"No," he says. "It's not. So what are you going to do about it?"

"Me?" I shake my head. "What can I do? I'm no one. The police—"

"No," he says. "You know how the police handle things. We're nobodies. A little girl dying in this neighborhood isn't anything new."

"The way she died is," I say. "And somebody has to pay attention."

His jaw tightens, and he looks away. "If only I weren't in this goddamn chair."

That makes me feel hot. I get a tingling in my fingertips, and I want to shake him.

"I hate to break it to you, Judah, but everyone in the Bone has a wheelchair. One way or the other, we are all fucked."

He glares at me, I glare at him. I wish I could glare at someone and look as if my cheekbones were carved out of marble. I look away first.

The tension between us is broken by Neveah's mother, who at that moment walks out of the blue house carrying a candle. There wasn't enough money to hand out candles to everyone, so people take lighters and hold them toward Nevaeh's picture. Judah lets me hold his lighter. It's a pink Zippo.

"My mom's," he says.

"No judgment."

He chews on the inside of his cheek; I've seen him do it a few times now. I sort of like it.

We all huddle around Nevaeh's school picture with our lighters and tears. Someone starts to sing "Amazing Grace," but no one knows the words to the third verse, so we just keep singing the chorus over and over. When the Grace runs its course, one of the local pastors steps up in front of the crowd. He hugs Nevaeh's mom and says a prayer.

"She isn't crying," I whisper to Judah.

"Shock," he says.

I look over at Nevaeh's grandmother. She has people on either side of her, holding her up. She can barely breathe, she's sobbing so hard. In the dim light of the streetlamp, I can see the tears smudged all over her cheeks and chin, the blue bandana on her head pushed crooked so the knot stands out above her ear. A grieving woman, her pain clear and sharp like the vodka I once tried at Destiny's house. I reach for Judah's hand. At first he looks surprised, his gaze passing over my face and then our clasped fingers. I don't look at him. I fix my gaze straight ahead. He squeezes my hand and looks back at Nevaeh's picture.

He does not ask me to push him home. He never does. Sometimes he needs help past the dents and ruts in the sidewalk, which I do without comment. Our relationship is seamless so that no one need feel guilty. I help him up the ramp to his front door, and he asks me to wait outside. I stand on the porch looking out over Delaney's yard, her pretty flowers and bushes a shock of beauty down an ugly street. When Judah comes back, he's holding a bottle of something brown.

"I'm too young to drink," I tell him.

"You're too young to have seen such ugly things, too."

I take the bottle from him, my only memory of alcohol being that one sip of vodka Destiny and I took from her father's bottle when no one was home. I lift it to my lips. The rum is spicy and sweet. I prefer it to the vodka. There is a pirate on the label. He reminds me of the Indian chief on my mother's healthy cigarettes. Indians and pirates—societal derelicts representing American addiction. I'd much prefer their company to the rest. We pass the bottle back and forth until I am too dizzy to stand up, then we sit quietly and look at the stars.

THE EATING HOUSE IS OPPRESSIVELY HOT. I carry my book outside and sit on the step. Mo is pushing Little Mo up and down the street in a hot pink stroller. He has his phone between his shoulder and his ear, and he's punctuating every sentence with the F-bomb. F-bomb this, F-bomb that. The stroller has a wonky wheel, so every time he hits a crack in the sidewalk, it veers to the right, and Little Mo is thrown sideways, a startled look on his face. I watch him circle the block, past the bad people house, past Mother Mary's house, right until he reaches Delaney and Judah's house, where he turns the stroller around and heads back. When he approaches the eating house for the third time, I jump up and block his path.

I mouth: *I'll take him.* Mo walks away without a word and leaves me with the baby and the stroller. I hear him F-bombing his way back to the crack house. I unbuckle the baby. He barely looks at me. I know there's something wrong with him, but they don't, and you can't very well tell people that their baby has a disability. His diaper is soaked through. I find a spare and some bottles in the basket at the bottom, and carry him inside. My mother is in the kitchen, leaning against the counter, smoking a cigarette, and looking out the window. *Look at you, wanting to see shit outside,* I think, as I kick the door shut.

"Whose baby is that?"

I'm startled by the sound of her voice, raspy from the healthy cigarettes. I haven't heard it in some time.

"Mo's."

"He shouldn't be in here."

I feel a tingle in my chest. *What is that? Anger?* "Why not?" I ask, holding him close to my chest.

She glares at me from her cloud of smoke. "He doesn't live here."

"But I do," I say. "And if you can have guests, so can I."

I don't know where that came from. But life has already made Mo feel unwelcome; I'm not going to let her do it, too. I carry him to the sofa in the living room, without checking her reaction, and lay him down. My mother follows behind me.

"What are you doing?"

This is the most she's said to me in months. I don't look at her when I say, "Changing his diaper." If I look at her, I'll lose my resolve. She'll bully me into leaving, and right now I just want to get this baby out of his piss-wet clothes. She leans over the back of the couch to look at him. I can smell the vanilla perfume she uses; it mingles with the stale smell of cigarette smoke.

"That baby isn't right," she says after a minute of staring at him. "I'll bet you anything that bitch of a girlfriend Mo has was using when she was pregnant." I don't know how my mother knows about Mo's bitch of a girlfriend, or that he even has a girlfriend. For someone who never sees the light of day, she appears to be well informed.

"There's nothing wrong with him," I say. He's kicking his legs contentedly, happy to be free of his diaper.

"No, of course not," she says. "And he doesn't have the worst case of diaper rash I've ever seen either."

She's right. His skin is inflamed. The worst part is, he's not even crying. My mother disappears from the room, and I think she's gone up to her bedroom when she strolls back in, her red robe billowing around her legs. She hands me a tube of A&D ointment. "Wash him over the sink. Don't use wipes. Dry him and leave his butt bare for a while."

She floats back to her cave, and I hold the A&D in my hand for a long time before I do what she says. No one comes to get Mo. I feed him one of the bottles I found in the stroller, and when it starts to get dark, I carry him home, dragging the wonky-wheeled stroller behind me. When adult Mo answers the door, he looks annoyed.

"Oh shit," he says when he sees the baby in my arms. "I forgot."

He reaches for him, but I steer my hip left so the baby is out of his reach.

"He has diaper rash. It's bad." I hand him the A&D. "Leave him without a diaper for a while so it can clear up."

Mo looks annoyed that I'm telling him what to do. I want to add, *And stop cooking crack in your basement before you blow him up.* But that's the type of shit that gets you in trouble around here.

"Where's Vola?" I ask, hoping Little Mo's mother is somewhere around to take care of him. Mo's eyes glaze over at the mention of her name.

"That buckwild bitch. Hell should I know?" *Ah, so they're fighting again.* I want to tell him that he can leave Mo with me until she comes back, but he's already slammed the door in my face.

I start to walk home, but I don't want to be there. She will find a way to punish me for bringing the baby inside—both her and the house. Judah is with his dad tonight, wherever that is. *Somewhere better than here,* I think. I walk up the street, then back down again. Mother Mary, who is sitting in a rocking chair on her stoop, waves at me. I wave back. The bad people house is throbbing with music, although none of the usual glassy-eyed inhabitants are outside tonight. Past the eating house there is a small path that leads through the trees and into the woods. It's overgrown now because nobody goes back there, but when I was little, and my mom left the house, we'd walk the path every day. My mom would say, "The leaves have varicose veins, Margo. Looky..."

I head there now, picking my way through the blackberry bushes, only half aware of the thorns nipping at my bare arms. I used to think these woods were mine, that they belonged to the eating house and whoever owned it. Now I know its part of the city. Protected wetlands, and trees, and birds.

Carpet growing up trees. Logs furred with moss. Leaves furled on the edges, burned brown by the sun. Most importantly there are flowers growing everywhere. Why don't I come here more often?

I walk for a long time. I'm heading west toward the water. If I keep walking, I'll come to the place where they found Nevaeh's body. I don't want to do that, so I head east. A little over a mile later I walk right into a wooden shack. It's a storage shack, just large enough for a lawnmower and some tools. What it's doing out here, I don't know. The door is unhinged, and it's mostly covered in moss. I step inside, brushing away cobwebs and the egg sacs that insects have left behind. It's empty, aside from a rusted shovel and a box of generic, unopened garbage bags that sit on a stool in the center. The box is so faded I can barely make out the writing. It's a place you could come to do secret things. It's a wonder the high schoolers haven't found it. They are always looking for a new place to smoke pot in peace. I pull the door closed and head back home, mentally making note of the fastest way to get to the shack. You never know when you'll need to use something like that.

MY FAT IS GONE AND NONE OF MY CLOTHES FIT. I don't care because they suck anyway, but you have to have shit to cover your flesh, because people will stare if you walk around fat and naked. My mother keeps a box of her fat clothes in the attic. I don't know when my mother was ever fat, but I go scrounging around up there for something to wear. She wore a lot of high-waisted, cut-off jean shorts, with the edges fraying and tangled, cut so short the pockets peek out the bottom. There are half a dozen flannel shirts in there, too, and a pair of bright blue Doc Martens. She said that after she had me her feet grew a full size, and she had to throw away all of her old shoes. I carry my spoils back to my bedroom and spread them out on my mattress.

"What were you doing up there?" My mother stands in my doorway, arms folded across her chest like she's cold.

"Up where?" I shake out the clothes and hold them up to get a good look. I'm shaken by the fact that she's talking to me, but I don't let it show. I don't hate her presence, just her lack of it.

"I heard you," she says. "In the attic…"

I ignore her, spreading, holding things up to my chest to check the size. If she looked closely, she'd be able to see the tremor in my hands.

"What is that?" She steps around me and looks down at the pile. Shock registers on her face, the lines that tell her age cut deeper as she frowns.

"Put that back," she says.

I spin around.

"Then give me money to buy clothes…" I hold out my hand like I expect her to palm me a fifty, but she's looking at the Docs like they're a ghost.

"You shouldn't wear things like that," she says, pulling her robe tighter around her shoulders. "Men will get the wrong idea. Even if you're not pretty, they'll think…"

"What are you talking about?" I'm holding up a T-shirt to get a good look at it. Nirvana. It still has the knot tied into the bottom. I glance over at her face and put down the shirt. My mother is the type who is always looking for a reason to be angry. She *tsssked* and huffed and stomped around the eating house over the slightest thing. Now she is angry I pulled her old clothes out of retirement. Like she could wear them anyway. She is a toothpick human, all bone and sharp edges, always buried beneath that robe.

"I was … my daddy, he—"

I lay the shirt down.

"He what?"

She shakes her head. "You shouldn't wear clothes like that," she reiterates. But I don't want to let it go. She was going to tell me something before she decided against it, and I want to know what.

"Did he do something to you?" I press. I try not to look intense; I don't want to scare her off. But my eyes are drilling into her.

She bites the corner of her lip, the most normal thing I've seen her do in years. It triggers memories of long ago—chilly nights under a blanket as we sat on the floor in front of the fireplace, it was her turn to tell a story; she bites the corner of her lip then starts. Helping me with my first grade homework at the kitchen table, biting the corner of her lip as she thinks of the answer. She snaps out of it, her old self.

"That's none of your business," she says.

"Who is my father?" I swear to God, this is the first time I've verbalized the question that plagues every child who has no memories of a father. The first time I care to know.

"That's none of your business," she says again, but this time she's slowly backing out of the room.

"It's my business," I say urgently. "It is. Because I have a right to know who he is…" I follow her—a step for a step. She shakes her head. I'm becoming more panicky. I feel my palms grow damp, the increased lub-dub of my heart. This is my one chance to get answers. I am eighteen. There are but a few breaths left in our relationship.

"Tell me, goddammit!" I grit between my teeth. I don't want to yell, but I'm not above it. My mother hates loud noises.

"Don't speak to me like that. I'm your moth—"

"You aren't a mother," I say quickly. "You hung my childhood by a noose. You don't even care, do you? Of course not. You don't care that I graduated from high school with honors, or that I got a job, or that the best kind of man likes to spend time with me. You're just an ugly, self-involved, guilt-ridden whore who refuses to even speak to the child you brought into this world. I can't even find the strength to hate you, because I don't even care anymore."

Her hand meets my cheek. It's an epic slap if I've ever seen one, and growing up in the Bone you see no less than half a dozen greatly administered slaps in a year. My cheek begins to sting before her hand even leaves it. My skin mars easily, so I can almost see the etchings of her fingers on my face. I begin to lift a hand to touch the spot where she struck me, but I don't want to give her the satisfaction. I drop my hand, curling it into a fist.

"Who was my father?" I ask again. This time my voice sounds more like me—flat and calm. The slap, the declaration of my ruined childhood makes it official. We will talk tonight, probably not ever again, but tonight is for answers. The kind people aren't usually willing to give.

My mother casts her bruised eyes to the scarred wooden floor. Her red robe is open, and her right breast has slipped from the material. The sight of it revolts me; the men whose hands have fondled it are on a carousel in my mind. Was one of them my father? I know it before she says it—the man who drives the restored mustang, the one with the LWMN license plate and the watch I'd now come to understand is a Rolex.

"His name is Howard Delafonte," she says. "Come downstairs. I need a smoke."

I follow her down the narrow stairs of the eating house and sit at the kitchen table while she lights a cigarette and pours a finger of scotch into a dusty tumbler she finds in a cabinet. She's doing things: pouring, lighting, sipping. I haven't seen her do anything but float from room to room in a long time. The movement looks odd on her, like a ghost mimicking flesh. When she sits on the only other chair across from me, she sighs.

"Poor me," she says. "I got knocked up by the mayor, but that was before he was the mayor, of course. He would have been much more careful. He was just a lawyer back then. At Markobs and Jacob. He left my first month there, but not before we had already slept together. He liked me, brought me gifts."

I think of the wrapping paper I find in her trashcan and wonder if he brings her those trinkets.

"Even after he left, he'd take me out. Wine and dine if I'd ever seen it." She takes a deep drag of her cigarette and drains her scotch before she's even blown out her smoke. "He had a family of course. Same old bullshit. Wife made him miserable. I saw her once—fat, cow-faced. She nagged the hell out of him." She stubs out her cigarette on the bare table, then uses the tip of her finger to play with the ash.

"I made him happy. He was going to leave her, but then she got sick. Said he couldn't do it."

I want to ask her what the fat, cow-faced wife of the mayor got sick with, but I know it doesn't matter. I need the end of this story.

"Howard kept seeing me, of course. Eventually the partners at the firm caught wind of it; someone saw us at the movies. Go figure," she says. Her tongue absently snakes up and rubs at her crooked tooth while she thinks. "By that time he was already running for mayor, and I was pregnant with you."

"Why does he still come?" I ask. "After all these years." Or maybe I should ask why Daddy doesn't talk to his daughter. Small talk even. *So what do you like to do with your free time? Haven't you ever wished you had a TV?*

Then it hits me. My mother had a television; she threw it out when I was little, told me it broke and that we didn't have money for a new one. And all these years there has been no new television. Not because we couldn't afford one with the piles of money she has lying beneath the floorboards, but because they haven't wanted me to see my father on TV. The mayor of Harbor Bone in his cherry red Mustang. I wonder what he really drives, probably a new Mercedes or BMW, something with dark, official-looking tints that smells inside of his cigars and cedar wood cologne. The mustang is his weekend plaything. He keeps it in his garage and drives it here because no one will recognize it. *Hey Dad, cool midlife crisis.*

"He loves me," she says.

"What about me? Does he love me?" I spit.

"It's not like that. He didn't want me to have you. He wanted me to have an abortion, but I wouldn't do it."

"So now he pretends that I don't exist? God. And you're okay with that because you do that same thing."

The eating house rattles around us, the panes on the windows humming from the pressure within. It agrees with me. The eating house knows what a corrupt deadness my mother has become. The insipid wasteland of a woman who gave her best years to a man who treated her youth like it was a weekend at the casino. It's seen her invite other men in while leaving her only child out. I feel a camaraderie with the eating house just then—a oneness instead of an oppression. My mother flinches away from the question. She glances at the rattling windows, probably wondering if I can hear it too. So, I pretend that I can't, allowing my eyes to bore into her sallow skin, making her fidget and squirm in her seat. *Let her think she's going mad,* I think. *Let her think she's the only one who can hear the eating house.*

"I have half brothers and sisters?"

"Yes."

"And my father is the mayor?"

"Not anymore. He's retired now." Her tongue reaches up to touch her tooth.

"And his ... children ... he's close with them?"

I want her to say no. That he's estranged from those children as well. That he didn't go to their baseball games, and ballet recitals, and sit around the breakfast table staring into their sleep-crusted eyes every morning.

"Yes," she says. And that yes is her last and final word on the matter. She stands up, and she looks a hundred years old. She's to the stairs when I call after her.

"If he comes here again, there will be no more silence from me," I say. "Let him know."

I hear the creaking of the stairs as she climbs back to her room. Slowly ... slowly.

age 19

IT'S SATURDAY, and I don't know what to do with myself. I cleaned the bathroom, then called work to see if they had a shift for me to cover. Sandy told me to stay home and live a little, but Judah is spending the weekend with his dad, and life feels dry when he isn't here. I study the peeling plaster in the living room for what seems like hours before I decide to cook a real meal. My mother has old cookbooks on top of the fridge. I pull them down and flip through the pages, sneezing when the dust crawls up my nose. I find a recipe I like and pull out my mother's notepad to make a list of the things I'll need. I've never cooked before, but there are a lot of things I'm doing lately that I'm new to. Judah, for example.

"Yo," I say to the stove. "You alive in there?" I kick the door of the oven with the toe of my boot and hear a crash. I have the eerie feeling that someone is watching me. But my mother is sleeping; I can hear her soft snores from upstairs. I shiver as I lower myself to my haunches and open the oven door. Inside is what looks like a metal box, sitting on a collapsed rack; the rack depresses me. I look over my shoulder just to see if she's there before pulling it out. Something is behind me; I can feel it. The box is heavy. I carry it to the table, my plans of cooking forgotten. Something shifts inside it—rough and smooth grating together— and suddenly the hair on the back of my neck is standing up.

Why would my mother put a box in the oven? And how long has it been there? I try to remember the last time I saw her cooking. Was it right after she lost her job and stopped leaving the house? I sit with both hands on top of the box and my eyes closed. *Put it back. Put it back. Put it back.* I want to. Hidden things should stay hidden. There are hinges and a latch. I lift the latch. My hands are shaking. My reaction is pathetic, like my body already knows what's inside of this thing, but it doesn't. At least not that I can remember. I push back the lid. Everything after that happens to someone who isn't me.

Bones. Tiny human bones. I am frozen. My hands claw the air above the box. I don't know how much time goes by with me looking into the coffin. I've seen this before. *Haven't I?* It feels familiar—the panic, the disgust, the slow numbing. All of it. Even as I close the lid and walk stiffly back to the oven, I have an eerie sense of deja vu. What am I supposed to do? Confront my mother? Call the police? I stare down at the oven door, the tomb to this tiny human. The box is heavy; I rest it on my hip and feel the bones slide around. I quickly adjust the box, instead cradling it in my arms like a baby. The doorbell rings, and all of a sudden I'm shaking.

I open the oven and carefully slide the child inside. I feel as if I am going to be sick. A knock at the door. I have to answer it before my mother wakes up, angry. I run to open it, glancing once more over my shoulder at the tiny coffin in the oven.

It's the mailman. He has never come to the door before, let alone rang the bell that hasn't worked since before I was born. *The eating house,* I think. *It's up to something.* My face must show my surprise. He rubs a hand sheepishly across his face and clears his throat.

"It wouldn't fit in the mailbox," he says. For the first time I notice the package in his hands. I make to tell him that it's not ours. We don't get packages, but he reads my mother's name off the label, so I unlatch the chain.

He nods at me before he walks away, and now I am holding a different box in my hands, my knees knocking beneath my white dress. There is a ball of tension inside me. It pulls tighter and tighter until I walk back into the house. I carry the box to my mother's door. I can hear her stirring inside her bedroom, so I leave it there for her to find, and tiptoe downstairs and out of the house.

When I talk to my father for the first time, I think he's going to fall backward down the stairs. I wait for him near the front door, on the usual night his cherry red Mustang pulls along the curb. He doesn't see me when he comes in, carrying a brown paper shopping bag, ignoring the lightless room to his left, which is usually empty. I sit on a threadbare piece of furniture, left from my grandmother's days, and wait for him to reach the stairs. I want to observe him without him observing me. When he's two up, I say his name. The sound of startled paper lets me know he's jumped in surprise.

"Howard Delafonte," I say. He stays where he is, the back of his heels hanging off the second-to-last stair. "I imagine I get my shoulders from you. Did you play football in college? Shit, what a waste if you didn't. I don't really know anything about football. I don't have a television, you know. Oh yes, you do know, don't you? Was that your awesome idea?"

I hear him setting down his bag, while the floorboards creak overhead. I imagine that my mother is the one with her ear pressed to the walls now. Too frightened to put a stop to our meeting, but perhaps a little curious as well.

He comes to stand in the living room, his eyes searching for me among the shadows. When he sees my form, sitting quietly on the couch, he clears his throat and walks over to turn on the floor lamp.

"May I call you Daddy? Or does it sound odd coming from a white trash girl like me?"

He says nothing. There is a greasy yellow light between us now.

"Never mind," I say, standing up. "I'll stick with Howard. Or Mayor Delafonte. That's what everyone else calls you, isn't it?" I get up and walk around the couch 'til we are standing face to face. It's the first time I've been this close to him, and I can actually see his features. He looks like me: broad face, eyes spaced too far apart, so lightly blue they almost blend into the whites. He's ugly, and strange, and striking, and I want to hate him, but I can't, because he has the same flaxen hair that I have. It falls in the same odd way around his eyes. I look into his eyes, hoping to see contrition, a fondness he harbored without words. But what I see there is fear of me. Fear of what I can say about him—how my words, if directed the right way, can reach his friends at the country club, his cow-faced wife at home who never did die of her illness, his legitimate children at their Ivy League colleges. The thousands of voters ... the news.

It'll be out of the bag now, Papa, I want to say. Except I don't make empty threats, and I have no intention of ratting out the secret life of Howard Delafonte.

I wait. I've daydreamed about this moment for so long, the moment my father says honest to God words to me. But, he says nothing. He's waiting for me to speak, and without that he has nothing to say. I feel a crushing truth that can't be reversed or unseen. It's a black hole that starts near my heart and moves outward. I thought that when I met my father—the obscure man who I pictured having a broad, smiling face—he would embrace knowing me. He'd be delighted at this new relationship prospect, the chance to know his offspring, a girl who got excellent grades and was capable of taking care of herself. In my daydreams, my father never rejects me. I am ill prepared for this reality. He has nothing to say. When I realize I'm not going to get what I want, which at this point is a simple acknowledgment, I take a step back. My insides feel oily. There are too many paths of disappointment, too many ways that this can make me disappear.

"All right," I say. And then again, "All right."

My backing off has unsettled him. I see his Adam's apple bobbing around his throat. *Say something.*

"Give me your watch." I am startled by my request. Probably more so than he is. I can see it glinting out of the corner of my eye, that heavy thing I once held in my hand. I hadn't known then that it belonged to my father, yet I felt strangely drawn to it. He doesn't move, still doesn't say anything. It's a standoff—a battle of wills. He's determined not to acknowledge me, even with his words. I stand there for a few more seconds before I am exhausted. I walk backwards to the front door, never taking my eyes from him. Committed to getting one last look at the man who was responsible for making me, yet responsible for nothing else.

The night air hits my shoulders. I feel the rain before I see it. My last glance before the door shuts is of my father, Howard Delafonte, walking back up the stairs, unperturbed.

The box, the box, the box, I think. Did the person inside belong to him? I go back inside to check on it—kneeling down in front of the oven and flicking on the oven light that has miraculously not yet burned out. It's there. *He or she,* I think, resting my forehead against the door.

I go to Judah's because I can't stand to be within the same walls as them. He's sitting by the window, his usual spot. I don't bother to go inside. I slide down the wall until I am sitting directly beneath the window. I can hear him messing with something that sounds like a plastic wrapper.

"I have Cheetos," he says.

"I'm not hungry."

"You don't have to be hungry to eat Cheetos, just depressed."

"I'm not…" and then my voice drops off, because who am I kidding? I was born depressed. "I don't eat that shit anymore."

"Well la-ti-da, fancy pants. Didn't know you were a health nut. Excuse me while I eat my orange-coated shit."

I smile. All of a sudden I feel like Cheetos, because Judah makes me want things I have no place wanting.

"Judah, you suck."

I hear him move away from the window, the clean squeak of his wheels on the linoleum. Then the door opens, and I feel something hit my arm. Judah leans out the door a little, and I catch sight of his wet hair.

Then the door closes, and he's back at his post.

I reach down for what hit me. It's a Ziploc bag of mini carrots. I smile as I open it. That's more like it.

"We are both eating orange-colored food. I feel all close to you and shit."

"And shit," he says. And then,"Why you all sad and shit, Maggie?"

"Eh, just life. You know."

"I know," he agrees. "But sometimes it's still beneficial to talk about it and shit."

"And shit," I say. "I met my dad tonight. He's the worst kind of cracker jack loser lobster."

"I've never met a cracker jack loser lobster. Is that like an asshole?"

"Yeah," I say. "Exactly."

"You know," says Judah. "I know you've never met my dad, but he's kind of a cracker jack loser lobster, too. He left my mom because he didn't want kids. Didn't even come see me at the hospital when I was born. Sent her the child support check every month though. The first time I met him was after my first surgery. He felt guilty and decided to start being a dad to his cripple son. Sometimes I wonder if he would have contacted me if I didn't get the tumor. Sometimes I'm even grateful to the tumor for giving me my dad. It makes my mom's life easier ... the help. And he's all right. But, I always feel like I'm disappointing him."

"I don't have anyone to disappoint," I say. "That's nice, I guess."

"You couldn't disappoint someone if you tried," Judah says.

The silence that follows is a black hole. It sucks all of the air from the planet ... or maybe just my lungs. I burst into tears. Girl tears. Foul, weak, stereotypical tears. I rub them away immediately, smearing them all over my palms, then rubbing my palms on the legs of my pants. I can feel Judah watching me through the screen that covers the window. I know that if it weren't there, he'd reach down and touch me. That makes me feel better. Knowing that someone cares enough. Everyone should have someone who cares enough.

"Maggie," he says. "People—our dads, our moms, our friends—they are so broken they don't even know that most of what they do reflects that brokenness. They just hurt whoever is in their wake. They don't sit and think about what their hurt is doing to us. Pain makes humans selfish. Blocked off. Focused inward instead of outward. "

What he's saying makes sense. But the potency of it hurts nonetheless.

"Just tell me one thing," he says. "Does your heart still beat ... with the ache and pain there? Does it still beat?"

"Yes," I say.

"That's because humans are built to live with pain. Weak people let their pain choke them to a slow, emotional death. Strong people use that pain, Margo. They use it as fuel."

When I go back to the eating house, I find his Rolex on the kitchen table. Tossed like the first day I found it in my mother's bedroom.

"Fuck you," I say, but I carry it to my room and hide it under the floorboards anyway.

I WAKE UP WITH MY PAJAMAS DAMP, and my hair stuck to my forehead. Before I have the chance to swing my feet over the side of the bed, my mother starts screaming. I run to her room, still disoriented, and fling open her door to find her standing at the foot of her bed, naked, her robe pooling around her feet. When she sees me, she points to the far side of the bedroom. I step around her, swiping at the hair falling in my face, almost tripping over the junk she has piled everywhere.

"What?! What is it?!" I ask.

My eyes search the darkness, seeing nothing, before I reach for her drapes and yank them open. Dust spirals in the air as light rushes into the room, hungry to devour the darkness. My mother lets out a little mewl of pain.

"Vampire," I say under my breath. But then my breath is yanked from my lungs as I stare at the bloody mess in the corner of the room.

I look at my mother, who is clutching her swollen stomach, rocking back and forth. I now notice the bloodstains on her hands and legs that I hadn't seen before. Shivering in the bright light, the blood on her pale skin looks garish and frightening.

"What is that?" I whisper.

She doesn't answer me. I take a few steps closer. My hand flies to my mouth as my esophagus swells with vomit. "What have you done?!" My voice rumbles through the small space. I sound demonic as I drop to my knees in front of the baby. A baby. Can you call it that? Tinier than anything I have ever seen, its skin is purple, matted with blood and a foamy white substance. I touch it, pull back, touch it again. No pulse, no breathing. It's too little. It— a girl. I groan and rock on my heels. How had she hidden it? How had I not seen? A billowing red robe. She no longer asked me to stay with her when she bathed. Had she done this on purpose? Rid herself of the baby. The answer is on her face, relief mixed with the pain. A baby, a little girl. I want to pick her up, carry her somewhere warm and safe.

My mother, gasping for breath and bleeding profusely, falls to the ground behind me. I take one last look at the little girl in the corner and walk out of the room.

I take my time walking to Judah's house. Delaney has a phone. My mother has a cell phone; I've always assumed it's how she makes her appointments with her various male clients, but there's a passcode on it. I'm not sure if it will let me call the ambulance. And I want her to die. By the time I reach Judah's gate, I am sobbing. Delaney opens the door. The smile falls from her face when she sees me. I'm sobbing so hard I can't get her to understand what I'm saying. I point to the cordless, and she runs to get it.

"Nine-one-one. What's your emergency?"

Suddenly, I am sober of the grief I was feeling. Sober enough to summon words, thick and clumsy.

"My mother," I say. "She's ... had a miscarriage. I'm afraid she might bleed to death." I hand the phone back to Delaney, who looks at me in shock, then repeats my address into the receiver. I walk home, soulless.

The ambulance comes; its wail cuts through the warm Wessex day like a thunderstorm, calling people to their windows and doors. I sit on the step and wait as the paramedics pound up the stairs to my mother's bedroom. I don't know if she will leave the eating house alive or dead. After I leave Delaney's, I don't go back upstairs. The paramedics leave.

They come to see my mother's body—two men in navy blue uniforms with stars on their chests. Policemen. I want to clean away the blood on her face and hands, but they tell me to leave it.

The morgue will take care of all of that after the autopsy. They're asking me questions, wanting to know if I'm the one to contact about the autopsy, and if I'll be making arrangements for her funeral.

"The autopsy?" I ask in a hollow voice.

"Standard procedure. You need one to be able issue a death certificate," one of the cops tells me.

I look at the bottles of pills next to her bed, overturned and empty.

"My mother wanted to be cremated," I tell them. My mother wanted no such thing. Or maybe she did, but she never told me. I don't want to deal with her body—coffins and gravestones. Give her back to me as ash in an urn, and I'll be happy. They ask me how old I am.

"Eighteen," I tell them. They ask to see my driver's license, but I don't have one. I show them my school ID, and they look almost disappointed that they can't cart me off to a group home. They won't be putting me in the system tonight, or any other. I've never been so grateful to not be a minor. They hand me a stack of papers, some brochures for funeral homes and crematoriums. There is one with a flower on the cover that is for a grief support group. I watch the police talk to the two guys from the morgue who have come for their bodies, leaning against the rotted siding of the eating house. Judah finds me there, his face drawn and concerned. "The morgue is here to pick up the bodies."

"My mom told me," he says. "She wants you to come spend the night at our house."

I look past him to the bad people house. All of the bad people are outside, drinking beer and waiting for the body bag. Some of them are shirtless; a man and a woman are kissing by the back door, coming up for air every few to look toward the eating house.

"That's the difference between the rich and poor," Judah says, following my eyes. "The rich peek through their drapes to see the neighborhood tragedy, while the poor don't try to hide the fact that they're looking."

"Thank you," I say. "But I'd prefer to stay here."

"I'll stay with you," he says quickly. "Just let me wheel home to get some of my shit."

I think about saying no, but, in the end, the idea of sleeping in the eating house frightens me. I nod. I watch him go, the muscles in his arms pressing against his T-shirt as they work the wheels of his chair. He stops when he reaches the bad people house. A couple guys swagger up to where he's stopped, giving him daps and offering him a beer.

Everyone likes that goddamn cripple.

I smile a little, but then my mother is wheeled out the door, and I have to use the eating house to hold myself up. There is a smaller bag for the baby. The second of the two morgue technicians carries that one out in his hands. He has gloves on, and he carries her, slightly extended from his body like an offering for some god who eats dead babies. It's her, that little baby girl, who I'll grieve for in the coming days. A child, wanted by her half-dead sibling, murdered by her already dead mother.

When they are gone, I go into the house to clean the mess the bodies left behind. The eating house is quiet. I wait for the grief, but it doesn't come. I want to feel something so I know I'm still human. But, I don't know how to grieve someone I didn't know. I knew Nevaeh. I didn't know my mother.

Delaney comes to help me, carrying buckets of hot water and Pine-Sol up the stairs. We work without talk, using my mother's sheets as rags, sopping up the blood until they are stained, and the smell of pine pervades the house. We carry the buckets outside, dumping the pink water into the grass. I hug Delaney, an ungainly hug, to thank her for not making me do that alone. Her eyes are pink-rimmed when she steps back. Her lips trembling. They share the same plumpness as Judah's lips, but hers are not sensual like his. They look almost clumsy now as she struggles to know what to say.

"No one should have to do that," she whispers. Her hair is damp and sticking to her face. I can see Judah in her features—the broad forehead and graceful slope of her nose.

"You children suffer too much."

As she walks up Wessex, I watch her, thinking about what she said. Children. Suffer. Yes, maybe more than adults. That's where we become broken, in our youth. And then we wear it like a shroud for the rest of our lives.

I name the baby Sihn, because she bore the sins of her mother and died for it.

I drag the big, wooden ramp from Judah's porch over to the eating house, and set it over the steps. When I push him up the

88

makeshift ramp, it wobbles and bends in the middle like it's going to crack in two. It's Judah's first time in the eating house. I leave the door open, letting the light stream across the living room, and I suddenly feel self-conscious of all the rubbish. Not literal rubbish, just the rubbish of my life—the old oldness. The damp dampness, the poor poorness.

The house hums around us, excited at the prospect of a new visitor. *You can't have him,* I tell it silently. *I know he's special, but you can't have Judah.*

I fiddle with the buttons on my shirt. "I'll drag down my mattress," I say. "You can have the couch. I mean, if that's okay?"

He nods. "Do you want me to heat you something to eat?" he asks. "My mom sent over shepherd's pie."

"I'm not really hungry." I shrug. He offers up the casserole dish on his lap, and I carry it to the kitchen. I stand at the fridge, out of sight, wishing I hadn't let him come here. This was what the kids called weird. Like taking a modern piece of furniture into an old crypt, weird; fried chicken in a vegetarian restaurant, weird.

Oh God, oh God.

"Margo?"

"Yes?"

Oh God...

"There's a man at the door..."

The casserole dish clatters to the counter. I march past Judah to the front door, where Howard Delafonte stands, just over the threshold, slipping off his raincoat like he belongs here. *It's Tuesday,* I think. *His regular day to come.* The eating house groans. It doesn't like him.

My angle is to hurt him.

"The baby," I say. "Yours?"

He says nothing. He doesn't have to; I already know. Whatever she took to rid herself of the pregnancy, he brought her.

"How do you know it was yours and not one of the other men's?" I ask. I mention the other men because I want to hurt him. Let him know he isn't the only one paying her for sex.

"She didn't make me use anything," he says.

I draw back, shocked. His confession is disarming. Intimate. I shouldn't know something that personal about my mother, but it tells me so much more about her than her words ever did. Did she want to get pregnant with his baby? Maybe she thought that she could have him all the time if she did? That he would leave his life to raise a human with her? My mother wasn't really into raising humans. Perhaps the eating house just made her crazy, and she didn't care if she got pregnant.

"The baby was a girl," I say quietly.

His face blanches.

"Where is she?" he says, heading for the stairs. By her I suppose he is referring to my mother, not his bastard baby. I allow him to run up the stairs. I trace the heavy *whomp whomp whomp* of his shoes across the floor. When he comes back down, there is a look of terror on his face.

"Where is she? What hospital?"

"What hospital," I repeat, laughing. I look at Judah, who is watching us cautiously, like he's wondering how to break up a fight if it starts.

"She's dead."

My father, by blood alone, stumbles—grabs onto the wall to support himself, and misses. It's like the eating house moves, shies away from his hands, contracting into itself. He falls, his face contorted and red like he's run a very long race. I watch impassively, the big hulk of a man on the floor, crying. He loved her. I am surprised. He doesn't love me, and I am from her. She did not love me either. As I watch him, I wonder if someone like me, who has never been loved, is capable of it—would recognize it if it came along? And then I think that I would rather not be loved than to be loved by a man like Howard Delafonte.

"Get out," I say. "Get out of my house, you murdering pig."

And, when he doesn't move fast enough, I scream it louder and louder until I am sure the entire Bone can hear me. *Get out! Get out! Get out!*

He crawls like a dog. Pathetic. I turn away, turn my back on him until I hear his car door slam, and the rev of his engine.

"You okay?" Judah asks.

"That was my father," I say.

Judah is quiet for a long time. I don't look at his face to gauge his reaction, though his emotions are so even, so fair and balanced that I hardly need to see him to know that he is frowning. Fathers should be fathers by Judah's account. Even if they don't want you, they should still provide for you. Like his did. Like mine didn't. Never would. *Do I have a daddy complex?* I think, as I watch Judah

90

watch me. *No.* I have a complex, sure. But it's more of an *I hate humans* thing. Disappointed. I am so disappointed in people. It's like they live without souls.

I feel it then—my mother's death. I start to cry. Great, big, gulping sobs. My knight rides his chair over to where I am bent in half by my grief. Folded like a piece of paper. He grabs me before I can blow away. Around the waist, pulling me into his chair until I am half sitting on his lap, hiding my face in my hands.

"Shhhh," he says. "You are worth loving. They just don't have any love to give. Forgive them, Margo."

I TAKE THE MONEY from the floorboards and lay it out in rows. There are piles of hundreds and twenties. I separate them and begin counting. My mother was a rich woman. Rich by anyone's standards in the Bone. Seventy thousand dollars. Her whole life amounted to a rickety old house, a daughter she never spoke to, and seventy thousand dollars.

"Bravo Mama," I say. I lean against my bedroom wall and stare at the money for a long time. Then I gather it all up and wrap it in her red bathrobe before stuffing it back under the floorboards.

Two gentlemen callers come that night. I send them away. Tell them my mama's dead, and unless they have a taste for necrophilia, they need to get the fuck off my porch. The news haunts them. I see it in the whites of their eyes. They'll be in a stupor tonight, going home to their wives with the knowledge that their whore is dead. Their wives will ask them if they're okay, and they'll make up some excuse about not feeling well, retreating to their offices or their bedrooms to ponder over my mother's death.

The next morning I dress in one of her old flannel shirts. I'm shorter than she was, so it hangs mid-thigh like a dress. I pull on her Docs and catch the bus to the funeral home to pay for her cremation. I pay with a wad of twenties, and the lady behind the desk looks at me like I stole it.

"What?" I say. "Haven't you seen a working girl's money before?"

Her eyes get big, but she reaches for the money with her age-spotted hands and stashes it somewhere I can't see. I can hear the clicks of disapproval she makes in the back of her throat.

"You get to choose her urn," she says, motioning to a shelf behind her. There are prices printed on paper and taped beneath each jar.

"I don't want her ashes," I say quickly. The thought of being in charge of her burned remains alarms me. Too great a responsibility.

"Well, neither do we," says the lady. "You're the next of kin. Unless you want to pay monthly for a storage cubby, you have to take the ashes with you." I sigh, glance at the urns again. I can't just leave her here.

"The green one," I say. It reminds me of the leaves she used to touch, before she became someone else.

The leaves and their varicose veins...

I squeeze her voice out of my brain.

"$78.21," she says. I hand her all dollar bills this time. I wander around after that, searching the eyes of the people I pass, looking for answers.

When it starts to rain, I catch the bus that Nevaeh and I used to ride together, and sit in the back staring out the window. I'm not ready to go back to the eating house and all of her ghosts—the bodies of babies and mothers filling her mouth. The bus driver asks me to leave or pay more fare when it gets dark. I haven't brought any more money, so I reluctantly climb off. I walk slowly, dread building.

When I get back, it's dark. Judah is waiting on the sidewalk in front of the house, his chair angled so he can see me walking down the scythe of Wessex.

"Nice legs," he says. I look down at my legs—so white they're practically glowing in the dark. I don't usually show them. Suddenly I'm self-conscious.

"You know..." he says, sensing my discomfort. "Because they work and all..."

I shake my head. "So inappropriate," I say.

"Yeah, I guess…" He rubs the back of his head, his mouth cocked up on one side. It looks like he's getting ready to say something that's going to make both of us uncomfortable.

"So, your mom—" he begins.

"I don't want to talk about it." I start walking past him, up the sidewalk to the front door.

"First Neveah, now your mom," he calls after me. I stop, but don't turn around.

'Yeah?"

"It's just strange," he says. "Like death is everywhere."

I don't know what he's getting at. I don't like the tone of his voice, the way I can feel his eyes on my spine.

"Night, Margo." I hear the wheels of his chair rolling over the sidewalk, back up the scythe.

Damn the Bone, damn my mother, damn Judah.

Three hundred dollars a night, three hundred and sixty-five days a year. She never left the house, never bought anything. Had she purposefully left the seventy thousand under my floor for me? *Fuck her for not leaving a letter.* You'd think if you ignored your kid for half her life, then overdosed, knowing she was the only one who would find you, you'd at least have the decency to leave her a note. I go to her room, find stationery in her nightstand, with birds of paradise in the margins. It is so old, the paper brittle and yellowing, water stained in some parts, like she'd been crying over the pages. I sit down at the kitchen table to write her suicide note.

> *Dear Margo,*
>
> *I'm sorry. First, for just ceasing to be your mom when you were eight and needed me most.*
>
> *I saw you desperately trying to get my attention, and I just didn't know how to come out of the fog I was in … for ten years. I don't know if you've ever kissed a boy, been in love, or what GPA you graduated high school with. I guess I don't even know if you graduated.*
>
> *I'm a prostitute and a drug addict. My heart broke, first when my dad left, then your dad left, then when everything in life kept leaving. I should have fought harder for you.*

You were worth the fight. I left you some money. Do something with it. Get out of the Bone!

Don't look back, Margo. GO!

Mom

In reality, my mother would never have written such an encouraging note. Even before she changed, she was a pessimist. Back then she would have told me to pray, but now she would have told me that there was no God, and we were doomed. Might as well strap in for the long haul of a miserable life.

I go to her room. It smells thickly of blood and flowers, and it makes me dizzy. There are dark stains on the wood where their bodies lay. They'll never come out, no matter how hard I scrub them; they've simply been absorbed into the eating house. I shiver. She was so hungry; she took two lives this time.

There is a box in the corner, the one the mailman delivered just a few days ago. It feels like more time has passed between then and now. I open it and look inside, but it's empty. I start putting her things inside of it. Bottles, books, slippers. I strip her bed and take down the pictures from the walls. Then I carry her things to the attic. The place where she stored her own mother's things when she died. The Irony. An attic full of dead mother things. I laugh, but it gets stuck in my throat, and I end up crying instead. It's just me and the eating house now.

I PICK UP THE ASHES OF MY MOTHER AND MY SISTER on a day so
dark it feels like the sun forgot to rise. The clouds are thick and
heavy, charcoal-colored. I walk to the bus stop and wait with my
hands pressed between my knees, the balls of my feet bobbing,
ebbing out my nerves. In a few hours I will carry two urns filled
with body—hearts and lungs and funny bones—all burned to a
fine dust.

Today we are here, and tomorrow we are gone, amounted to a
handful of memories. It's freaking depressing. I don't feel my grief
anymore, not really. It was sopped up the night Judah pulled me
into his arms and told me I was worth loving. I am only numb
now, doing what I ought: walk, talk, eat, pick up ashes. *Check!
Check! Check! Check!*

On my way home from the funeral home, I stare at the urns—
one small, like a bottle of perfume, and one large, like a bottle of
milk—both sitting in an unmarked paper bag on the seat beside
me. I consider putting them on the floor, but then think it
disrespectful. I wonder if when I die someone will put my ashes
into a jar or bury me in the dirt.

The rain doesn't come; it seems the sky will be all threats
today. I carry my sister's urn to the garden. I can hear music

pounding through the open windows of the crack house—
something angry and fast paced. Looking around, I see that the
trees are mostly bare—nowhere pretty to put my sister. I am
wearing short sleeves, and I shiver as I search the yard for
somewhere nice. There is a bush near the back of the garden, close
enough to the woods to be considered wild. There are some
blackberries and bright, bell-shaped leaves still clinging to the
branches. I lean closer to examine it. Is that...? Judah calls to me
from the sidewalk. I look back over my shoulder, and he waves.
He's wearing a red shirt; it's bright against the gray of the day.

"Let me be with you when you do this," he says when I walk
over to him. I press my lips tight and nod. *Sure. Yeah.* Who wants
to say goodbye alone?

I wheel him over the rough patches in the yard; we hit a ditch
that almost rocks him out of his chair. He is quiet when I crouch
down and empty the smaller of the urns around a tree whose leaves
bloom red in the summer.

There is still a body in my oven. I want to bury that one, but
before I do, I want some answers. I want to search the house to see
if there are more. Maybe it was the first of us—my mother's
unwanted babies—but why had she put in in the oven? Why not
bury it, or ask the father to bury it? The baby in the urn would have
grown into a sister. We could have been friends. I do not empty my
mother's urn near the baby's. She does not deserve to be put to
rest.

"What are you going to do with her?" Judah asks.

"What would you do with her?"

He frowns scratching the back of his head, and then looking
up at the rain clouds. A raindrop has landed on his mouth and he
licks it away.

"I like my mom," he says. "I'd want her to be somewhere
nice."

"And if you didn't like your mom?"

He thinks for a minute. "Leave her somewhere in the house.
Seems like punishment enough, right?"

I laugh. "Yeah..."

"Hey, Margo," says Judah. "You're pretty tough you know
that?"

"Tough?" I repeat. "No. If I were tough I'd be a normal girl. I
turned out all crazy and shit."

"And shit," he smiles. "Well, whatever. I like you anyway."
"Go home," I say, standing up and dusting off the back of my pants. "It's starting to rain."

He blows me a kiss and wheels himself back on home.

I like that kid.

I bathe, and eat a little of what Judah's mother brought me. I am still thinking about the berries I saw when I climb into bed. I have dreams filled with corpses and hollow-eyed humans stuffing blackberries into their mouths 'til they choke. When I wake up ... I know.

I am in the kitchen when I find my mother's last correspondence. On the last Tuesday of every month, she'd leave four envelopes on the kitchen counter; three of them were for me to take to the post box: the power bill, the water bill, her cellphone bill. The last envelope was blank. Inside was always a list, written in her near-perfect handwriting, of the things she wanted for the month. Sometimes the list would have things like: *shampoo, Advil (large bottle), crackers, bananas.* Other times it would say: *New Stephen King novel, tweezers, mascara (brown/black).* She'd tuck a fifty in the envelope, and that would be that. I finger the envelope. What had she wanted this month? Did I even care? I rip a thin strip off of the top of the envelope and pull out the notebook paper inside.

There are only three things on her list this month. I look at the first: laxatives. Not an unusual request, but there were girls in my school who used laxatives early in pregnancy. The rush of wet bowels flushed out the barely fertilized egg, or that's what they believed anyway. You could often see a bottle of MiraLAX being passed from hands, shoved in a backpack. A home remedy that never worked. Also on her list is a request for a birthday card— *(something masculine)* she writes next to it. I wonder if it's my father's birthday, or one of the others. Who would she feel is special enough to receive a paper acknowledgment? My bitterness causes me to temporarily fold the paper. No birthday card for me. No acknowledgment. When my bad feelings subside, I unfold it to see what her last wish was. Written in different color ink than the first two items is something that makes the hair stand up on the back of my neck. Tell Margo. That's it.

Why would my mother write this on her shopping list she'd know I'd see? What does it mean? Had she meant to write more and forgotten? Tell Margo about...the baby? Maybe she thought I didn't know about the money underneath the floorboards. I bury my face in the crook of my arm.

Howard Delafonte had his offices on Main Street. And when I say offices, I mean both the law firm and the wine bar five doors down that he'd opened a year earlier. Someone else ran the wine bar for him, and he had partners at the firm, but the ex-mayor was keeping himself busy. "Busy, busy like a bee," I say under my breath as I watch him walk into the bar, a paper latte cup in his hand.

It is amazing what you can find out on the internet. A little trip to the Harbor Bone Public Library, and bam, more information than you know what to do with. There is no such thing as not airing your dirty laundry anymore. Anyone's shit-stained knickers are just a web search away nowadays. Howard Delafonte's knickers had a divorce smeared across them. I guess the Missus finally left him. And, according to the internet, his oldest son is addicted to heroin, while his youngest has an arrest record for battery. Between my mother and Howard, I was part of a pretty nasty genetic cesspool.

He's in the wine bar for a good thirty minutes before he comes out—a paper bag in his hand. He's whistling, though I can't hear the tune from my bench across the busy street. I wait until he's almost to his car before I stand up and follow him. He hits the electronic button to open his car—not the Mustang, I notice, but a shiny, white Mercedes. He puts the paper bag in the backseat, then opens the door to the driver side. That's when I make my move. I sprint across the street and grab onto the passenger side door, sliding into the car at the same time he does.

"Hey Dad."

His face blanches. I expect him to leap out of the car, but after giving me a long, hard look, he buckles his seat belt, and the engine purrs to life. It's raining. The wipers whip water back and forth as he pulls out of his space and onto the road. I feel slightly uneasy. I am at his mercy, and he can do anything he wants with me buckled into his front seat. I won't give him the upper hand. I relax into my seat and wait for him to speak first. I want him to ask me why I'm here. I had to take five buses to get to the quaint little town he calls home, and I wonder now if he's paranoid about one of his small town people seeing us together.

"Your mother ... did you bury her?"

"Cremated," I say.

He nods.

"Did you give her the Misoprostol?"

He nods again. I clench my fists and stare at the side of his face. It's a strange thing, looking at your father. Knowing that you're somewhere in his face—maybe the curve of a cheek, or the dip of a nose—and searching so hard for it that you want to cry, because you're ashamed and desperate.

"You killed my sister. Why did you let me live?"

"How do you know ... how do you know it was a girl?" he asks. He glances at me briefly.

"Because I found her on the floor."

This seems to make Howard uncomfortable. He wipes a meaty hand across his face, then slams it down on the steering wheel. His gesture reminds me of why I'm here.

"She wanted you," he says. "I tried to get her to have an abortion, and she wouldn't do it."

"She told me my father left..."

"That's what I wanted her to say," he says quickly. "We knew each other for a long time. I gave her the job at the firm when she graduated high school. It was different in those days. You could get a job based on competency rather than a degree. She was a very competent woman. Saved my ass a bunch of times when clients went haywire. I used to send her in to talk to them, calm them down."

"I didn't come here to reminisce about my mother," I say.

"So why are you here?"

"I want to know about your regrets."

He pulls into the parking lot of a diner—Peppered Pete's—just off the highway. There are a couple of semis parked in the lot, a trucker's diner. Before turning off the car, he says, "Let's get something to eat." I nod reluctantly. This will be my first official dinner with my father. I follow him out of the car and through the parking lot. He's making things way too easy for me. He doesn't wait to see if I'm tagging along.

When we get to the door, he holds it open for me. A real gentleman. The air in Peppered Pete's is loaded with grease. But I can't even remember the last time I was in a restaurant, so I feel charmed. We sit in the back by the bathrooms where every few minutes I hear a toilet flush. I don't comment on Howard's choice of table, or the fact that he positioned himself with his back to the door. I leave to go to the bathroom before the waitress can come over. "Whatever you have," I tell him.

When I get back, there are two steaming mugs of coffee on the table. I hold my cup, but don't drink anything.

"I loved her," he says. "I wanted to marry her. My wife got sick…"

I think about my mother. Had she loved him? Had she been using him?

"But you didn't want your children with her?"

He picks up his knife, sets it back down. "I have children."

"If you loved her, you should have wanted *her* children."

"You think it's that simple, but it's not," he says. "You're just a kid. You don't know how hard things can get. Complicated."

I smile wryly.

"Excuse me," he says. He disappears into the restroom. The timing is perfect. It's like the universe mapped it all out for me. I see our waitress turn the corner with two plates in her hand. I get up and go to the restroom again, making sure to leave my purse on the seat so she knows we didn't run out on her. She can't see my face. I come out a few seconds later. Blueberry pancakes, eggs, and bacon. I dip my hand into my purse and pull out the Ziploc baggie I brought.

Then he's back, sliding into the booth, his hands still damp from washing.

"Margo." It's the first time he's ever said my name. It makes me feel empty. Sad. My eyes dart around, looking for the waitress. She will be back in a minute to check on us … bring more coffee.

He takes the first bite of his pancakes. Then the second. I watch, mesmerized as he eats what I put on his pancakes.

"She wasn't in the right frame of mind to have a baby. I don't know what she was saying to you, but she was depressed. She spoke about death a lot."

"She didn't speak to me at all." I still haven't touched my food. He looks up at me, his fork still cutting through pancakes. It looks like he wants to say something, but then changes his mind.

"I loved her," he says again. "I don't regret that."

"You killed her … and the baby."

He wipes his mouth with a napkin, and it leaves a purple smear. "No. That was … she wanted…"

"You gave her the drugs that killed her, ex-Mayor Delafonte. What will people think about that?"

"What do you want?"

I smile. "Nothing. Nothing at all. I have everything I need now."

And with that, I get up and leave, keeping my head ducked.

I don't know what happens after that. I don't check. But I fed my father nightshades and hoped to hell he died.

THERE IS NOTHING in the news about the former mayor, Howard Delafonte. I look and look, but I can't find it. If the nightshades I gave him stopped up his black disgusting heart, no one was reporting it. Unlikely. I decide to take a bus out to Cress End, the town where he lives—larger than mine, but still smaller than most. I have an address for him that I found in a notebook in my mother's bureau, scrawled in sharpie across the page. I wonder what she intended to do with it? If it ever crossed her mind to go to his home and confront him with his family watching. It was his old house I was going to see, the one where his children grew up. I walk the two miles from the bus stop and stand across the street under a sickly looking tree. The Delafonte house is a white colonial with plum shutters. The lawn is neat—evergreen bushes trimmed to ovals and smooth white stones lining the path to the door. I wonder if politicians always choose this style of home because it gives them a sense of the White House. I can imagine his children running across the lawn, and Christmas twinkling through the front window. I can imagine it all because it is the quintessential life.

I've been standing on the corner long enough to not be able to feel my toes, when the former Mrs. Delafonte walks out of her front door and heads down the path. It's a quarter 'til three in the afternoon. She opens her mailbox and bends her head low to look inside. I am shocked. She is the opposite of my pretty mother—round and sturdy with a helmet of iron-colored hair. She is wearing the ugliest sweater I've ever seen, which makes me smile. She likes ugly things; she might like me. She is about to turn to go back into the house when she spots me standing across the street. I stand very still as she crosses the two-laner, her head swinging left then right to check for traffic. She throws me a cautious smile that lights up her plain face.

"Hi there," she says. "You from around here?"

I shake my head. She looks me curiously up and down, not the way rich people do when they're assessing your net worth, but almost sweetly like she's seeing what she can do to help.

"You okay, honey? You look like you've seen a ghost." And I have, haven't I? The ghost of mayor Delafonte's past.

"I'm okay," I say. "Just a little lost." That is true, isn't it?

"Lost in life, or in the technical sense of the word?" she asks.

I just smile.

"Very well then…" She pivots her body toward the main road I walked down to get here and says, "Highway's that way. You can also find the Greyhound station and the bus stop." She turns so she's facing the opposite way. "Over yonder is the pathetic excuse for a town—I'm more of a Seattle girl—but there's a couple restaurants, the post office, stores that sell shit you don't need, yada yada." She turns to face me again. "Do you need some money? Do you have a way to get home?"

I nod my head, though my eyes are burning from the salt water fighting to escape my tear ducts. She wasn't supposed to be so nice.

"Can I ask you a question?" I say. She stops her rundown of Cress End and blinks at me. There's flour on her sweatshirt; I wonder what she's baking.

"Yes," she says. "I suppose you can."

"Are you happy?"

She presses her lips together 'til they burn white. "Well, that's a strange question, isn't it? I haven't been asked that in a very long time…"

She stares out at nothing, her eyes narrow slits as she thinks. "I'm happier than I've been in a long time. It's not the happiness I imagined for myself as a young girl, but I'm alive, and no one has broken my will to live."

She looks directly at me then. "You have to be willing to be happy. Despite the mess of your life—just accept what's happened, throw away your ideals, and create a new map of happiness to follow."

It's the best thing anyone has ever said to me. The best advice. I'm so sorry for what my mother and father have done to this woman that a single tear trickles down my cheek. I nod my head and turn to leave. If I were her daughter, I would have been good to her.

I am half a block away when she calls out, "Goodbye, Margo. Live well."

I don't stop walking, and I don't turn to look back, though every hair on my body is standing up in a surprise salute. I can't stop myself from wishing she had been my mother. A woman so kind, she takes the time to speak to her ex-husband's bastard— probably the reason for her divorce in the first place. My mother wouldn't even acknowledge me, and there she was, a stranger who had every right to hate me, speaking to me with incredible kindness.

My last stop is the wine bar my father owns. I want to see if he's there, or if not, there should be someone who can tell me something about him. There's a young man polishing glasses behind the bar when I step through the doors. He glances up and away quickly enough to let me know I've been dismissed.

"We're not open 'til six," he says. "And you look too young to be in here anyway."

"I'm looking for someone," I say. "Mr. Delafonte…"

He looks up suddenly, and I realize I'm seeing my brother. He is the very image of his mother, with a little of Howard in his shoulders and around his downturned mouth.

"Whaddoyouwanthimfor?" His sentence comes out tinny, slurred, and strung together like a party banner.

"That's my business," I say. "He here?"

"Nah. He's taken a leave of absence…"

I cock my head, shift my weight from one leg to another. I am agitated. I want to snatch the glass from his hand and scream *'Out with it!'*

"Is he sick?"

He sets down his glass and wipes his hands on a towel. "Who's asking?"

I can't help the smile that creeps onto my face. I try to bite it back, but, in the end, who cares?

"His bastard."

Paul—that's my half brother's name—freezes. And then all of a sudden he's polishing glasses again.

"Ah," he says. And I wonder if everyone in the family knows about me.

"You want money?" he asks.

"Nope."

"Then what? A reunion? Because that ain't gonna happen."

"I wanted to see if he was dead."

The glass slips out of Paul's hand. He catches it before it can meet the floor. He walks around the counter, heading toward me.

"What's your name?" he asks.

I smile. "Tell him I said hello," I say. "It was nice to meet you, Paul."

He stops just short of where I'm standing. I give him one last look before I head out the door.

Mission failed, but at least I made him sick enough to take a leave of absence.

When I get back to the eating house, the box in the oven is gone. I slide down the wall until I am sitting, and squeeze my head between my knees. A leave of absence my ass.

I CAN HEAR A BABY CRYING. I curve my way down Wessex, pulling my raincoat tighter around my body. My face is dotted with rain, and every few minutes I have to lick the water from my lips to keep it from running down my chin. The crying gets louder the closer I get to the eating house. My steps slow as I lift my head to catch its direction. It's not at all unusual to hear an infant wailing in the Bone. The people here are conditioned to concentrate on survival rather than happiness. Parents let their babies cry while they bicker and yell; a single, ragged mother lets her baby cry so she can catch a few hours of sleep. Grandmothers let their grandchildren cry because a little crying never hurt no one. But the crying that I hear is not that of an unhappy baby; it's the cry of a child in pain; frantic and high-pitched, it's almost a scream. *Mo.*

I can hear the asphalt beneath my shoes, the *shush shush* of the rain, and the humming of cars on the nearby highway. I try to concentrate on those sounds—sounds that are my business. But something is whispering to me; it's a cacophony of heart, lungs, and mind, topped by the anguished screams of a baby.

I follow the cries to the crack house. Not to the door, but to a window where I can see yellow light escaping from between the drapes. I know that Mo is beneath my feet, cooking meth in the basement. That's what he does at night. Meth which he does not use, but sells, which is probably the smartest way to go about it. Except his baby is upstairs screaming, and he can't hear him. Maybe the baby hurt himself ... Maybe...

I press my gaze between the curtains; the sliver of space doesn't afford me much of a look around the room. I can see a bed, and for a moment I feel relief. Little Mo is not alone. His mother is kneeling among the rustled sheets, her narrow back to me, a long braid trailing down her back. Her name is Vola. She is slender and exotic, Polynesian, Mo once told me. She is always screaming at Mo, and Mo is always screaming at her. Sometimes they take their screaming to the street; Vola always has the car keys in her hand as she threatens to leave Mo for good. Mo throws her clothes on the lawn in armfuls: yellows and purples fluttering onto the weed-stricken lawn, like confetti. He screams to get the fuck out of here, and that she's a fucking slut, and that she's going to fucking get hers if she tries to leave him. Her response is always silence. It seems more profound than Mo's yelling, like she's better than his cheap, slovenly used swear words. And Mo seems to get her message, because after that he starts to yell '*What? You think you're better than me, you bitch? Get out of here.*' Sometimes she leaves for a while. Goes to stay with her mother in Seattle. But the next week her car is back, and they're groping each other in the driveway—his hand up her shirt, her grinding into him with such force it looks like she's trying to wrestle him to the ground.

Vola is not from the Bone. You can tell. Mo met her at a bar in Seattle. None of us really know her, and she has no desire to know any of us. I tilt my head to get a better look at the bed. My breath is frosting the window. I wipe away the condensation carefully, and then steeple all ten fingers against the glass to steady myself as I lean in. Mo is playing music from the basement. It rattles the windows, but even that is not enough to drown out the cries of the baby. Maybe he's sick. Maybe he's...

At first I don't understand what I am seeing. My brain takes a moment to catch up—sluggish, processing through thick confusion. And my view, so obstructed! I could be wrong. Then everything goes too fast: my breathing, my heart, my thoughts. All jumbled, slamming into each other 'til I feel dizzy.

Vola's head is bent over something. I watch as she lifts her hand again, and again, and again. She's hitting something. *A pillow,*

I tell myself. She had a fight with Mo, and she's hitting a pillow. I've done that, exacting revenge on a pillow in the name of a school bully or my mother. Beating and beating until my knuckles were tender and my anger felt dry. But I know it's not true, because I can't see the baby through the slats in his crib. Vola leans back suddenly, and I can see Little Mo. He's lying on his stomach, his head lifted, his face red from the screaming, wet from his tears. He cries so hard that he exhausts himself and stops crying, resting his head on its side and closing his eyes, his little back moving up and down as he takes big, gasping breaths.

As soon as his eyes close, Vola reaches out a hand and pinches him on the leg so hard, I flinch. His head rears up, and he starts again, his face shiny and swollen. I am frozen. I watch as Vola lifts a pillow and slams it into his head. His face bounces off the sheet, and he jerks up, his belly carrying the weight as his head and feet lift. He is shaking, and she is so calm. I don't understand. I feel as if I am missing something, but there is nothing to miss. I am witness to something sinister. As soon as Little Mo has recovered from the pillow, Vola slaps him again, this time with so much force he rolls onto his back.

I can't … I can't…

I fall back from the window, gasping, my heart struggling behind my ribcage like a wounded animal. I hear a noise, and look up, trying to regulate my breathing. A crow is perched on the roof of the house just above my head. Its oiled feathers melt into the darkness of the sky, but I can see its outline, the sharpness of its curved beak. It's looking at me, cocking its head this way then that. It caws at me as if to tell me something, then lifts its wings and flies away.

My soul reacts. It's a deep awakening of something I thought was dead. My brain says: *You're going to lose control. You're going to lose control. You're going to lose control.* And my brain may be right, but what do I care? How has keeping control ever benefitted me? Something else is speaking too. There is another voice—primitive, soft, foreign. The words don't make sense, but then they also do. *Go, go, go.* It says. *Do, do, do.* Soul speak. I look for the crow to see what he says, but he is long gone. The longer I linger out here, the more she hurts Mo.

My heart roars. *Lub dub, lub dub.* I am at the front door. *Lub dub, lub dub, lub dub.* I test the knob. *Why is it open? Lub dub, lubdublubdub.* I step inside. Close it softly. *Lub dub, lub dub.* The baby's car seat is abandoned on the floor, lying on its side, and her keys are on the floor next to it, like she dropped them there in a hurry. In her hurry, she forgot to lock the door—something Mo would not take kindly to. His business needed locked doors, and guns, and thugs. Where were his thugs? The house is empty. *Lubdublubdublubdub.* I walk through the kitchen. Messy counters: food, plates, cat hair. A giant spider scuttles up a bottle of vegetable oil and sits on its lid. The house smells like pot and cigarette smoke and mold. Same as the eating house, minus the pot. A steak knife covered in mayo lays on the counter. *No.* Too messy. I follow the hallway to a door I believe is Vola's and Mo's. I'm emotionless, calm. For a moment I stare down at the brass knob. I can see my reflection on its surface. It's warm when my hand touches it. It's smooth when my hand turns it. She doesn't see me right away; she's too focused on what she's doing—beating the crap out of a baby.

I lunge forward as her hand is suspended mid-air. I have no plan, no choice of action. In fact, I feel as if I'm not acting at all, just watching my body from a far removed corner of the universe. I grab her braid. It's long and thick. She's not expecting my attack, so she starts to fall backward. Half my weight, and a foot shorter, she feels hollow and light. I yank her off the bed, her braid wrapped around my hand. She falls on her rear, her cry of surprise drowned out by the baby and the music. Her mouth is open, her eyes wide as she stares up at me. I glance up at the bed to make sure Little Mo isn't about to roll off. His eyes are open, and he's sucking his fist.

The sight of him trips a switch in me. I can almost hear it. *Click.* My brain suddenly stops warning me that I am going to lose control, though I do not in fact lose control. I am about as calm as I've ever been. A smooth river. A sleeping baby. The melody of a harp. My body moves naturally. I don't just want to stop what's happening. I want vengeance. The same voice that urged me in here is telling me that she needs to pay for what she was doing to Little Mo.

I drag her by her hair to the dresser, chipped and old with sharp edges. There are bottles of nail polish lined up on top of it— blues and turquoises. Vola is over her initial shock, struggling to get away from me. I wind her hair tighter around my fist and lift her knees off the ground 'til she's in a half-standing position. Her mouth is moving, her lips curling over words that I can't hear. Her fists slam into my sides and stomach, anything that she can reach. She's ineffective, a light breeze trying to move a tree. I look down in her empty eyes for long seconds, trying to drag answers out of them. No answers. She's sick. Demented. Physically beautiful. Not worth the life she was given. A predator. A bully. I see my mother in her gray ghost irises. And then, as hard as I can, I slam her left temple into the corner of the dresser. She falls at my feet. Limp. Flesh and bones, but I took her soul.

I smile gravely, and somewhere deep, deep inside of me I know that what I am doing is not normal. I look over at the bed. Little Mo's unfocused eyes are on me. I calmly walk to him and pick him up, holding him against my chest, rocking him side to side. "Shh," I say. I rub his little back, kiss his temple. How long had she been doing this to him? I thought there was something wrong with him mentally, but now I know that's not true. His unfocused eyes, the limpness of his body when you hold him, the way he doesn't really hear your voice—it's all her, what she's done to him.

When he's asleep, I lay him in his crib. There is a stool in the corner of the bedroom. I drag it over to the dresser and place it in between the wall and Vola's body. Then I go to the closet to look for a shoe. I find a plastic flip-flop from Old Navy.

Then I go to the kitchen to find the spider. It's on the wall above the sink, not far from the bottle of oil where I first saw it. A furrow spider. I cup it in my hands and carry it to the bedroom. I let it crawl up the wall above Vola's body, watching it zigzag a path. I never once think about the grown-up Mo, downstairs cooking his crack. At any moment he could walk into the bedroom, but I am not afraid. I do not care about anything except the spider. When it's almost to the ceiling, I climb onto the stool and hit it with the flip-flop, making sure to smear it across the wall. A dramatic death. Poor spider. I wipe the flip-flop clean of fingerprints, and position it in Vola's limp hand. Then I turn the stool on its side, glance at Little Mo one last time. He sighs in his sleep, the deep and raspy sigh of someone who spent the evening crying.

I close the bedroom door softly behind me so as not to wake him, and rub my sleeve over the knob just in case. On my way out,

I straighten the car seat, put the keys neatly on the kitchen counter, and lock the door from the inside.

I smile halfheartedly at the crescent moon. Some people see a thumbnail clipping, but I see a curved mouth. The moon is wicked, jealous of the sun. People do bad things in the dark, under the hollow gaze of the moon. It's smiling at me now, proud of my sin. I'm not proud. I'm not anything. An eye for an eye, I tell myself. A beating for a beating.

THE RAG is full of muted colors. Everything faded, plaids and flower patterns rubbed on the knees and elbows, an ink stain on a sleeve, a coffee stain where a woman's breast had once been pressed. It is depressing to touch the things that people do not want—the washed out, misshapen, frayed. But today, the day after I killed a woman in cold blood, everything in the Rag seems overly bright. I want to close my eyes against the onslaught of colors and patterns. I want to be somewhere still and quiet to go over the details of last night.

I think I'm crazy. Not the crazy that most people are proud of: *Girl, you are so crazy!*

I'm the kind of crazy that no one knows about. Jeffrey Dahmer crazy, Aileen Wuornos crazy, Charles Manson crazy. All the people I've Googled at the local library, and then subsequently read books about, crazy. Had they known the extent of their insanity? Or had they justified their behavior? Narcissists. At least I know. Right? I am not justifying what I did.

I fold clothes, I put cash in the register, I carry a bag of trash to the dumpster out back. I do all of the day-to-day things, trying to grasp a sense of normalcy, while my hands tremor, and my stomach rolls itself into a knot. At any moment I expect the fat, greasy cops of the Bone to come storming into the Rag to arrest me. But the most I see of the police are a couple cruisers stopping across the street to get lunch from the food truck.

Sandy shoots me looks throughout the day, asking me what's wrong, bringing me a bagel from the food truck. I smile and shake my head. Feign a headache. I fold clothes, I dust shelves, I empty bags, I push buttons on the register. I go to the bathroom and lean against the wall, trying to imagine what prison will be like.

I am only nineteen. I had a life ahead of me, and I had to go ahead and ruin it. I try to imagine last night going differently. I come up with dozens of scenarios in which Vola lives, and Little Mo is taken somewhere safe. All I needed to do was run to Judah's house to call the police. But then what? Mo would have come after me. Not because he didn't believe it was true, but because that's just what you did. If someone upset your family dynamic, you made them pay. I could have shown him video of Vola beating his son, and he still would have punished me for being the messenger. And what if the police hadn't taken Little Mo? What if Vola convinced them that he had fallen or he was sick? Would she have taken her anger out on him when they left? And if they did believe me, and they took the baby to a foster home, would they have been better to him than his own crack-cooking, psychotic parents? No matter how hard I try, and no matter how afraid I am, I cannot convince myself that I did the wrong thing. That's the part that makes me like the others: Wuornos and Dahmer and Manson. I do not regret my choice; I stand by it.

There had barely been any questions after they found Vola, limp and cooling on Mo's bedroom floor, her eyes open and staring off into a corner. The police had come and gone, their flashing blue lights bringing the neighbors to their windows and lawns. All ten inhabitants of the bad people house, smoking cigarettes in their wife beaters, making the small lot look like a prison yard. And then, when the paramedics declared her dead, the morgue van had come—old and white, rolling down Wessex like a stately, timeworn gentleman. Had the scene staged in the bedroom been that convincing?

I heard people talking around the neighborhood and in the Rag. The spider turned into a rat, the rat turned into a possum, but there was no alteration to the story in regard to Vola. She had tried to kill whatever vermin was in her bedroom in an effort to protect her baby, and in the process had hit her head and died. What was there for the police to investigate? My little setup had worked. That both mortified me and delivered a sick sense of power. I could do something like that in a place like the Bone and get away with it. Had Vola been someone else, somewhere else, there might have been an investigation. But, here in the Bone, where fathers cooked crack in their basements, someone could hit their head on the corner of a dresser, in an attempt to kill a spider, and die.

Before he called the police, where had he hidden the drugs, his cooking equipment? Had he thrown them away? He had an alibi for the time Vola died. He was listening to music in the basement with two of his buddies, smoking pot and drinking vodka and Red Bull. None of them heard the thud Vola's body made when it hit the ground because the music was too loud.

He found her when he came upstairs for another bottle of vodka, and called down to his friends to call the police. The police searched the house, I saw them do it, but by that time, Mo had already gotten rid of anything that could incriminate him. Slimy bastard. But I was glad he hadn't gotten caught. If he had known what Vola was capable of, he might have killed her himself.

At eight o' clock I lock up the Rag and walk home. I am too sick to grab my usual cup of coffee, so I bite my nails instead. I expect to see a gaggle of police cars outside the eating house, but when I turn down Wessex the only thing different is Vola's car is missing from Mo's driveway. I stop by the crack house, my hand hesitating for a moment before I knock.

Mo opens the door. His eyes are puffy, and it looks like he's been drinking.

"I don't have nothing today," he says. "Had to get rid of that shit before the police came.

"I'm not here for that," I say quickly. "I wanted to see if you needed some help with the baby. I can take him for a bit if you need some time."

Mo's expression softens. "Yeah, thanks," he says. "He's sleeping now, but maybe in the morning. He was messed up today. I think he misses Vola."

"Yeah," I say flatly. "That's expected." I can hear music pounding from the basement, and I wonder how many people are down there while the baby is upstairs alone.

"I'll come back in the morning," I say.

117

As soon as Mo closes the door, I sneak around the side of the house to peek in the bedroom window. The lights are off, but I imagine the baby curled up. Asleep. Safe. And, for a little moment, I feel sated. I did the right thing.

22

WHEN I KNOCK ON MO'S DOOR THE NEXT MORNING, a woman answers. She is heavily perfumed and wearing gold bangles all the way up to her elbows. Little Mo is perched on her hip, his mouth open and emitting wails of discomfort as he tries to pull away from the jewelry digging into his side.

"Yeah?" she says, running her eyes over my jeans and tank top. "Who you is?"

I draw back at her use, actually misuse, of English, wondering if this is Mo's side pony. Vola had been very well spoken, rarely using contractions, even when screaming swear words across the front lawn. *YOU ARE A FUCKING LAZY ASS NOBODY. WHAT YOU NEED TO DO IS GET A REAL JOB, YOU DRUG-DEALING LOSER, AND TAKE CARE OF YOUR SON THE HONEST WAY!*

"I'm here to take Mo for a few hours. Mo the baby," I add. She hands him over without further question and calls over her shoulder. "Your babysitter is here." Mo yells something back about a diaper bag. She reaches into the kitchen and hands me a paper sack with a diaper and two sweaty bottles. I take it from her without a word. She seems relieved to be free of the baby, dusting off her shirt, and pants like she regrets touching him.

The baby stops fussing once he's in my arms. I feel a strange satisfaction that he feels comfortable with me. I walk him down the driveway and over to Judah's house. Once in Judah's living room, I lay him on the couch and start stripping off his clothes.

"What are you doing?" Judah asks, glancing over his shoulder to where Delaney is washing dishes.

"Looking for bruises," I say.

"Why?" He wheels his chair to where he has a good view of what I'm doing.

My hands pause briefly before I pull off Mo's onesie; maybe I imagined the whole thing. Then I step back, giving Judah a view of his chest.

Dark, plum-colored bruises mark his ribcage and arms where I saw Vola pinch him. The rest of his body looks unscathed despite the beating I saw him take. *Slaps,* I think. *Not hard enough to leave lasting marks.* Wasn't that typical of child abuse? Put marks where you can hide them—under clothes. Slap and punch just hard enough to hurt and not stain.

"What is that from?" Judah asks. He reaches out a hand and touches the marks with his fingertip.

"Bruises," I say. "I think his mother ... I think someone hits him."

Judah draws his hand back like he's been stung. "He's a baby..."

"And you think people don't hit babies...?" I wonder after Judah sometimes. How having a more loving mother than the rest of us seemed to increase his naiveté.

I glance at him sideways. His mouth is pinched like he's tasted something terrible, and his eyes stay glued to Mo.

"Do you think Mo—"

"No. I don't think it was his dad."

"Then ... you believe his mother...?"

I grit my teeth. He's putting things together pretty fast. At this point he'll have me pegged for first-degree murder by lunchtime.

"I just noticed these. The other day. I wanted to see if he had new ones."

I gently put his clothes back on and lift him into my arms. The entire time I was examining him, he never made a sound, just stared up at me with those darkly unfocused eyes. I hold him close to my chest, wanting to hug away the first eight months of his life, but as soon as I do, he stiffens, pressing his little hands against my chest and pushing away.

I read an article once about orphans in China, who were left so long in their cribs without human contact that people actually flew there from other countries and volunteered their summers to hold them. Those babies were unused to touch. But Mo associates touch with pain, which is why he stiffens and pulls away when I hug him. It makes sense now. What I had thought was a disability was actually a consequence of abuse. I rub his back and feel the muscles there stiffen and retract.

I suddenly have the urge to tell Judah everything: how I heard Mo crying as I walked home from the Rag, what I saw through the bedroom window, how I walked into the house with not even the slightest falter in my step, and how I slammed Vola Fields's head into the side of the dresser. I want to tell him that I'm glad she's dead, and how I want to take Mo and run away from this place forever. I open my mouth, the entire confession ready to fall off the tip of my tongue, when Delaney walks in, drying her hands on a dishtowel and shaking her head.

"Poor little guy," she says. "Everyone needs their mother." She realizes, too late, what she's said, and her face turns red. "I'm sorry, Margo ... I—"

"Don't worry about it," I say. "She wasn't much of a mother."

I am shaking, just my hands. My mother is dead, and despite the fact that she was lousy at the job, she was it for me. I am alone now. I pull Mo close to me and smell his head. I don't want him to be alone.

LYNDEE ANTHONY is a liar. I am standing behind her, chewing on a piece of my hair as she pays for her Virginia Slims at the Quickie Mart. Knick Knack is hitting on her in that pothead sort of way, where he laughs at everything she says and punctuates his sentences with 'damn.' He sees the SpongeBob fob on her keychain and asks if she has any kids.

Oh my God, Knick Knack, I want to say. *Don't you watch the damn news?* I wait for her to break down; I even hold my breath as I imagine her tear ducts opening, releasing the full force of her pain. Instead she laughs and coyly shakes her head no. *No?* I am still in shock and trying to work out her angle when she leans over the counter to grab her change from his hand. Maybe she doesn't want anyone to know she's Nevaeh Anthony's mother. Maybe she's tired of the looks, and words, and the pity. Knick Knack holds her change just out of reach so that she has to jump for it. He's watching her chest with the rapt attention of a man watching his dinner approach. She seems to be enjoying the play—doe-eyed Lyndee Anthony, who can make Bambi look like a stone cold killer. Playing and flirting like her little girl isn't dead.

That's the moment I decide she's a liar. And if she can lie about not having a kid, a kid who's goddamn dead, what else is she lying about? Maybe I'm being too hard on her. I entertain the thought that she's pretending to be someone else to escape. When Knick Knack has his fill of her bouncy breasts, he hands her the change, and she giggles all the way out the door.

"That's Nevaeh Anthony's mother, you shit," I tell him.

He plucks a box of healthy cigarettes off the shelf and scans them under the gun.

"I know," he says.

I balk at him. "Well, she lied about having a kid," I say, handing over my money.

"I know."

"So the flirting and the questions?"

Knick Knack shrugs. "Why not?" He hands me the pack. "You want to know my professional opinion?" he asks, lowering his voice and leaning his elbows on the counter so that he's close to my face.

"She got rid of her kid. Wasn't no stranger that took her."

The pothead gas attendant is the first one to voice my thoughts. I glance over my shoulder to see if anyone else is in the store.

"Why do you think that?" I hiss, tucking the cigarettes into my back pocket.

"My cousin works with her at the car wash," he says. "My cousin has a little girl, you know. About the same age as Lyndee's kid. My cousin was saying that she couldn't go to this party her friend was having because she didn't have anyone to watch her daughter. Lyndee told her to slip the kid half a sleeping pill. Said it's what she did when she wanted to go out."

I stare at Knick Knack, sour dread curling in my stomach.

"I gotta go," I say. I am halfway to the door when he calls out to me. "Hey, Maggie!"

"Margo," I say.

"You look good, girl! I'd hit that."

I roll my eyes, but there is something so deeply satisfying about that, *You look good girl,* I have to smile.

I am walking down Wessex when I realize I bought cigarettes, and my mother is in a jar in the corner of her old bedroom.

The Bone has one grocery store, two gas stations, and a peppering of small businesses like Fat Joe's Burgers and the FUN! FUN! ARCADE. You're bound to run into the same face more than once a week; at least, that's what I tell myself as I follow Lyndee up and down the streets of Bone Harbor.

It's not until I follow her from the bus stop to Wal-Mart one night that I realize the extent of my obsession. I trail her through the brightly lit aisles with a blue basket looped on my arm, as she piles things into her cart in a hurry: a package of bologna, two liter bottles of Pepsi, a giant jar of pickles, and a bag of green apples.

Every day she eats her apple as she sits at the bus stop, thin slices in a plastic baggie that she pulls out of her purse. I walk past her on my way home from the Rag, studying the bag of apples beside her on the bench. Watching as she sits hunched over her cell phone, her thumbs darting across the screen.

Lyndee was with her boyfriend, Steve, the night Nevaeh went missing. They made dinner and stayed home to watch a DVD: macaroni and cheese—the Kraft kind—and *Transformers*.

The more I see Lyndee Anthony, the stranger I feel. I see her on her porch some nights when I walk home, drinking Mike's Hard Lemonade with Steve, music pounding from the overly juiced stereo inside. I watch carefully for her grief, but it never comes. At least not for my eyes. But I can't tell anyone, not even Judah. My mother had the same look about her—the deer in the headlights vulnerability. I buy a box of Gushers, like the ones Nevaeh used to eat on the bus, and take them to Judah's house. We eat them on his porch as we watch the rain.

"I've never seen her cry," I say about Lyndee.

"Everybody deals with their pain differently," Judah says.

I suppose he's right.

"But shouldn't you cry? Just a little. Or at least look sad?"

He sucks the candy off his teeth and looks at me seriously.

"They found my tumor when I was five. I had to have surgery to remove it. The doctor did a shitty ass job and there was nerve damage."

He runs his hand over his face, and suddenly the cocky joker is gone, and I can see all of his shadows. "God, the therapy ... no little kid should ever have to be that sick. My mom was there all the time. Every day. They had to make her leave to sleep and shower. But, not once did I ever see her cry. That didn't mean she wasn't suffering."

That's the most Judah's ever said about what put him in the wheelchair. It wasn't a car accident like the kids at school had guessed. I remember him as a little boy. He used to run around the front yard naked, shrieking until Delaney would catch him from behind, and tickle him into a fit of laughter. Sometimes I used to see him working in the dirt with her, planting things.

Then one day he just stopped being in the yard. I never thought much about it until school started. He would have been in the same kindergarten class as me, except he never showed up on the first day of school, or the second, or the third. Then a few months later, when I was walking home from school, I saw the chair. It was on the porch, empty, but spoke volumes. Something had happened. *Something.* But what?

When I asked my mother, she said that he'd been sick. He had to go away for a while, and now he was crippled. I didn't know what cripple was until I went to school the next day and asked my teacher, Mrs. Garret. Then the wheelchair made sense. Judah couldn't use his legs anymore. I tried to imagine what it would be like. His house didn't have stairs like mine, but how did he get in the bath? Get out? Who put his pants on in the morning if he couldn't stand up to do it himself?

I imagine his mother does it for him, my mom said when I asked. I watched him really carefully from then on, not because I thought he was a freak like the other kids. Because I didn't know how he could be so different and still always be smiling.

I finish my bag of Gushers and crumple the wrapper in my fist. How did I even end up here, on Judah's porch? We'd never spoken a word to each other, and now, here I was every day.

"Hey," he says.

"What?"

"You look different lately."

I laugh a little. "Lately? As in the two months you've known me?"

"Awe, come on. We've lived on the same block since we were little. We might not have known each other's names, but..."

"Different how?" I ask. My palms are sweating. I look like a murderer, that's what. But what does he see? Can he see the blood on my hands?

"Like you don't give a shit anymore," he says.

I don't.

"I remember watching you walk to school. Every day. First grade through twelfth. You reminded me of a rat."

"Whaa?" I spin around, and he pretends to flinch like he's afraid of me. He's laughing when he says, "You scurried around like you were afraid of everything. Hiding behind the hood of your raincoat, sneaking looks at the world like you expected it to take your cheese."

"It did take my cheese, fool." I laugh.

"Well, you don't do that anymore. You're gangsta now, with your Groceries & Shit bag, and your blue Docs, and your defiant walk."

"You're dumb," I say, though inwardly I wonder how right he is, and when exactly I stopped being a rat?

"I like this new look on you, Margo the lion," he says.

What Judah doesn't say is how much weight I've lost since I broke up with Little Debbie and her crew. Fat rat lost a few pounds. And I stopped chopping my hair off every time it grew past my chin. So, now it's shoulder length, and it reminds me of dying grass—pokey and yellow.

I wonder if he saw *those* changes, and not just the ones that happened on the inside. The fact that my lips aren't buried in the dough of my cheeks, or that I actually have long legs once the cottage cheese deposits melt away. Or maybe he's one of those saintly people who only looks to the inside of others and doesn't see their doughy arms and freckled double chins. *He's just a cripple kid*, I think. *Who cares what the poor, cripple kid thinks of you?* But I do. Because pot-smoking, Judah Grant is the best human I've ever known, and I can't even pinpoint why. I listen to Alanis Morissette on my headphones all night and pretend I don't have a crush on that smiling fool.

"You listen to white girl music," Sandy tells me the next day. I'm singing "Uninvited" as I empty garbage bags in the stock room. "And on top of it, *old* white girl music," she says.

"I am a white girl," I say, putting an ugly ass shirt into the ugly ass shirt pile.

"Yeah, but you have to stay current and shit. Listen to some Miley Cyrus or somethin'. That bitch is a 'Wrecking Ball'!" Sandy cracks up, and I frown. I don't have a radio, car, or television. I use my mother's old CD player and listen to my mother's old CDs.

"And why you singing anyway? You in love or something?"

"Ugh, Sandy! Go away and manage something."

"I'm managing you, girl," she laughs. "You're different lately. I like that."

I stare at the wall after she walks away. Why does everyone keep saying that? And yet no one ... NO ONE has said anything about the fact that I'm not a walking Honey Bun anymore.

I make it two more weeks, covering Lyndee Anthony's shortcomings with Judah's words. Everyone grieves differently.

But it's her laughter that changes everything for me.

I no longer see her as Nevaeh's mother, because, after all, Vola Fields was Mo's mother, and that didn't give her a minute of pause when she beat him. I see her instead as a possibility. Is there a possibility that she is tied to Nevaeh's death? Her boyfriend? Her negligence? Her hands?

Nevaeh looked at me with years in her eyes. She had the young, fresh face of a child, the kind that should always be suntanned, and dimpled, and kissed, but instead her eyes held all the years of a seriously damaged adult. I hated the world for her. I wished someone had seen the years in my eyes when I was her age, and loved me for them. I hate that her father didn't claim her, not even when she went missing, and then only when he could get something out of it. I hate that nothing can be done about the suffering of children, and that most of the world blocks out their suffering to cope with their own inability to help. The few who carry the burden, like social workers and teachers, become weary, burning out after only a few short years, forced to carry the weight that should be shared by a society. Children are vastly overlooked. Their importance underestimated by their size.

In my eighteen years I've heard the phrase *children are resilient* in passing, half a dozen times. But in books they tell you that a child's personality is set by the time he is four years old. That gives parents a four-year window to mold and love accordingly. And thank God that my mother still loved me when I was four, that she only kept her distance later in my life, with the sum of who I was already set like a wobbly Jell-O mold. I can be shaken; I can have a mother reject me over and over, and still I remain someone who is accustomed to love, enough to still seek it out. I desire a deep connection because I have had a deep connection. Reject me, and I'll look elsewhere. I'll just cast less and less of my pearls before swine each time.

THE POLICE ARREST LYNDEE ANTHONY on December 27th. Delaney saw it all go down. She says that when they brought Lyndee out of the house—handcuffed and in a T-shirt with her daughter's photo on it—her face was as peaceful as if they were escorting her to Sunday lunch. Her arrest sent the Bone into a rage. Lyndee had already lost her child, now the police were bringing murder charges against the bereaving mother. The Bone was sick of the persecution of the poor. Sick of not being seen, then being seen for the wrong thing.

Within hours of her arrest, someone had graffiti'd the side of the Wal-Mart that faces the highway with 'Lyndee is innocint!' I cringe when I see it. I have my doubts about her innocence, though no one else seems to. I remember what Knick Knack told me about the sleeping pills. And there's something about her face when no one is watching. But to everyone else, she is a representation of the system trying to hurt you, and all of those who have been hurt rally behind her. Sometimes I wonder if half of her supporters even know what she is being accused of, or if they are just looking for a reason to be mad. Either way, T-shirts pop up all over the Bone. Green ones that say 'Lyndee is Innocent!' I am relieved that someone got the spelling right this time.

But you can't convict a woman based on her facial expressions, and the police seem to have found evidence enough to arrest her. To keep up to date on the case, I buy a small television from the Rag and put it on the kitchen counter. It only gets three channels, but one of them is the news. I watch, like everyone else, as one news station then another picks up the story: *Little girl murdered, her body burned and left in a field.*

It makes us sick all over again, especially when the photos begin to emerge. The police are building a case against Lyndee, the news says. Their evidence is a footprint that matches Lyndee's left in the mud near Nevaeh's body. They found a sneaker in her closet with the same dirt crusted on its sole. The news has been showing a picture of the sneaker in an evidence bag. Different angles of the same shoe, so we know how important it is. It is purple and white, and I wonder if they are making a big deal about the shoe because it is all they have.

We are all on the edge of our seats, waiting. Lyndee's boyfriend provides her with an alibi, as do two other people—their roommates—who saw the couple that night. They release Lyndee on insufficient evidence, and the Bone rejoices. *She is innocint!* And who could blame anyone for believing that with her sweet, childlike face. All across the nation, people make fun of Bone Harbor's shit poor police work. The handling of the crime scene was a joke; they didn't even bag the evidence correctly. The media focuses its attention for a little while on her boyfriend, Steve, who disappeared for a bit and now is back. But since his alibi is Lyndee, they come up empty-handed. This is a case with no evidence.

A little girl went missing on her way home from school, and was murdered, and all they have is a sneaker in a plastic evidence bag. I wonder if the rain had something to do with it—if it washed away something the police could have used.

One afternoon, when I have the day off, I walk to the crime scene. The eating house has been strangely quiet since my mother died. It only speaks when I am trying to sleep—groaning and heaving like it is displeased. Its silence is what really bothers me. So, I escape. Judah is with his father, and I have nothing to do. The day is still. Everything frozen in place without the mountain wind. I take the path through the woods, climbing over fallen trees, and rocks, stopping briefly to pick some blackberries that grow wild along the river. *Even the animals are quiet today*, I think as I listen for even a bird song in this incredible stillness. But, there are no birds singing, only the sound of my shallow breathing as I push through the undergrowth. When I arrive at the place where they found Nevaeh's body, I am surprised to find the yellow police tape still stretched between the trees. The plants have been flattened, stomped down by too many boots. I can see the water from where I stand, peeking lazy from between the trees. I wonder if Nevaeh saw it before she died—if she was conscious and if it brought her peace, or became something ugly because of what was being done to her.

I cannot feel her in this place. I came here looking for her, hoping her presence would kick-start something in my heart. A decision. Now I feel cold and lonely, worse than before. There is a tree with broad, thick branches overlooking the area. I decide to climb it, throwing my leg over the lowest branch and pulling myself up. The bark digs into the exposed skin on my arms and legs, but I don't care because there is something I want to see. I climb higher and higher without stopping. When the branches have thinned enough for me to know that my climb is becoming dangerous, I stop. I can see far into the woods. Most of the trees are below me. Over to the left, the mountains rise, snowcapped, framing the Bone in a wild beauty. I can see some houses on the hill; two of them have red roofs so bright they look like splashes of blood amidst the green. And there it is, what I was hoping to see. The little shack I found weeks ago. It's tiny; you really have to know what you're looking for to be able to spot it. It's a straight shot from here—a place someone could stop if they were hauling a body around in the woods—especially if they were coming from town. I scramble down the branches, careless, and almost lose my footing and fall twenty feet to the ground. When my feet are on the forest floor, I take off running. I hear voices now—laughter. People are in the woods, probably a bunch of kids going to see the crime scene. I flinch when I hear their loud swearing and the high-pitched screams of a girl as she calls out to her boyfriend to stop messing with her. I make a broad circle, hoping to steer clear of their path. I want to see the shed ... the shed ... the shed.

The door to the shed is open. Wide. I stand in between the half-unhinged door and forest, uncertain if I want to step inside. I could be disappointed. I could find everything I need. I step through the doorway and suddenly get the sense that someone is watching me. The inside is much the same as when I last left it—musty, faded. The box of garbage bags is still there ... has it been moved? I can't tell. Piles of leaves lay across the floor—more than before because the door has been left open. I search the corners, kick the leaves aside. There is nothing unusual. I wonder if the police came here when they were searching the woods after they found her body. There is nothing here, but I still get the feeling that there should be. I leave the shed, walk west toward the eating house. The moss is thick on the tree trunks, bright lime against the black bark. It's because of that stark contrast that I see it. The pink among the green. I bend down to retrieve it, half-buried in the moss. A pink hair tie. One that I used to tie off the end of her braid that last day on the bus. I clutch it in my fist, my eyes burning from the tears. *There you go,* I think. *You found what you were looking for.*

I hope Judah comes back soon; when he's gone I start having very bad thoughts.

JUDAH GOT A NEW WHEELCHAIR. One of those electronic things that move around with the press of a button.

"Someone donated it to the center, anonymously" he says, swiveling it in circles until I feel dizzy watching him. "I don't like it, but the director looked like she was going to cry when she presented it to me. I feel like a lazy ass pushing a button to move." I glance at his old chair, which looks mournfully abandoned on the lawn.

"Maybe you can lift weights," I offer. "You can't let your guns go; they're a thing of beauty."

"My arms!" He pretends to be offended, but I can see that he's pleased. "You treat me like a piece of meat," he complains.

"Let's see if it can handle both of us." I ignore him and climb onto his lap without being invited.

"You're crushing me," he groans dramatically. For a moment I remember the fat jokes in high school, the embarrassment I felt being the owner of my own skin. But Judah is joking, and I'm no longer fat.

I spin around to look at him. "How do you figure? You have no sensation in your legs."

"Oh yeah," he says playfully. "Let's do this shit."

"Onward!" I lift a fist into the air, and we surge forward on the sidewalk. It's only when you're pushing a wheelchair, or hitching a ride in one, that you notice how shitty sidewalks actually are. We are gliding forward at a snail's pace, but I hold on for dear life, afraid I'll be thrown by one of the cracks or the general unevenness of the sidewalk. There is a couple sitting on lawn chairs outside the bad people house. They cheer and hold up their drinks as we scoot by. I am conscious of everything during our painfully slow ride up the street—the way his arm wraps around my waist, his head peering around my arm to see where we are going, the sun warming our skin. We stop when we reach the eating house. I feel self-conscious being this close to the house while sitting on Judah's lap. Judah looks up at the sagging, decrepit house. His eyes linger on the newspaper that covers the hole in my bedroom window.

"It's kind of scary looking," he says. "It feels like it's looking at me, instead of me looking at it." He moves his chair back and forth in absent little jerks, while I stand beside him, admiring the monster house. I hate the eating house, but I feel somewhat unsettled by his comment, like I need to say something to defend it.

"It's ... not that bad." But, even as I say it, I can smell the mold and feel the relentless chill that creeps through the walls at night. "It is that bad," I admit. "At night I always get the feeling that someone is watching me. And the wood floors give me splinters and shit."

"And shit," Judah says. "All right! Hop on, we're going back!"

Despite his offer, I walk beside him, the hum of his chair reminding me of distant helicopter blades. As we pass the bad people house, Judah points to a twenty-dollar bill on the pavement. I bend to pick it up, glancing at the house like someone is going to come charging out, demanding their money back.

"Finders keepers," says Judah. The bill is slightly damp. Someone had drawn horns on Andrew Jackson's head and written *Fuck you America* underneath his picture in red ink. Suddenly, the memory of the last time I saw Nevaeh comes rushing back to me.

Neveah went missing with her backpack. The Hello Kitty backpack with the teddy bear stuffed at the bottom, and her matching wallet with her ten one-dollar bills folded neatly into the bill flap. The ten dollars that she never got to spend because she didn't live a week past getting them. I remember her pulling out a purple marker from her pencil case and drawing a heart in the corner of each of the dollars her grandmother had given her. I remember thinking that it was an odd and endearing thing to do. Before the bus reached her stop, she had straightened the dollars into a pile and carefully placed them back in her wallet. I left her at the bus stop that day wondering what she would buy with her ten dollars, and imagining what I would have bought when I was her age. How exciting was the prospect of ten dollars to a little girl.

Had she died the same day she disappeared? It was something I thought of almost every day. I hoped so. I hoped that whoever took her didn't make her suffer. To think of Nevaeh suffering caused a tightness in my chest that wouldn't go away. I hope she died quickly, and that she didn't know it was happening. Sometimes I fantasized about finding her before the sick bastard killed her. In my daydream, I would strangle the perpetrator, then pick Nevaeh up from the floor and carry her to Judah's. There we would devise a plan to get her out of the Bone, together. We'd go somewhere bright, where the sun never stopped shining. I'd come back to reality, lying on my mattress and staring up at the ceiling, convincing myself that it was too late, and that she was already dead.

There were suspects who the police were questioning. That's all they told us: suspects. I saw them in my mind as dark, shadowy figures without faces. How the police were finding these *suspects*, and who they were questioning, nobody knew. But Nevaeh was still making national headlines, and everyone was looking at the Bone, so the news had to say something positive about the case. Leads ... detectives were always following leads. There were even reporters wandering around the Bone, wearing pressed khakis and Oxford shirts, carrying fancy messenger bags. They always wore a look of careful determination, like they were going to be the ones to unearth Nevaeh's killer. Sometimes I saw them talking to the locals, trying to extract little bits of story here and there. I avoided them. They didn't have a look of despair on their faces. I couldn't trust that.

A few days into January I pass a man reading the paper as I walk to work. The charred remnants of Nevaeh's Hello Kitty backpack are on the front page. The picture is grainy, and I glance at it for just a moment before I quickly remove my eyes, my heart pounding. The last time I had seen her, she'd been wearing that backpack, shiny and clean, and now the plastic on the backpack was bubbled and black. I remember her braids, and I wonder if they were still in her hair when the police found her body. I'd touched her hair, and then she died.

A week later I watch Lyndee Anthony count out five one-dollar bills, and hand them to cashier at Wal-Mart, the gallon of milk she's buying tucked under her arm. Each dollar has a purple heart in its corner. I reach up to touch the pink hair tie on my wrist. That's when I know I'm going to kill her.

IT TAKES TIME TO PLAN SOMEONE'S MURDER. There are a lot of things to consider; for one: you have to ask yourself if you are trying to kill an innocent woman. Two: how do you want this potentially innocent woman to die, and should you establish absolute non-innocence before reviewing your options? Three: if she were innocent, how did she get those dollars?

Poison is my first choice—clean and easy. But poison can be traced. And I don't know Lyndee well enough to offer her an arsenic-laced bon bon, and there is always the chance someone else could eat it, then I really would be responsible for an innocent death. That would make me just like her.

There is strangulation, which sounds more appealing than poison, but takes more work. The risk that something could go wrong is bigger—I could be overpowered, or even caught.

I can buy a gun; there are ways. But guns are messy and loud. There is no art in a bullet. No class in a knife. I want her to die in the right way. A way that serves the most justice to my little Nevaeh.

Lyndee Anthony told police that the last time she saw her daughter was on the morning she disappeared, when she sent her off to school with her backpack. Nevaeh got off the school bus that afternoon, walked the two blocks to the bus stop on Bishop Hill, where she caught the 712 with the intention of going to her grandmother's house. And on that rainy day, I braided her hair—cuffing the braid with the pink hair tie I now wear around my wrist—and bid her farewell, reminding her to be careful in the briny Bone. Which means Nevaeh went missing with her backpack, her hair in the pigtails I braided, and her ten one-dollar bills tucked safely away in her wallet. There was, of course, the possibility that Nevaeh drew that same purple heart on her mother's dollars. It might have been her trademark. That's what concerned me the most. Deciding a woman was guilty of murdering her only daughter based on a purple heart.

My worries about Lyndee being innocent are put to rest one evening in November when I decide to take the bus home from the Rag. In winter it gets dark around four o' clock. The chill creeps in from the Sound, blowing over the Bone, then skirting on to Seattle. The early darkness paired with the dragging rain is enough to chase an avid walker to the bus. I stand huddled underneath the shelter, my jacket soaked from the short walk over. My limbs, which have become accustomed to the walking, long to be stretched and pushed up hills. But, as I climb onto the bus and choose a seat in the back, I am glad to be out of the nasty weather. I wonder what Judah is doing tonight, and if he wants to watch a movie. When I look up, I notice Lyndee sitting across from me. Her short hair is plastered to her forehead like she was caught in a bad downpour. Aside from being wet, she looks quite happy, smiling down at her phone every time the chime of a text sounds. She's not wearing the T-shirt with Nevaeh's face this time, but a low-cut top and a cheap-looking necklace that spells out SEXY. When we arrive at her stop, she reaches for the backpack that has been sitting between her knees. Unzipping the top, she pulls out a bottle of water, upsetting some of the contents inside. Her keys come falling out, and I am given a glimpse of a small, pink bear—Bambi. My heart hammers.

I look away quickly. Too quickly. Lyndee sees my reaction and zips up the bag, her eyes fixed on my face in a bold challenge. *Does she know who I am? Does she know I was one of the last people to see Nevaeh alive, and that I gave my statement to the police?* I look out the rain-speckled window; I look at the ripped seat next to me. I cannot look at her face. Everything I'm feeling is naked on my face. She had something to do with it. My heart feels sore, like it's tired and bruised. Mothers hurting their children, mothers giving up on their children, mothers loving something more than their children. I watch her sling one strap over her shoulder and climb off the bus in a hurry. To get away from me? I follow her down the stairs. When we reach the pavement, we head in opposite directions. For several minutes I keep my eyes straight ahead, pointed toward Wessex and the eating house. But, as I pass the corner store, and Knick Knack waves to me from the window, my curiosity gets the best of me. I stop walking and turn just my head, just enough so that I can see her. She's already looking at me, paused on the sidewalk, her whole body facing my direction. I am racked with chills. She turns on her heel, quickly, almost running now. I watch her with the bitter look of conviction. I've convicted her in my head. Me, the jury of one. And I've issued her a death sentence. I decide to burn her, the same way she burned her daughter. An eye for an eye.

I COLLECT THINGS. It's an art to buy weapons and not look suspicious. Rope, a hunting knife, arsenic, sleeping pills—my mother has a myriad. I won't use most of them, but it's become a compulsion. I think about burning Lyndee every day. I don't buy a new lighter because I have the pink one and also a book of matches. That's what I'll use. I wonder if I'll be able to watch, or if it will make me squeamish.

Some days, when I see her around town, laughing and flirting, I decide that I'll watch every moment—the bubbling and crackling of her skin, the charring of her pretty white flesh. And other days—days when I feel sad and sluggish—I just want it to be over: fast and clean. She shouldn't be here, walking around ... living. It irks me. When I watch her, I pick at myself—the skin around my fingernails, the sides of my mouth. I have little scabs on the back of my neck and behind my ears. But I watch her every day. Just to be sure. You can never be too sure.

In the time not spent watching Lyndee, I search the house for my birth certificate. I get it now. Why my mother wouldn't let me see it. She didn't want me to see who was listed as my father. But I want to get a driver's license. Open a bank account. I find it one day as I'm searching the attic. It's stuffed in the middle of a book tossed with all my mother's things. It's one of those travel books that people get when they're going to Europe. It's yellowed, turned up at the edges. Well worn. I wonder if she was planning a trip before I was born. Perhaps with Mayor Delafonte. But who cares? I have my birth certificate. She listed him as my father. I can't imagine why except if she was keeping it to use against him. Ammunition. My mother wasn't stupid; she was just mentally ill.

I call from the Rag and make an appointment to take the test to get my learner's permit. That will have to do for now. I need a way to leave if I have to. I stress for weeks about how I'm going to get Lyndee alone. Should I drug her? Lure her somewhere? Would she come alone? I planned for every possibility. Plan A. Plan B. Plan C. That's what you need: a dozen plans in case something happens to change Plan A. I can't sleep at night when the eating house is awake, making noises around me. I catnap during the day and stay up most nights—planning, thinking about the tiny coffin in the oven, the little body in the corner of my mother's bedroom. Bones and blood, all in the eating house. Children died because of the evil inside of grownups. Selfish evil. The only time I don't think about killing Lyndee Anthony is when Judah is near. He takes all of my vengeance away. Replaces it. But he's not around very often anymore. His father comes to get him in his big, shiny truck, wheelchair folded into the cab, Judah's face smiling. I am jealous, and I am not. I want him to have things, be happy.

I am in bed. I squeeze my eyes shut, block out the shadows that are dancing across my ceiling. Next to me, on the floor, is a bottle of chloroform that I paid Mo to make. Five hundred dollars for ten measly ounces. But Mo doesn't ask questions, and that's worth every penny. I open my eyes and pick up the bottle, lifting it to my face. I sniff, but there is no odor. Everything is sealed so there won't be any accidents. Chloroform seemed like the boring choice at the time, but sometimes a choice needs to be boring to work.

When the sun comes up, I sleep. Just for a few flat hours while the house is still. Lyndee Anthony is up, eating the strawberry yogurt she buys from the market—have some in the fridge downstairs—putting on her uniform for another workday at the carwash. Today will be her last day. Today will be a good day.

At noon I get up, dress. I go to the shed first, to get things ready, then I stop by the carwash to make sure Lyndee is there.

I see her through the window, talking to a customer. She hands him his change and points in the direction of the coffee machine, where customers can sit and drink muddy caffeine while their cars are pushed through the washer and dried by two meth heads named Jeremy and Coops, who I went to school with. I touch the rubber band on my arm as I watch her, and suddenly I am struck by what I am about to do. It's like I am looking at myself from some high vantage point outside of my body—a stranger. I remember the girl, who, just a few months ago, was timid and afraid. Now she is something else. Something deadly. Determined. I am scared of her. I go home to wait out the afternoon. At six o'clock it begins to rain. That was not in my plan. I worry about the rain making it difficult to drag Lyndee's body through the woods. But, in the end, I know that I will get her to the cabin ... rain or not.

Two blocks over from where Lyndee lives is a small park bordered by the woods. It's a decrepit excuse for a park—a patch of dirt with a swing and a grungy yellow tunnel slide jutting from a wooden platform. The neighborhood kids don't really play there anymore. There are swear words spray painted down the slide, and you can always find a used condom inside of the slide. Teenagers come here to drink—late at night normally. I will be gone by the time they arrive.

For three weeks I've been leaving Lyndee love notes. Sometimes I put them in her mailbox—a plain white envelope with her name—or I leave them in her cubby at work when she has a day off, sneaking into the break room when the girl at the desk goes to the bathroom. In the notes, I pretend to be a man named Sean, who lost a son to drowning four years ago. Sean is empathetic to Lyndee, complimenting the poise with which she handles the negative media attention. He tells her about the ridicule he received from friends and family as they blamed him for his son's death. At first it was just Sean writing her all the notes, but then he gave her the option of writing back to him ... so they could really get to know each other. *You can leave a note taped to the bottom of the slide at the park on Thames.* Within a day of his last note, Lyndee left a three-page response taped with duct tape to the underside of the slide. Her handwriting is childish, little circles dotting each "i." She does not speak about Nevaeh in her letters, instead detailing her own suffering, the injustice with which she's always been dealt. It makes me hate her more that she won't talk about her dead daughter. I test her, writing long details about Sean's son, telling her stories, and in turn asking her to tell me about Nevaeh. She ignores the topic of her daughter altogether to talk about herself, over and over. I become angrier at each bubble-dotted letter. More sure.

Judah would defend her—say that she's lonely and has trouble talking about Nevaeh. But her letters are too sensual in nature. She's flirting with Sean, playing the part of the vulnerable, grieving mother. Steve had broken up with Lyndee shortly after they let her out of jail, saying she brought too much drama to his life. He moved out of the house they shared with their roommates, and in to a house with Genevieve Builo, his high school sweetheart. Lyndee, scorned and still under media scrutiny, needed a hero. I decided to be that hero. During the first week or two of us exchanging letters, she would wait at the park to see if "Sean" would show up to collect her note. But eventually she would grow tired of waiting in the rain, and walk home, my note stuffed in her backpack. I am still astounded that she didn't question things more. Become suspicious. But the truth of the matter—as I've come to understand it—is that people will ignore every warning sign when blinded by their thirst for something. It's better to not be thirsty.

It's dark when she arrives. She's told no one she's coming; she's afraid of the media finding out. *They'll say awful things about me if they hear I'm happy*, she said in her last letter. I agreed, saying we should meet in secret. So we agree. The shed in the woods. Take the path by the park, walk half a mile. I smile when I see the yellow glow of her flashlight through the trees.

THE NIGHT IS COLD. I can see my breath—human steam disappearing into the night. I wait for Lyndee to wake, blinking languidly at the space on the floor where I've laid her. I have no sense of urgency, no need to move, and fidget, and do. I'm content to wait. My thoughts are delicate, forming frail arguments of why I shouldn't be doing this, then breaking apart in the firmness of my resolve. So, I watch Lyndee, I watch my breath, I wait. In the early hours she stirs, mumbling something under her breath and rolling onto her back. Despite her impending death, I've brought a blanket and spread it across her body. In her sleep she pulls it tighter around herself. I shift on my stool, sighing deeply. It was easy—so easy. She fell right to the floor, the rag pressed to her nose.

Lyndee awakes disoriented. She sits up, struggling against the ropes I've tied around her ankles and wrists. Slowly she takes in her surroundings. Her hair is sticking straight up on one side. I wait, perched on the stool, my hands folded in my lap. I imagine I look like a schoolgirl gone wrong, straight-backed and intense, a can of gasoline between my boots. When she sees me, she doesn't look surprised. Not even a little. It feels right, like this is all supposed to be—her and me here, in a shed with a can of gasoline.

"I'm Sean," I say cheerfully. She flinches.

I open her backpack, the zipper loud even among the singing of the night creatures. From it I pull Bambi, Nevaeh's pink bear. I hold it up to Lyndee. "I was on the bus with Nevaeh the day she went missing. This was in her backpack." Lyndee's eyes travel from the bear back to my face. Her expression reveals nothing, though her hands appear to clutch the blanket a little tighter.

"She disappeared with her backpack. Except she didn't really disappear, did she? She was with you."

Lyndee at first shakes her head, her eyes zoned in on the bear. But, when I say, "You killed Nevaeh." She becomes defensive, her face contorting as she tries to form an argument. She sees the gas can, and something changes in her movements.

"It was an axe-dent," she says, scrambling backward until her shoulders hit the wall. One of her breasts has slipped from her shirt; it hangs limply over the floral material. *I sold her that shirt at the Rag*, I think. When Nevaeh was still alive. She came with her mother, and hung out with me at the register, counting the pennies in the "extra jar" while Lyndee shopped. I can see the beads of sweat on Lyndee's brow, brewing slowly then slipping down the side of her face. She reeks of sweat and fear, but not regret. If I smelled a hint of it on her, I might think twice about what I'm about to do. But Lyndee is a narcissist. She's convinced herself that killing and burning her daughter's body was an accident.

"You could have sent her to live with her grandmother."

"I know, I know. Don't do this, please. Let me go. I'll turn myself in to the police. Is that what you want? I ain't got no problem with you." She's holding up her hands as if she can ward me off with her dirt-stained palms. Her nail polish is blue, painted perfectly like she took the time to get it right. This makes me angrier, that she could be so meticulous with her nail polish, caring that there is no overlap onto her fingers, that there are enough coats to make it smooth and thick. All for Sean. Caring about fingernails while she cared so little for her girl.

I ease up, relax my shoulders, and readjust my face to pretend I'm thinking about it.

"Why did you do it?" I ask.

She's cowering on the floor. I can see the whites of her eyes as she claws at the dirt.

"My boyfriend," she says. "He didn't want no kids. He wanted to move to Portland, he's got family there and a better job waiting.

I told him Nevaeh was a good girl, but she didn't like him. Always used to make trouble for me by saying stuff to him. When I told her we was leaving, she said she wasn't going, she wasn't moving away from her granny. Her daddy wasn't paying me nothing either," she finishes, as if this justifies everything.

"How did she die?" My voice is neutral, my face impassive. I am afraid that if I show emotion, she won't tell me what happened, but I need to know what they did to Nevaeh.

I expect her to answer me, but she turns her face away.

"It was him, wasn't it?"

She nods, her jaw clenched. "We went to pick her up, caught her on her granny's street. She wouldn't get in the car…"

I think of Nevaeh. I'd never seen her be defiant, never seen her disrespectful.

"Steve got out to grab her," Lyndee says. "He was … rough. She screamed real loud and tried to run. We had to drive off real fast."

I have to close my eyes, the scene playing out graphically in my mind. A little girl's terror, her need to run to her grandmother who gave her a sense of love and permanence. Her mother's boyfriend, always resentful, always watching, wishing she weren't there. Nevaeh knowing and living with the fact that her mother chose someone else over her daily. Sent her away as often as possible to salvage her relationship with a man who couldn't tolerate her child.

"What then?" I say, impatient for the story to be over. I want to know how she died, so I can bring Lyndee Anthony to justice.

"He gave her some juice, to calm her down. Didn't tell me there was sleeping pills in there until after. He was just gonna make her sleep 'til we got to Portland. We went back to the house to get some things before Tom got home from work. Tom owns the house, he's Steve's friend. We wanted to be out before the morning so we didn't have to pay rent. We owed a couple months, you know. We packed up the car with our shit. Before we left I looked back at her. She looked funny. When I reached back and felt her neck, she was cold. And she wasn't breathing." She lets out a pitiful sob. "I ain't meant for her to die!" Her story is wobbling from "he" to "I," and I wonder how much of her account is truth. How much of it was her plan, and how much of it was Steve's?

"Why didn't you take her to the hospital? There could have been time to save her. She could have been in a coma!"

Lyndee's eyes shift from side to side, trying to find an adequate excuse, or perhaps a way out of the shed. She is trying, I realize, to answer me in the way she thinks I want.

"It was too late," she says. "There was no heartbeat." I know that's not true by the look on her face. Nevaeh's heartbeat may have been barely discernible, but there was still time to get her to a hospital.

"So you drove her to the woods and burned her?"

My heart rate is rising as I realize Nevaeh could have been alive when they burned her. Trapped inside her own mind, in a coma. Lyndee and her idiot boyfriend too high and stupid to know that a person's heart rate can drop so low that even a stethoscope can struggle to pick it up.

"Steve said the mistake was already made. We could make it look like someone took her. I didn't want to go to prison because of an accident!" She's so insistent. So desperate for me to see her broken reasoning.

"An accident?" I ask. "What about the rest of the days? Not just the day you killed her. All the days you chose your piece of shit boyfriend over her, the nights she put herself to bed because you were too drunk to stand up, the nights she made herself dinner, the days she had to take care of YOU. You were her mother!"

Lyndee is temporarily stunned, her lips moving without sound.

"You knew her," she finally says. "Did she tell you that?"

She did. Stories on the bus. Little things Nevaeh would say. Never accusatory in regards to her mother, just simple facts that slipped in during our conversations.

"Bambi was scared last night. She cried 'til she fell asleep."

"Why was she scared?"

"We were home alone."

"Where was your mom?"

"Somewhere with Steve…"

"I ate brownies for dinner, and I felt so funny after."

"You did? Was it someone's birthday?"

"Naw. It was dinnertime. Mama was asleep, so I ate the brownies I found. But after that I felt dizzy and weird…"

"It was my birthday this weekend."

"What did you do? Did you go somewhere special?"

"No. Mama had to go somewhere important with Steve. She said we would go to a movie next week."

"So you didn't do anything for your birthday?"

"They sang to me at school, and Granny brought me over a cupcake."

I try to find my humanity. There is forgiveness, even in the hardest human heart. I could hand her over to the police, but there's no evidence. If they pushed her, perhaps she'd confess like she did with me, but if she didn't, then what? Without proof, they'd have to let her go. Judah is right. There is no justice for the poor.

"I'm sorry," I say. "I can't do that. From one murderess to another, you should understand."

She whimpers. She was a little girl once. Just like Nevaeh, with pigtails and innocence and hopes for a life of love. Maybe if I picture her like that, I can forgive her. I try, but all I see is a murdering whore. She was born to be a murderess, just like me. Plus, I like the way this feels. Cleaning up. The satisfaction is deep. A warm shower when you're cold. I pick up Bambi from where Lyndee dropped her, and tuck her under my arm.

Murderess!

Murderess!

I empty the gas can around her; it splashes on her arms and legs, the smell of petroleum burning my nose and making me light-headed. She yells and begs, brilliant, thick tears streaming down her face. All I can think is how she never cried for Nevaeh, not once, but here she is crying for herself. She stands up and rushes me, but the chain around her ankle yanks her back. She falls, but for a moment she is suspended in the air. I slip the book of matches from my back pocket. Heat flares across the shed. Lyndee screams. I close the door behind me. I burn her. One match from a book that I bought from the Quickie Corner—the ones with the teddy bear on them—and a locked room soaked in gasoline. An eye for an eye. A burn for a burn. Vengeance for Nevaeh.

I am a monster. I am just like her. One day I'll burn, but not now. Now I'll burn her. I am not five steps out when I see the crow. A dark blur on a branch. It caws at me. I lift a hand, wave to the bird, then carry on.

The smoke curls into the sky behind me as I pick my way back through the woods. I take my time, touching the leaves and listening to frogs and crickets. I am relaxed, lulled by her screams.

"Do you hear that, Nevaeh?" I say to the woods. "Vengeance is mine."

I WAKE UP IN A COLD SWEAT. I am shaking so hard I bite down on my tongue and taste blood. There was a dream, horrific and violent, in which I burned Nevaeh's mother alive. I swallow the blood in my mouth and stare down at my hands. My fingernails are dirty—ripped, jagged, and caked in dark dirt. I run to the bathroom. I don't care if my mother has a man in her bedroom. I don't care that I'm not supposed to be out here before seven so that he can leave in peace. I need to see myself. My face is dirty, my eyes big, panicked. There is blood on my chin and long scratches on my cheeks. I fill the sink with hot water, and grab the old rag from its hooks. Dipping it in the water, I scrub my face, then my fingernails.

"Oh my God. Oh my God..." I say it over and over to fill the silence of the eating house. Her body burning. Her screams. They were all real. I did that. Again. And it wasn't an accident. Not the first time, not last night. I killed. I bend over, breathing hard, and then not breathing at all. I don't know whether to breathe or not breathe. I don't know whether to stand, or sit, or cry, or run. It wasn't like this the first time. I killed Vola on instinct when I caught her in the act of beating her child. I planned Lyndee's murder, agonized over the details, but I never saw her hurt

Nevaeh. I could turn myself into the police. It's then that I remember my mother is dead. It all comes back in a flash of memory: blood, the body bags, the tiny body in the corner of the bedroom. I straighten up, blinking at myself in the mirror.

Someone is pounding on the door. I stumble downstairs, blinking at the light streaming in through the windows. My mother kept the upstairs dark in hopes that her customers wouldn't notice the fine lines starting to etch their way across her face. Sometimes, when you were up there, you forgot if it was day or night. I make a mental note to pull down the newspaper she used to block out the light.

I look through the peephole and see Mo on the porch, irritated. My blood runs cold. I take a step back, wring my hands, lick away the beads of sweat on my upper lip. He couldn't possibly know. Unless someone saw me...

Why is it so goddamn hot in here? Hiding is bad. Hiding makes you look guilty. I lunge for the deadbolt and turn it before I have the chance to overthink things.

"What the fuck took you so long?"

"I was fucking sleeping."

Mo is looking at his phone, his fingers moving across the screen in hyper speed.

"That's bullshit," he says. Except he pronounces it bool-sheeit.

"What do you want?" I fold my arms across my chest, to hide the fact that I'm not wearing a bra, and lean against the doorframe.

"I need you to watch my kid," he says. "Vola's ma don't want him, and I got shit to do."

My heart jumps at the prospect of seeing Little Mo. I'd been too afraid to go over there since ... I did that thing. Afraid someone would see her death on my face.

"Yeah, whatever," I say. "But I'm not your babysitter."

He looks up from his phone. "Chill out, giiirl. I ain't asked you to be no babysitter. Just watch him for me as a favor. I'll hook you up."

I shrug. *Lubdublubdublubdub.*

He starts to walk away, then suddenly turns to look at me. "Sorry about your moms. We both lost someone. 'S fucked up." It looks like he might want to give me a hug, so I back up a few steps.

Out of habit, I glance at the stairs, expecting to see the bottom of her red robe. The eating house is mine now. If I want to use the bathroom before seven, I can. If I want to stomp around and yell at the top of my lungs, I can.

"I'll be okay," I say. "...will you guys?"

Mo shrugs. "Don't have no choice but to be."

I wonder what Mo would do to me if he knew about Vola. Maybe, in some ways, Mo is relieved she is gone. Like I am about my mom. But he'd probably lodge a bullet in my skull and call it a day. That is the way of things here: revenge over reason.

He comes back with the baby ten minutes later. There is no diaper bag, no food, no bottles, no instructions. Just Little Mo in his too-big-for-him stroller, his velvety brown eyes blinking slowly like the world has no appeal.

"Let's go shopping," I tell him, watching through the window as his father slams the door to the crack house. I mess with the wheel of the stroller for twenty minutes while Mo lies on a blanket on the floor next to me. In the end it's too hard to fix, so I sling my Groceries & Shit bag over my shoulder and carry him. He's so still in my arms that every few minutes I peer down to see if he's fallen asleep. I hear Judah calling my name. When I turn around, he's wheeling himself down the sidewalk quicker than I've ever seen him move. He went back to his old chair, said the other one made him feel lazy.

He slows down when he's next to us, and keeps pace.

"Where were you last night?"

I stop. "What?"

"Last night," he says again. "I saw you walking home. You looked ... strange."

"Work," I say, starting to walk again.

"Something keep you late?" he asks. His hands are moving quickly across the wheels of his chair to keep up.

"Huh?"

"It was midnight when I saw you."

"Oh ... yeah. I was late." I look out at the field across the street. The leaves on the trees are turning.

He's quiet for a minute, then he says, "They found a body near the harbor this morning."

"Whose?" I ask. My mouth feels dry. I try to keep my eyes on the road ahead of me, but everything is blurring in and out of focus.

"They don't know yet. It's on the news. Someone reported a fire in the woods near the harbor, so the police went out there to check it out, and there was a body."

"Hmm," I say. "Whose was it?"

"You just asked me that," he says. "I told you they don't know."

'Oh," I say dumbly. I switch Mo to my other hip.

"Let me have him," Judah says, holding out his arms.

"He doesn't know you," I say, squeezing Mo a little tighter.

"And you two are on a first name basis?" He wiggles his fingers impatiently. I reluctantly relinquish the baby to Judah's arms. My arms are starting to get tired, and I'm not even to the end of Wessex yet.

"You can push me, and I can hold him. Doesn't he have a stroller?"

"It's broken," I say. "The wheel…"

"Bring it over later, I'll take a look."

"Ugh, you're so helpful it's annoying," I say.

Judah turns the baby around so they're facing each other. I notice that Little Mo pulls his legs up instead of stiffening them when held under his arms.

"You don't look like a Mo,'" he informs the baby. For the next forty minutes I listen to Judah discuss various name choices with the baby, who looks right through him. By the time we reach Wal-Mart, my arms are aching, and the baby is fussy. Judah has somehow renamed him Miles. "Mo Miles, Mo Miles," he says, and I swear Mo gives him a little smile like he's approving. Mo's smiles are rare. I feel jealous.

"I think he needs formula," I say. We make our way to the baby aisle. I grab diapers, formula, and a pack of bottles. When I turn around, Judah has a colorful toy in his hand; he's moving it left to right, letting Mo follow it with his eyes. There is a brief moment where Mo lifts his fist as if to touch the toy, and my heart does a little jump.

"We're getting that too," I say.

"Your mom leave you some money?" he asks me when I pull a hundred dollar bill from my pocket.

"You could say that."

"Here," he says, holding out his hand for my Groceries & Shit bag. "He needs a bottle."

I hold Mo while Judah makes him a bottle. Two scoops of formula, a bottle of Aquafina, then he shakes it and holds out his arms. I place Mo is his lap, and Judah sticks the bottle in his mouth. As I watch Mo eat, I wonder how Judah knew how to do that. I would have struggled to read the instructions for fifteen minutes, and probably would have dropped the whole container of powder on the ground. While I watch them, I hear Lyndee's screams. I smell the smoke. I feel her blood. I killed a woman. I planned it all out, and I killed a woman, and here I am at Wal-Mart the next day with my hot cripple friend and the neighbor's baby. I don't know which person is the imposter. I am either Margo of the Bone, or this new thing, this murderer. Or maybe I've always been her, this vile, wicked person; she was just there, simmering beneath the surface, waiting for me to act on my impulses.

"How did you know how to do that?" I ask.

"Work."

"You work with babies?"

"I work with children of all ages."

"Where do you work anyway?"

"Are we friends now?" he asks. "Officially?"

"I guess so," I say. "We see a lot of each other. We're either friends at this point or we're married."

"Margo Grant," he teases. "You can be Miles Grant," he tells Mo. Mo pauses for a minute in his sucking to smile at Judah, while I blush profusely.

"Don't you buy into his charm," I tell Mo. "He's a big flirt."

The sun heats our shoulders with little mercy. I am wishing I had sunscreen for the baby when Judah suddenly decides to answer my question.

"I work at Barden's School for the Disabled," he says. "It's also where I went to school. My mom got me a scholarship, somehow convinced them to put me on their bus schedule even though they have to drive all the way out here to this evil corner of the universe. When I graduated, they offered me a part-time job working with the after school kids and as a teacher's aide."

I glance down at the top of his head, impressed. It seems exactly like the sort of thing he should be doing. I am just about to say so when he says...

"I hated going there. I already felt so different, then I was forced to go to a school where everyone was different. And all I wanted to do was experience some normalcy."

I think about my high school experience—the kids with their guarded, worn eyes. Wanting someone to notice you all the while praying no one does. The urgency to find likeness in your peers and knowing you never will. The desperate and clumsy attempts to dress, and speak, act and tolerate what is deemed acceptable. It was the most humiliating, desperately lonely four years of my life. And yet, had Judah's body been whole, his legs undamaged by the tumor that stole his ability to walk, he would have stood tall, probably played football on the school's team. Handsome and popular, he never would have been the kind of boy to exchange words with me. How lucky did that tumor make me? How blessed? To get to know a man like Judah Grant without the social barriers dictating our roles.

"You didn't miss out on anything," I tell him. "People are mostly just assholes in high school."

Judah laughs. "Don't swear in front of the baby," he says.

"Sorry, Mo," I say dutifully.

"Miles," he corrects.

"Sorry, Miles," I say. "Mo Miles, Mo Miles…"

All three of us are smiling. *So rare,* I think. But I am happy. I feel it all the way to my toes, even though yesterday I killed someone.

30

JUDAH KNOWS SOMETHING. I realize this one day as I am hanging clothes on hangers, and arranging them around the store, the musty smell filling my nostrils and making me feel sick. He's been different with me ever since that afternoon with Mo. At first I told myself it was in my head—the assessing looks, the silence, the strange questions, but they come too frequently. He's on to me. He's been spending more and more time with his father. I don't like the look of him, or maybe I'm jealous. He comes to get Judah, patiently lifting him into the passenger seat before carefully loading his wheelchair into the back. I wonder how he and Delaney met, as I watch him climb into the driver's seat, his russet hair lifting in the wind. He isn't the type to shoot the breeze and smoke a joint on someone's front porch. He is a serious man; you can tell by the way he hardly smiles, the pristine condition in which he keeps his truck. Even the care with which he handles Judah's wheelchair says something of the way he lives. Judah is like him. It is strange to realize that the boy I feel most connected to doesn't really belong here. His only tie being Delaney, probably the only reason he hadn't left. My eyes follow the truck and the boy out of Wessex, until they burn from brine.

I wait for him to come back, checking out the window, looking for his dad's car. But he doesn't come home until three days later, and he looks different. When I see him after that, he is distant. He locks eyes with strangers more than he does me. He peels the skin off oranges, and does not eat them. He picks up a joint and does not light it. He smiles at Mo, and it does not reach his eyes. Where has Judah gone?

At first, I wonder if it's because of how much I've changed. I've lost almost fifty pounds. I'm not the girl he met in either shape or mental form. Perhaps my ability to make this change bothers him. While he is stuck in his wheelchair, I am free to walk off my weight. But, no. That's not Judah. The fortune of others does not turn him melancholy. He doesn't wish for what he cannot have. That's what drew me to him in the first place. So I move on. *When did it start?* I think. *When did he start pulling away?*

Was it after I killed Vola? Lyndee? I remember the way he looked at me that day after I came back smelling of smoke, with dirt smeared across my knuckles.

I must have reeked of it that night—death and smoke. I hurried back to the eating house and sat at the kitchen table, staring down at the scars on the wood until I eventually climbed the stairs to my bedroom. The next day it all felt like a dream. Sometimes, I almost forget it happened.

The following week Judah tells me that he's moving to California. I feel all the blood rush to my head.

"What? Why?"

"My dad is going." He hands me the bowl of popcorn and wheels himself into the living room. "He said I can live with him while I go to school."

I trip on the rug by the front door, and popcorn goes flying everywhere.

"Jeez, you okay?" Judah bends down to grab my hands. I pull them away from him, my face burning. "You can live with your mom and go to college, too." I try to say it casually as I scoop kernels from the floor, but there is a slight tremor in my voice. The idea of the Bone without Judah is unbearable. Some days I'm not even sure how I made it through eighteen years of my life without him.

"My doctor thinks it will be good for me to be there. I'll be in Los Angeles," he says. "Everything will be easier, even getting from one place to the next without getting soaked."

"It's just a little rain," I say limply. I make to eat a piece of popcorn I find on the floor, and Judah knocks it out of my hand.

"Stop it," he says. "We can make another bag." I watch as he goes back to the kitchen. I want to cry. I want to beg him to stay. I eat the rest of the popcorn I find on the floor. When he comes back, I am slipping on my coat to leave.

"What are you doing, Margo?"

"I'm going home." I reach to open the door, but he throws an un-popped kernel at my head. It bounces off my forehead, and I glare at him.

"We had plans!" I yell at him, and then I cover my mouth with my hand, hoping Delaney didn't hear my outburst from her bedroom.

"To get out of the Bone," Judah says.

"Together," I insist. "I can't do it alone."

He stares at the blank TV screen, absently pushing pieces of popcorn into his mouth. I want to confess about eating the popcorn on the floor, but I know he'll be really upset with me.

"You have legs," he says finally. "I have to go where I have an extra pair of legs to help me. At least for now … until I'm done with school."

"I can be your legs."

"You need to be your own legs, Margo. Look, I don't want to be a burden on anyone's life. I want to be able to do things for myself. My dad has money. He said that if I come out to California with him, he'll pay for my school. He wants to buy me one of those custom cars that I can drive. A cripple's car."

When I don't say anything, he glances at Delaney's bedroom door and lowers his voice. "He stopped paying child support when I turned eighteen. I suddenly became really expensive. I can't be a burden to her. I have to be able to work, carry my own weight."

I look down at my legs, and suddenly I hate them. I hate that they give me an advantage over Judah.

"Stay," he says, as I turn back to the door.

"Why? You're just going to leave. Why should I waste my time?"

"You think it's a waste of time to be with me?"

I don't know how to answer him without sounding pathetic.

"You can leave too. Anytime you want. I know someone in the city who will give you a job."

"And where will I live? How will I know where to go and what to do?"

"You learn those things," he says cautiously. "You don't have to be trapped here."

I don't want to learn those things without him. He's stolen my dream, and I feel stupid for ever having it. Of course someone like Judah would never run away with someone like me. Of course he wouldn't want to share a life with an ugly, unaccomplished girl from the Bone. It was all talk to lift our spirits, and now he is going to move away and leave me with a brain high on ideas that will never be fulfilled.

"When are you leaving?" I ask.

Judah looks away. "Tomorrow."

"Tomorrow?" I repeat. "That's why you've been so weird lately."

I break our connection. It happens in the blink of an eye. I snap it in two and forget it was there. He calls after me when I leave his house, but I keep walking. I survived eighteen years without Judah Grant. I didn't need him. I want to be fireproof. Nothing should have the power to break my heart.

The eating house is quiet when I let myself in. I sit at the kitchen table with a glass of milk, staring at the gas stove and entertaining the idea of leaving the Bone. If he can, I can. My milk grows warm, the condensation on the glass long gone. My fingers stay wrapped around the glass, my brain rifling through my options. Every possibility seems bleak without Judah: staying, leaving, living. But, no. I won't be the type of woman who lacks in courage. I didn't survive just to fold to the familiarity the Bone offers. I push my untouched milk aside and stand up, my chair scraping loudly against the wood. The house stirs around me. The floorboards above my head creak with the weight of invisible feet, the refrigerator begins to hum, the light bulb on the porch starts flickering in the early dusk. *It's awake,* I think. *Just like that.*

I imagine my mother's ghost walking into the kitchen, standing over my shoulder, trying to push my back into my seat. *Stay in the Bone, stay in the Bone, stay in the Bone.*

I feel like my lungs are constricting, like everyone who has ever lived in this house is ganging up on me, filling me with their fear. I walk backward to the front door, looking accusingly at the air around me. My hand reaches behind me for the doorknob. I can feel its grooves, its rust, its connection to the house. I try to turn it, but it jams, moving neither left nor right. I yank at it. The ghosts are moving in. If they reach me, they won't let me leave. I am crying without tears, but then I hear my name on Judah's voice. The knob is unstuck; I fling it open and stumble out into the night air. Judah is at the bottom of the three steps, calling my name. I run down to him and find myself kneeling at his chair, crying into his lap. He touches my head, warm hands and compassion, which only makes me cry harder.

"What is it, blondie? People are going to think you're giving me a blow job." He makes no move to disturb me. I feel his fingers massaging my neck and scalp as he lets me cry. My hurt is compounded. I'm unsure from which direction to approach it. It feels like everyone is leaving me, like everyone always has, and yet I'm not sure I care. But, I do care, because I'm crying, and it hurts. I don't blame them, that's the difference. I've grown to expect it.

"I'll come back for you, Margo. I promise."

I shake my head. No, he won't, but that's okay too. This is our goodbye.

"Judah," I say, pulling my head back to look at him. "I'm only nineteen years old."

"Yeah," he says. "I kind of already know that."

"I've only really known you for a few months."

"If you want to think of it that way..."

I stare at him. The way he's looking at me is causing me shame. But I'll say it. I'll say it all, despite the wrongness of my feelings.

"What are you saying?" he asks.

"That I love you. That I love you deeply. I'm in love with you."

The smile falls from his face. For a moment, he's exposed. Horrified. I pull back, but his hands are on my arms, holding me prisoner in his lap.

"Let me go," I say.

He does. I step back, out of his reach.

"Don't come back here. No matter what happens. Promise me."

"Margo…?"

"Just promise me."

"Why? Why would you make me promise that?"

"Because," I say. "If you come back, I'll come back."

He stares at me for a long time.

"I'm sorry," he says finally. "I'm sorry for all of this."

I'm backing up again. It feels ironic, familiar. Back into the eating house I go, the word goodbye eating the flesh of my lips. Wanting to be said, wanting to never be said. *Get it over with,* I tell myself.

"Goodbye, Judah." My voice is clear and strong.

"I can't say it, Margo."

"Don't," I tell him. "Just remember one thing. You left me."

And then I'm back in the house, and I've closed the door on Judah, and on the small chance I thought I had at love. And what an idiot I was to think I had that chance.

"It's just us now," I say to the eating house. "You can have me."

A REPORTER IS SPEAKING about a baby koala born at the zoo near Seattle. I focus my whole attention on that story—the birth of a koala on the day Judah leaves the Bone. It's only after he leaves that I look out the window at the empty street, but all I can think about is the koala. I want to see it. I want to go to the zoo, just like Judah promised me we would. As I leave the room and walk up the stairs, the news story switches to the murder of Lyndee Anthony. The clear voice of the reporter travels with me for a while, and then my thoughts drown it out. "Police are still searching for—"

When you start life, you have high hopes. Even if you're born in the Bone, with a mother who wears a red, silk robe all day long, and sells her body to men for a nice crisp hundred dollar bill. You believe in the unbelievable. You see fairies in your empty pantry where the cans are supposed to be, and the rats that scramble across your bedroom floor are messengers from the gods, or your own personal spirit animal. And, if you're really creative, you romanticize the rags you're wearing. You're Cinderella, you're Snow White, you're…

You're a dead girl walking. But, for a time, you're blind to it, and that's a good thing. And then it's taken—slowly … slowly … slowly. The loss of innocence is the most severe of growing pains.

One day you believe you're Cinderella, and the next all your imaginary glimmer falls away, and you see yourself as just another poor fuck, sentenced to live out your days in the Bone. Your innocence leaves so violently. It hurts to understand that no one is going to rescue you. No one can give you freedom. No one can give you justice, or vengeance, or happiness, or anything. Anything. If you're willing, and if you're brave, you take it. I have to get out of here.

The day after Judah leaves, I take six thousand dollars of my mother's money, and I buy a car from an ad I find in the paper. It's the first time I've ever bought a paper, and it takes me ten minutes to find the section where used cars are sold. An impulse buy, but I trust it because it's what I need right now. It's an open top Jeep, black and older than I am, but in pretty good shape. The owner is Mr. Fimmes, a rickety old vet with arthritis and a set of dentures that he pops in and out of place with his tongue. The Jeep belonged to his son before he died in an accident climbing Rainier. He's not the sentimental type, he tells me. He kept it around because his wife wouldn't let him sell it.

"She died of cancer six months ago, so I figured now's the time…"

I tell him I'm sorry for his loss as I poke around in the glove box. I find a moldy box of cigars and a pocketknife that looks expensive. I pull out the knife and offer it to him. "You might want to keep this." He shakes his head. "Told you. Not the sentimental type."

"Oh," I say lamely, thinking of all the boxes of my mother's things in the attic. Would I be able to give those away as easily?

"I hardly drove it, and it's in pretty good shape." He pops his dentures in place to tell me this, then pops them back out again. It's tough looking and impractical since it rains so goddamn much. But I don't mind the feel of rain on my face, and it's better than buying a beat-up, gang-banger car from Alfie's Car Lot. Everyone knows Alfie deals everything Mo does not. The lot is just a side business. Cars traded for drugs, cars bought to hide cash. Those cars have bad juju. I hand Mr. Fimmes the cash and drive away. I go slowly, my foot hovering nervously over the brake. I watch old Mr. Fimmes in the rearview mirror, thinking at any moment he's going to figure out I can't drive and call the whole thing off. I've only driven once before, when Sandy let me drive her car around the Rag's parking lot after hours. I'd been good at it then, but there had been no other cars around. So this is it. I'm teaching myself. I take the back streets, slamming the brakes too hard at the stop signs, and almost knocking over someone's mailbox when I make a turn.

I'll be the only person on Wessex Street, besides Mo, who owns a car. This makes me a target. Judah was suspicious of me, so why wouldn't these strangers be? Either way, I don't want anyone to know I have it. Sandy says I can leave in in her garage for a few days. I drop it off at her house and catch the bus home. It feels good. I bought a car. I'm a total grownup.

I rent the eating house to Sandy, who finally left Luis and is seeing a new guy she met in the vitamin aisle at Wal-Mart. He's nice enough; I met them at a bar once, but soon after arriving, I felt like the awkward third wheel and said I had to go.

I go to the library and print off a lease agreement I find online. Four hundred dollars a month, and she is responsible for the utilities. She says she is going to get a roommate and charge them six hundred dollars a month to live with her. I don't care. I tell her so. This response seems to illicit excitement from her, and she rushes off to put an ad on Craigslist. I don't know who Craig is, but as I toss my things into garbage bags, I pray he doesn't send a psychopath to live in my mother's house. Then I remember that I'm much worse than a psychopath, and that shuts up my mental fretting.

I get a driver's license, and then I open a bank account, depositing most of my mother's money and a stack of my paychecks. I keep five thousand dollars in a rolled up sock in my purse. On an almost sunny day in late August, when the wild blackberries hang heavy and ripe on their branches, I climb into my Jeep and leave the Bone behind forever.

HOW DO YOU JUST LEAVE the place you've always lived and not know where you're going? HOW DO YOU JUST LEAVE THE PLACE YOU'VE ALWAYS LIVED AND NOT KNOW WHERE YOU'RE GOING?!

I jerk my steering wheel to the right and cross two lanes of traffic, cutting off a Subaru and a semi before the Jeep groans to a stop on the shoulder of the highway. I flick on the Jeep's emergency lights and hop out. This is crazy. What am I doing? The gravel crunches beneath my shoes as I race to the opposite side of the car and lean against the passenger side door, bending at the waist. I just need to … breathe … without … anyone … seeing me. I try to look calm, even as my heart rages. I am nothing. I have no one. The world is big, and this is all I've ever known. I cover my eyes with my hands and feel fear crushing what courage I worked so hard to cultivate over the last few weeks. I'm following signs to a city I've never even visited. I have no idea where I'm going to sleep tonight. God, I'm stupid. Following a pipe dream that Judah laid the foundation to. Before he left me.

What makes me think I can live this fray?

And then there is a voice that comes from deep inside me; it is what I imagine the eating house sounds like: rumbly and old. *"You've killed people. What makes you think you can't?"*

I say it out loud, with car engines roaring behind me, and suddenly I'm sober. Sober as the night I smashed Vola Fields's head on the side of her dresser for beating her baby. Sober like the day I used Gassy the gas can to douse Lyndee Anthony in two dollars worth of premium before I tossed a match her way.

Of course I can do this. I'm deranged. I am capable of murder. I'm like my grandmother who pushed my mother's head under the murky bathwater and tried to drown her. Surely, somewhere inside of me dwells the ability to survive in a city larger than the Bone. I survived aloneness, I fed myself, I clothed myself, I graduated high school, I read books to make myself smarter. I'll do it all again, because that's what I do. *Right?* Right.

I am almost put back together when a highway patrol car pulls up behind the Jeep. *Fuck.* Running my hands through my hair, my mind immediately goes to the contents of my car. Is there anything in here that can get me in trouble? I think of the knife set that I took from the kitchen when I was packing up, and the pink Zippo that I never gave back to Judah. No. I can't get in trouble for having those. But Nevaeh's bear sits on the passenger seat. The bear from the picture that was on every news station in America. The bear I took from Lyndee Anthony's book bag before I burned it along with her.

I straighten my spine.

"Hello," I say. I notice that his hand rests lightly on the hilt of his gun as he walks over. Something they teach them to do in the police academy? *Just so you know, I have a gun! Hey there, I can blow your head off!*

"Ma'am," he says. "Are you having car trouble?"

"It's overheating," I say quickly. He bends down to peer into the Jeep, even though the removable top is off. "Are you headed somewhere?"

"I'm moving," I say flatly. "To Seattle." I eye Bambi. Why didn't I stuff it into one of the trash bags?

He eyes the bags stuffed into my trunk in a hurry, then opens the driver's side door.

"Seattle," he says. "Big ambitions. See your license and registration," he says. I fumble in my wallet, then the glove box, and hand them over. I study him as he looks them over, carrying them back to his cruiser to run my plates. I consider putting the bear away, but if he's already seen it, it will look suspicious.

"Start her up," he says. "Let's see."

I walk past him, my hands clammy and shaking. *You're fine!* I tell myself. *He's trying to help.*

I slide into the driver's side and turn the key. The Jeep grumbles to life. The officer eyes the dashboard. "Seems to be fine now," he says. "But you might want to turn around and head back into town to get it checked out."

I nod, pull my door closed, and grip the wheel 'til my knuckles burn white.

"Do you have children?"

"What?"

His eyes are on Bambi. I can't read them because he's wearing sunglasses. Big, reflective things like a fly's eyes.

"No," I say. Just a childhood toy. Can't bear to let it go, you know?"

"My daughter has one of those," he says. "She's eight. Didn't know they've been out that long." Bambi has bulging eyes. I didn't know that she was a *type* of toy that people could recognize. That was stupid to assume. I breathe a sigh of relief when he steps back, allowing me to pull forward and back onto the highway.

"You have a nice day," he calls over the engine. I wish I could see his eyes. I lift my hand in half a wave and pull away. *My heart, my heart, my heart.* When I look in the rearview mirror, he's still watching me. People have looked at me like that before: Judah, Lyndee, even my own mother. Maybe there's something about me that others can see. I try to imagine what they think when they look at me that way. *A strange girl. Something about her ... She creeps me out.* I laugh at the last one.

Now I am determined. I have to leave. I was stupid to think that I could stay. A town the size of Bone Harbor can't hold what's inside of me. I turn on the radio to drown out my thoughts and drive, drive, drive the speed limit all the way to Seattle.

I DRIVE TO A MOTEL on the outskirts of Seattle and check in. The room is dingy, but it's clean. At forty dollars a night, I am grateful for that at least. I lie quietly under the humorless fluorescent light on the ceiling and listen to a motorbike on the street. It grunts and farts probably as loudly as the middle-aged crisis who is driving it.

My entire life is a crisis, and I am glad that no one has paid enough attention to it to notice that something is off about me. The bike revs loudly one last time and then guns off down the street. Tomorrow I will find a paper, or perhaps use the computers at the library, to find a place to live. Then I will have to find a job, preferably not one at a thrift shop. I switch off the light and roll onto my side so that I can see the flashing neon sign of the strip club next door. *IRLS!*

I'll be different. I'll never go back to the Bone or the eating house. I have come this far, and I will go farther—running from who that place made me be. But before my eyes close and my mind drifts into sleep, I already know I'm lying to myself. The eating house will never stop calling to me, and I will never cease to answer.

The city burns my eyes, glinting demon, like under the rare winter sun. It isn't like the pictures I've seen of New York City. It is industrial, hard metal hanging over clear, crisp water. Shipyards and skyscrapers outlined by the blunt, graphite sky. My small town eyes are accustomed to space and squat, colorless buildings. People who look soft to the touch and clothe their bodies in faded cottons and fleece. Here, the women wear bright, gem-colored coats and glossy rain boots. Their bodies look hard and strong. I don't know how to drive amongst cars that seamlessly weave and wedge themselves into small spaces of road. People honk at me, their horns loud accusations that I don't know what I am doing.

By the time I find the parking garage I am looking for, my shirt is damp with sweat and my hands are numb. I get lost in the garage, and during the twenty minutes it takes to make my way down to the street, I already doubt my ability to survive here. The apartment I am coming to see is on Sixth Avenue in a high rise. The website has pictures of a tiny kitchen and bathroom with black and white checkered tile, and a closet-sized bedroom. But it is affordable. I stand on the street, backed up against the window of a paperie, clutching my backpack to my chest. The people here don't acknowledge the rain. They move through it like it's a part of them—an extra leg or arm they're used to working around. I am made breathless by the efficiency in their step, the impassivity on their faces. I can't make myself move, because I can't move like them.

It's a crow that puts me back into my skin. It lands on the sidewalk a few feet away from where I am cowering, and caws at me, tilting its head from side to side. I blink at the street, then back at the crow. I am the essence of evil. Most of these people who are passing me have not taken someone's life. They have not planned a murder, or poured gasoline over a woman's body and lit a match. They may have thought it, thought murder, but by acting on my impulses, I have separated myself from the rest of the world. Released a beast from its cage. And here I am, so paralyzed by fear that I can barely move.

It is the crow's caw that reminds me of who I am, and it sets my feet moving. Electric blue Docs and the splash of puddles. I make my way toward Sixth Avenue, imitating the facial expressions of the people around me. People I can never be because of what I've already done. But, I realize, I can watch them and pretend. I can buy a raincoat and learn my way around these streets. Piece of cake. I just have to get this apartment.

The apartment isn't as nice as it looked on the internet. I feel like a woman who's arrived to a date with a man she met online, fooled by his outdated picture. I take it anyway, because the owner takes me. The longer I wait to find a place to live, the longer I'll be sleeping in my car. We do everything right there, on the peeling Formica countertop of the outdated kitchen. *It's not worse than the eating house,* I tell myself, as I sign the lease and hand over a year's worth of rent. The year's rent is the reason I get the place. No questions asked. I don't have references or credit. I feel lucky he's giving me a chance.

The owner is a balding, thirty-something man, named Doyle, with a gut that nudges over the top of his pants. He smells of Old Spice. I walk the apartment one last time before we leave, taking in the familiar smell of cigarette smoke and the lingering stench of grease that clings to the wallpaper. The windows face other windows, but, from the living room, I can see a patch of sky, and that is enough. We make arrangements to meet at a coffee shop later, where he will bring me the keys and the sticker I'll need to use the building's parking garage. As I walk out of the building, I feel accomplished. I want to tell Judah what I've done, so I go to a store and buy a phone. They want my address. I give them the address of the eating house, and plan to change it later. I fill out the paperwork, pay them, and when I walk out and head down a deeply sloping street to the coffee shop, I have one of those fancy things that can do anything and everything.

Finding a table near a window, I watch the people and the traffic, a growing sense of excitement bubbling in my chest. I wait for four hours in the coffee shop before I get up and ask the man making coffees behind the bar about Doyle. He looks at me with his eyebrow cocked, his pierced lip pulled up in impatience.

"How am I supposed to know who Doyle is?" he says, sliding a beverage across the counter to a waiting customer.

"Doesn't he come in here?" I ask.

"Sweetheart, do you know how many people come in here every day?" I glance around at the dinner crowd, people freshly clocked out of their jobs, stopping by for an espresso with their coworkers before they head home for supper. He eyes my clothes, the insecurity with which I cling to my backpack. "I don't know where you're from, but this is Seattle. We don't know our neighbors." I think about my neighbors, not nice, plaid-wearing folk, who make jam and bring you over a mason jar with a handmade label. My neighbors were druggies, thuggies, and murdering mothers. And their neighbor was me: a cold-blooded killer. Poor old country folk. I look at the pierced-lip barista and roll my eyes. We were a lot tougher than he thought. *I don't know where you're from, but it sure ain't the Bone.*

I back away from the counter and go stand by the window, convinced that I've done the wrong thing by coming here to this proud, undeterred city. I'm already sick of that thought, the back and forth of my decision. Judah would tell me to own it. My eyes blur in and out of focus as I watch for Doyle, unable to accept the deception. It's a mistake. I'm at the wrong coffee shop. He was held up by something: a car accident, a family emergency. I am willing to entertain anything but the sad, stinging truth that I was scammed. I handed twelve thousand dollars over to a stranger without so much as asking his last name. A naive girl with a wad of cash—an easy target. As the sky darkens, I watch the pedestrians, imagining the spaces they are going home to—the warm kitchens and the sofas facing the televisions. The children throwing themselves at their daddy's legs, the mothers wiping their hands on dishtowels to come fetch a kiss on the lips.

I walk to the library and search for the ad on Craigslist with Doyle's phone number. It's gone; however, if my suspicions are correct, it shouldn't be long before another pops up just like it. Probably with a new number that Doyle has acquired. A pay-by-the-minute phone bought at a gas station. There will be a new name on the ad. I find the number from the ad scrawled on a piece of paper in my wallet, but when I use my new phone to make the call, it rings and rings until I finally hang up. My situation becomes more discouraging as the library announces it will be closing in five minutes.

Back into the rain, back into the march of people who know where they're going. I make my way toward the apartment building eight blocks away. The cold is locking into my joints, and I have a headache. When I realize that I haven't eaten all day, I buy a bowl of noodles from a food truck and carry it with me to the apartment building where Doyle stole my money. I sit on a bench across the street and watch the entrance. The food falls to my belly, but I don't taste it. This is what happens; everything becomes black and white. I see only injustice. The man who chose the moniker Doyle, who will continue to prey on the innocent, must be held accountable. The building looks different without the glow of hope around it, dingy and mean-looking. I walk to the front of the building and stare up at the oppressive, little windows. Doyle had opened the main door with a keycard that he pulled out of his wallet. He had access to the building, which means he either already lives here, or he had pulled his scam before and somehow managed to get keys to the empty apartments. He can be anything from a maintenance man, to a friend of the real owner's. I sit for a while longer to look up at what was almost mine. It's all right. I'll wait. When the time is right, Doyle will repay me—one way or another.

THERE IS AN APARTMENT FOR RENT across the street from the building where I was supposed to live. The landlord takes me up four flights of stairs because the elevator is broken. The stairwell smells like piss, the rent is more expensive, the apartment more dingy, but the light is better. From my living room window, I have a straight on view of Doyle's building. I take it. Not because I can afford it, but because I can't afford not to have it. I can move in in a week. I sleep in my Jeep in the meantime, a sweatshirt rolled beneath my head, not wanting to waste money on a hotel. I sneak into a fitness center and use their shower a couple of times, promising myself that one day I'll get a membership to make it up to them. During the day, I wander the streets of Seattle—Pike Place Market, the pier. I take the ferry to Bainbridge Island; I ride the elevator to the top of the Space Needle. I eat in a restaurant that has thousands of oysters piled into icy silver bins. When I pour the silver meat into my mouth, I can taste the ocean. I'm instantly hooked. I've never seen the ocean, but on the banks of the Sound and in the exotic, salty meat of an oyster, I can taste it. I sit on the bench outside of Doyle's building and watch for him. I write everything I spend in a notebook, so I know how much I have left.

Loaf of bread and peanut butter: $4.76

Socks and shampoo: $7.40

Toilet wand: $3.49

Coffee: $5.60

Aspirin and milk: $6.89

This week I spent 137.50. Try to spend less next week! I write in the margin of the notebook.

I think of the places I'd take Judah if he were with me: to the market, and across the Sound on a ferry, a stroll on Bainbridge Island, a lunch at my favorite oyster bar. I call him once, but hang up when I hear his voice. I don't know what to say to him, and I'm afraid he doesn't miss me. When the day arrives for me to pick up my keys, I carry myself into the rental office, sure something will happen. They will decide I'm not good enough to live there, they'll find out I killed a woman and burned her body, they'll know what I am and send me to prison instead. When the landlord sees me, he exclaims, "It looks like you're here to identify a body, not pick up your keys!" I laugh at the irony and relax. If he's in this good of a mood, he's not prepping to tell me that I won't be moving in today. In the end, the landlord hands me my keys and shakes my hand, congratulating me on my new home.

I carry my garbage bags of possessions up to the fourth floor and deposit them in my living room before I wander around. It's beautiful. It's mine. I want Judah to be here. I want my mother to be proud. I wipe both of those thoughts away quickly and pack my few possessions into the closet. *A job,* I think. *A job, and Doyle, and life.*

I buy things: a chair, plates, knives and forks, a blowup mattress, and a blanket with a large, black crow on it. A coffee maker. During the day, I walk the streets, looking in store windows for HELP WANTED signs, and speaking to bums who assume I'm one of them. I take that as a bad sign and buy some new clothes, the type of things that may get me hired. I practice facial expressions in the small mirror in my bathroom. I smile, laugh politely, and keep my voice even and demure. I try to be the type of person someone would want to hire.

And, then, on an unusually sunny day, I am eating a small lunch of salad and soup at an all night diner in Capitol Hill, when the manager jokingly asks if I am looking for a job.

The diner is called Myrrh, and serves everything from waffles to crab legs. They let me work the graveyard shift because I am one of the few who is willing to do it. I start my shift at nine when the dinner crowd is thinning, and the servers who have worked all day are moody and short tempered, eager to go home for the night. I help them wrap their silverware in napkins, and sweep their sections, just as eager to see them gone. There is another girl who works the late shift. A pretty Asian girl named Kady Flowers. She keeps to herself, and so do I. We work together seamlessly, communicating with painfully short sentences: *Refills for table five. Ran your food for twenty-three. Taking bathroom break.* It works well for both of us. I sometimes wonder what Kady is hiding. Did she kill someone, too, or did someone kill her?

My shift ends at five, right as the sun is coming up. There is something both deeply demeaning and deeply satisfying about waiting tables. The jostling in the dining room, the blank-eyed stares that make you feel like an intruder when you're just refilling a water glass, the yelled-out orders, minus the thank you. You are just a face, a nametag. It gives me the anonymity that I need, and an emptiness that I perhaps deserve. Mornings, when my shift ends, I walk to my tiny apartment and make myself tea with bags I steal from Myrrh. I sit at the window and think about Judah, and Nevaeh, and Little Mo. I think about my mother too—the way she used to be when she loved me. I am bone deep lonely.

When I have lived my new life for six months, I fill out the application and have my transcripts sent to University of Washington. I start with two classes a semester: Psychology 101, Comparative Animal Behavior, and then Behavior Disorders, and Human Development. I ask plenty of questions in class, my hand shooting up twice as much as any of the other students. My professors favor me, as they mistake my self-exploration as a hunger for the business. They think I'll go far. They suggest master's programs, they offer to write letters of recommendation, and invite me to sit in on their other, more advanced classes. I play along, because who knows?

I take long walks, and eventually long runs. Before, when I lived in the Bone, I lost weight. Now, I build muscle. It juts out of my body in hard, ugly cords. When I look in the mirror, I can almost see what I'm made of—the tightly pulled muscle, the bone, the marrow that Judah so often spoke about. There are days when I miss the Bone, and that is when I think about my marrow the most—the who I am, the what I am. You can leave, but it never leaves you.

I write letters to Judah, but he seldom writes back, and when he does, it's just a page of scrawled words I have to work hard to decipher. He's busy with class ... life. I get it. So am I, right?

I sleep little—four hours a day, or night, depending on my work schedule. My eyes resemble darkly bruised moons. I often catch Kady looking at me strangely, like she's wondering the same thing I wonder about her. One night she slips a tube of something into my hand and then walks away. When I go into the bathroom to examine it, I find that she has given me under eye concealer. Something to wipe away the look of exhaustion. I use it, and it makes a difference. I feel less dead. My customers must think so too, because I get better tips. After a few more weeks, Kady slips a tube of lipstick into my apron pocket. I put it on in the bathroom. It makes me look ... alive. When the lipstick and the eye concealer run out, I ask Kady where to buy more. It's the longest conversation we've ever had.

"Where can I buy the makeup you brought me? I couldn't find it at the pharmacy."

"I'll bring you more ... my mother sells it."

Kady Flowers becomes my makeup dealer; concealer and lipstick first, then blush and mascara. She will not let me pay for anything; instead, she lets me roll her share of the silverware. When she suggests one night that I let her cut my hair, I shake my head. "I've never cut it," I say. Her look is one of such grave disappointment that I immediately agree to have her come to my flat the next day. She arrives on what happens to be my twenty-first birthday with a little black backpack in her hand that makes her look like an old fashioned doctor. She takes a cursory look around my four hundred square feet, before setting me in front of the window in my only chair, and pulling out a sequined pouch that holds her tools.

"I go to the beauty school in the city," she says quietly. "Just in case you're wondering if I know what I'm doing." I hadn't wondered, of course. If someone wants to cut my hair, who am I to stand in their way?

"Is that why you work nights?" I ask.

Kady nods, then says, "You take classes. At UW."

When I look at her with question in my eyes, she rushes on, "I saw you there once. While I was visiting a friend. You were coming out of a lecture hall I think."

We are both quiet for a while, soaking in these new details. Kady is touching my hair, lifting it in places like she's sizing it up.

"Take it all off," I say suddenly. "As short as you like." I suddenly feel emboldened by my twenty-one years. The fact that I made it this long without anyone helping me. I might as well have new hair to go with my new face and body. I've been here a year, in this city, in this culture.

I close my eyes.

I am not the Margo of the Bone. I am a new, tightly shaped Margo of Seattle, my white lashes painted dark like spider legs, and my iridescent skin blushed. I wonder if my mother would still find me ugly if she saw me now. I should look like a boy with my short hair, but the makeup softens me. Makes me feel tough and feminine all at the same time.

35

EARLY ONE MORNING, as the fog rushes in from the Sound, I am walking home from work an hour earlier than usual since the restaurant was dead, when I spot a scuffle down an alley. I linger along the street, wondering if I should do something. There is no one around to call to for help. Sometimes there are fights among the homeless—a strong possibility right now. It's four in the morning; the late night drinkers have long stumbled home, and the working class has not yet risen. I strain to see the struggle, my breath fogging the air around me. I am cold. I want to wash the restaurant off my skin and crawl into bed. I should leave them to it, and I'm about to when I hear a woman's scream. Short, like it was cut off before it could gain volume.

I start down the alley, my hesitation trimmed away by the sharp cry for help. I run on my toes—long, quiet strides. He doesn't hear when I approach from behind, his back to me. A strong, broad man in a leather jacket. Pinned against the wall is a girl younger than I am. Her eyes are bleary and unfocused as she wriggles from side to side. Her attempts are futile. He is three times her size.

One hand is clamped over her mouth, the weight of his shoulder holding her against the wall, and, with his free hand, he is struggling with his pants, urging them down over his thick hips. I watch for a moment, my rage building. It's a slow boil, but I let it climb—wanting the full force of my anger to be intact before I act.

In my mind I have already killed him. I've ripped him off her and slit his throat with the knife I keep strapped to my ankle. But I know I can't kill him. There is a witness, there would be police, a long day answering questions, and eyes. I don't want them to know I exist.

I have to be careful; he's bigger than me. I wait until he's slipped his pants lower. They hang mid-thigh. He's taken the time to rip his belt free of the loops and toss it aside. I bend to retrieve it, grabbing one end and dragging it toward me, never taking my eyes from his back. The girl has spotted me. Her eyes are on my face as I approach. I lift a finger to my lips, signaling her to be quiet. It just takes a second—my arms lifting, the belt around his neck. His yelp of surprise is cut short as I pull the belt tight.

"Run," I say to the girl, before he pushes me backward. His pants restrict his movement, something I was counting on. I do not loosen my hold on the belt, but pull tighter as he repeatedly slams me into the wall. His fingers pull against the belt, but my boot finds leverage against a large metal dumpster, and I wedge it there and hold on tight. I can barely feel the brick bite into my skin, the adrenaline coating my nerves like a nice, rubber sealant. I manage to loop the belt. I hold it with one hand as I reach down for my knife. He almost knocks it from my hand, and, in the process, I slice open his thigh, which causes him to buck more wildly than before. I lose my grip on the belt, and he stumbles free, hissing and gasping for air. He uses his seconds to pull the belt from around his neck. I use my seconds to plow him into the wall, bending at my waist and rushing forward like I'd seen football players on television do. He hits me once, in the face, and I think I'm going to throw up from the pain. He grabs my arm and pulls it behind my back. I think he's going to rip it from the socket when I swing my free hand up and slash with the knife at his cheek. He lets me go, and I clutch his face. I swing around and press the blade to the soft spot on his neck. His hands come up in surrender, though I know they won't stay there. Another few seconds, and I'll be in the weaker position. That's the thing women don't get; if you want to keep the upper hand, you have to act faster than they do. So I stab him. Press the blade through his skin until his blood warms my fingers. I didn't intend to kill, but I did.

Three lives, I tell myself. I stumble back as he collapses into a pile at my feet. That's when I see the girl. She ran, but not far enough. She waited to see what would happen, or perhaps she stayed to help. She doesn't really look committed to any one thing, even her socks—which are pulled up over her tights—don't match. We lock eyes, hers considerably less bleary than when I'd last looked into them.

"You killed him," she said.

I wipe a hand across my forehead, unsure of what to do next.

"Who is he?" I ask.

She's staring at the body, and I have to repeat my question.

"Who *was* he," she corrects me. "He's dead."

She's a little thing. Not even legal. I eye her too-sexy clothes: a leather mini skirt and a tight sweater, and want to change my question to 'who are *you?*' But we are running out of time. Things must be decided. My fingerprints are all over this man. She's seen my face. We can't just walk away anymore. Someone might have already seen or heard us and called the police.

"Jonas. I met him online," she says, in a flat, bored voice. "He told me he was eighteen. We were meeting for the first time tonight. I even snuck out." Her last sentence she says with surprise.

"How old are you?" I ask. If I can get her to go home now, maybe she'd never talk. I could wipe down the area...

"Sixteen."

"What's your name?"

"Mary," she says.

"We have two choices, Mary," I tell her. "We can call the police—"

"They'll tell my parents," she rushes. "They'll be so pissed." She wrings her hands, and I notice the smudge of mascara under her eyes.

I blink at her for a minute. "Well, yes, they'll be angry. There's a dead man at my feet, and he tried to rape you. They'll probably be happy that you're okay," I add. I lick my lips. My skin is itching underneath my clothes. I just killed a man, and this girl saw me do it.

"What's the other option?" Mary asks. Her nose is running. She does nothing to wipe it away. *She's in shock,* I think.

"We walk in opposite directions, and we never talk about this again."

She turns without a word and heads out of the alley, hugging her arms around herself. "Hey," she calls. I glance over my shoulder. She's walking backward. "Thank you." And then she sprints out of the alley, her hair whipping the air around her.

I want to tell her to be smarter next time. To stay away from men who want to meet up with her in alleys. To definitely stop sneaking out of her parents' house in the middle of the night. But she's gone, and I just killed a man, his blood cooling on the tar at my feet. *There will be fibers*, I think. My DNA will be all over him: hair, skin, perhaps blood. Thank God for the rain. That's the key right there: commit a crime in the rain, and your chances of remaining a free man or woman significantly goes up.

"Jonas, my ass," I say, slipping my hood around my face. Try Peter Fennet. And he was thirty-one. *Pervert.* I pocket his ID and prop his body against the side of the dumpster and pull the cash out of his wallet. Eighty-six dollars. I slip his watch off his wrist too—make it look like a robbery. *I'll dump it in the Sound later*, I think, slipping it in my pocket. I look down at the body one last time. I don't feel a single thing. Strange. I crack my neck as I leave the alley. I have to stop fucking killing people.

I throw Peter the Pervert's watch in the Sound later that day. There's a little plop, and it sinks gracefully into the gray. I wait until I know for sure that it's not going to resurface like a demon to haunt me, then I walk over to the market. I buy fruit and spiced orange tea, and make my way home—body aching. I am black and blue under my clothes; I look like abstract art. Peter the Pervert whipped me good. But not good enough. He is dead, and I am alive. I was just there at the right time to punish him, but anyone else would have done the same. I make tea and carry the mug to the bath where I soak in hot water until my fingers are puckered. I wonder if Mary will tell anyone. If she'll think of that night and always wonder what would have happened if I hadn't heard her scream. Or maybe she's like my mother—a shut-down-and-don't-think-about-it kind of girl. Either way, I doubt I'll ever see her again. And I'm okay with that.

I pull my laptop from underneath my mattress. I am afraid of someone stealing it. I hide it in a different place every day, even though if someone really wanted to, they could ransack the apartment and find it tucked somewhere fairly obvious. I search the news to see if anyone has reported a murder in Seattle. I wonder how long it will take to identify Peter Fennet and notify his family. I wonder who found him propped against the dumpster.

And there it is, the headline: "Man's body found near Pike Place Market." Except it wasn't really near Pike Place. The media just wants you to know there is a killer in Seattle. *An ugly blonde girl from the Bone,* I think. The article is boney, just the basics. An unidentified male found dead. Late twenties to mid-thirties. Stab wounds and signs of a scuffle. It ends with the typical urge for information from anyone who saw or heard anything.

I bite my nails and think of Mary. She didn't know my name, but I bet she could pick me out of a lineup. It was stupid, impulsive. I could have fought with him and given her time to run off, then perhaps gotten away myself. Unscathed , no ... but perhaps not being sought by the police. I put my laptop away and crawl into bed. I sleep, but I have nightmares of being chased by headless lions down long alleyways.

Around four PM, I wake up and brush my teeth. I eat an orange over the sink and check my computer again. There is nothing else about Peter the Pervert. Some of the tension leaves my chest.

36

I REMEMBER WHEN I FIRST MOVED TO THE CITY; I thought I was very different from the people around me. I told myself that I was the one pretending to fit in, but life has taught me that we are all pretenders. Every single one of us. We are born ready to cultivate ourselves, find a place where we feel comfortable. Whether that is to fit in with the geeks, or the jocks, or the cold-blooded killers. There is nothing new under the sun. Nothing new we can invent or make up. We grapple with our likes and dislikes, who we want to please, what we want to wear and drive. Our interests, whether they include drawing Italian sunsets, playing video games, or thumbing our way through erotic novels, they are all handed to us by a society that produces them. No matter how hard we try to invent ourselves, there have always been druggies, and tattoos, and ambitious men who take over the world. There have always been artists, and hippies, and meatheads, and that beautiful, single Mother Teresa, who lights up the darkness. There have always been murderers, and mothers, and athletes. We are all pretenders in life, finding a patch of humanity that we relate to, and then embrace it. We come straight down the birth canal and our parents start telling us who to be, simply by being themselves. We see their lives, their cars, the way they interact, the rules they set, and the foundations for our own lives are laid. And when our parents aren't molding us, our situations are. We are all sheep, who get jobs, and have babies, and diet, and try to carve something special out for ourselves using the broken hearts, and bored minds, and scathed souls life delivered to us. And it's all been done before, every bit of suffering, every joy.

And the minute you realize that we are all pretenders is the minute everything stops intimidating you: punishment, and failure, and death. Even people. There is nothing so ingenious about another human who has pretended well. They are, in fact, just another soul, perhaps more clever, better at failing than you are. But not worth a second of intimidation.

Seattle is my city. Washington is my state. It's mine, because I say it is. And I take lives, because I want to. And I fear nothing, because there is nothing left to fear.

I'm reading on a bench one day when I see Doyle walking down 2nd Street, a wiry young man with glasses trailing behind him. Doyle's latest target. He looks limp, like a kite that can't quite catch the wind. He glances constantly at his phone, then back up at Doyle who is chatting and pointing to things along the way. Same as he did with me. He pointed out breakfast bars and corner stores, telling me the best places to buy bread and fresh fruit. All meant to make you feel comfortable, get you used to the idea of living in his building and impaling yourself on this neighborhood. I watch them from behind my novel, clucking my tongue at Doyle.

When they have passed me by, I set my book down, forgotten, and follow them. "I told you I'd find you," I say under my breath, as I duck around a corner. I am their shadow as they move down 2nd and onto Madison. And they don't look my way, even though I am wearing a bright orange shirt and leather pants. They are headed for the building. I wonder if Doyle is taking him to the same unit he showed me. I wonder what he used my money for. Drugs? Rent? A car? *Who cares?* A thief is a thief no matter what he does with the money.

Doyle uses his card to open the main door to the building. The man looks once over his shoulder before he follows him in. I dart from my hiding spot, and grab the door before it can close. Doyle won't recognize me; I look different now. But I lurk in the shadows, listening for their voices in the hollowness of the building. They take the elevator. I take the stairs. I think about what I'm going to say to Doyle ol' Boyle as I trot upward, climbing the stairs two at a time, remembering when I couldn't walk up the stairs of the eating house without getting winded. Doyle takes the young man to a different unit on the same floor as the one he took me to. I linger outside the door, listening to their exchange. He wants first month, last month, and a two thousand dollar deposit. He's cutting this guy a break. A scam at a fifty percent discount. The man, who Doyle calls George, sounds unsure. He wants to speak to his girlfriend. He needs to ask his parents for help with the deposit. Doyle says he needs to hurry. There are other people interested. I push open the door.

"Like me," I say.

They both turn to look at me at the same time.

"Hey," I say to George. "This guy is actually a scam artist. You probably don't want to give him your money."

George laughs at first, like I've told a really good joke. But, when I don't laugh with him, his too-thin eyebrows make sharp triangles over his glasses.

"Go, go," I say. "Unless you want to be out twelve thousand dollars like me."

He gives red-faced Doyle one last look before scurrying for the door.

"Hey George," I call. "The best place to buy bread is on Union and Fourth. Don't listen to this joker."

As soon as I hear the ting of the elevator, I close the door and smile expectantly at Doyle.

"Oh hey! Remember me?"

His eyes are darty, like a cornered rat. He looks dumb. I can't believe I ever bought into this guy's sales pitch. Doyle the Dope. He looks at the door while I look around the apartment. It's nice. Really nice. Better than the one I was scammed out of. The kitchen is small, but there are granite countertops, and the cabinetry looks new. I breathe in the scent of fresh paint and newly laid carpets.

"Who owns this place, Doyle?"

He walks for the door, *a shit don't care* look on his face. But, I pull out my part-time gun. I don't like to use it; it's such an ungraceful weapon: loud noise, silver bullets, pretentious. I carry it with me on the nights I work late, stick it in my purse, which I keep in the manager's office, then transfer it to the back of my jeans in the bathroom for the walk home … just in case. You can never be too careful with all these psychos walking around.

Doyle sees the piece of black metal in my hand and stops short. Amazing what a little gun can do to people. I've burned a woman alive, but no one gets all watery-eyed over a pink Zippo.

"Doyle," I say. "Is something wrong? You look a little green."

He shakes his head. I can see a thin line of sweat brewing on his forehead. I hate forehead sweaters. So gross.

"I definitely asked you a question, Doyle. I am the girl holding the gun, so you might want to answer me."

Doyle's Adam's apple bobs in his throat before he says, "Yeah, it's mine."

I nod, pleased. This will make things easier.

"How many do you own in this building?"

"Three."

"And in between tenants—your real tenants, that is—you scam people into believing you'll rent to them?"

"Well, my dad owns them," he says. "Look lady, I'm just trying to make an extra buck. My old man rents them out, and I don't get shit. But he has me do all the work for him."

"Oh boo! Doyle. Did you really just tell me that story and hope I'd feel sorry for you?"

Stupid fuck.

I walk around the living room, peer out the window. There's a nice view of the city. "How much does your old man rent this out for?"

"Three thousand a month."

"Oh boy. But I heard you tell George you'd give it to him for a thousand."

Doyle blinks at me. He's obviously not following my game.

"I'll take it for a thousand," I say. "And give me George's number; I'll need him to sublet my current place. I obviously won't need a deposit because you took twelve thousand dollars from me."

I start mentally arranging my furniture around the room: the castoff sofa from my neighbor, the kitchen table I bought from Target and hauled up the street in its box, by myself. That's when Doyle decides to decline my offer with a shaky, indignant, helium-soaked voice.

"You're fucking crazy."

I giggle.

"Oh man, Doyle. Yeah. I am. But you stole twelve thousand dollars from a crazy person. What does that make you? You're the real crazy motherfucker. You know what I'm saying? I'd hate to be you right now, Doyle. Because I have the gun, but even more importantly, I have this really vindictive personality. God, you should see how vindictive I am."

Doyle doesn't seem to be absorbing what I'm saying. He's looking for a way out, his pint-sized brain churning up ideas to manipulate me. I can see it in his watery eyes. I walk a few steps toward him.

Whack.

I hit him in the face with the butt of my gun.

Doyle's cry is muffled as he grabs his nose, which is spraying healthy amounts of blood through his fingers, and bends over at the waist.

"What. The. Duck."

"What the duck, indeed. You didn't even see it coming! You need to pay attention."

I let him calm down a bit while I wait by the window. I like the view here. It's very Seattle: water, fog, ferry boats, bobbing umbrellas. Peaceful. I'll enjoy living here. It's so different than the eating house. I find a deep contentment knowing it will be mine.

"So, Doyle," I say. "Tell Daddy Doyle that the place has been rented for whatever he rents it for. Then figure it out. Give me your license," I say, waving the gun at him. I get tired of holding the gun. I'm not cut out for the gangster lifestyle. Doyle digs in his pocket and pulls out a Batman wallet, still trying to plug the flow of blood with the sleeve of his fleece. I roll my eyes. He tosses it to me, and I catch it, flipping it open. *Indeed! His true name is Brian.* Brian Marcus Ritter. He lives on 22 Sycamore Lane. I read all of this out loud for him. What a stupid, stupid fuck.

"Now I know where you live, Doyle," I say. I pull out a business card from his wallet. Ritter Enterprises. His daddy is a contractor. I stick the card in my back pocket without taking my eyes from him.

"I'll have to go to the police, and of course Daddy Ritter, if you can't comply with my request," I say cheerfully. "I'm sure I can find some other scammed humans to solidify my story. Fraud will get you at least seven years!"

Doyle—or Brian—looks … cornered. He also looks like he's about to cry, the forehead sweat thickening like a flour mixture. But he's stuck. Stuck like Chuck. And I'm the one who stuck him.

A FEW WEEKS LATER, Judah sends me an e-mail. He wants me to visit him in California. *Screw the evergreens,* he says. *Come see the palm trees!* But I'm not interested in the palm trees; I just need to get out of Seattle for a few days. Sometimes I feel like the ghost of Peter Fennet is following me around town.

I spend a lot of time wondering why this time is different—why, after I killed Lyndee and Vola, I never had nightmares. I wonder if it's because I killed Peter Fennet *before* he had the chance to commit the crime.

I tell Judah I'll come, and he buys me a ticket. On the third weekend of June, I board a plane to Los Angeles with my newly purchased duffel bag. I have never flown before and have to ask strangers what to do.

"Where is the B gate?"

"Do I wait in line now? Or will they call me by name when it's time to board?"

"Can I put my bag anywhere, or is there a space assigned to me?"

The flight attendants are frustrated with me, and passengers look on with sympathy when I ask if there is a separate bathroom for women. It's all a nightmare until I disembark and walk down to baggage claim where Judah is waiting for me. I run to hug him, dropping to my knees and throwing my arms around his neck.

"Hey Margo," he whispers into my hair. "I missed you."

"Take me to your home," I say, standing up. And then, "How are we getting there?"

"Cab it," he says. "My place isn't far from here."

He says, *my place,* but there is something in the tone of his voice that says it is not just *his* place.

Judah has a girlfriend. Her name is Erin, a horribly androgynous name with too many hippie dippie spellings: Aaron, Eryn, Errin, Erinn, Aryn. I hate her on sight—all slender, feminine five feet six inches of her. Though, as it turns out, she spells her name the regular old way: E-r-i-n. She is lithe and thin, the bones in her wrists so frail and dainty I could break them with one meaty squeeze of my hand. I envision myself doing it every time she touches Judah. She has tattoos and an eyebrow and tongue piercing, and wears clothes whose only purpose is to say: *I am a free spirit.* I eye her pitch-black hair, which she keeps in a charming messy knot on top of her head, and hate the white blondness of my own hair. Erin is a nurse, so she has that naturally caring thing going on. Very annoying. Her brother is blind, so I suppose she has a soft spot for handicapped men.

She pretends not to see his wheelchair. That's what really bothers me; she acts like he's just this regular guy, with regular guy legs. "Let's take Margo to the farmer's market today. Let's go for a walk on the beach. Let's ride the Ferris wheel." To which Judah has to remind her that he doesn't have the right wheels on his chair to ride the sand, and that the boardwalk near the Ferris wheel doesn't have good wheelchair access, and that the farmer's market is so crowded on Saturdays, that the last time they went they had to leave for lack of sidewalk space. She whispers to me that Judah can do anything we can do, but he just needs encouragement, and then winks conspiratorially. *No, he can't,* I want to say. *That's why it sucks.* I'm not saying treat the guy differently; just treat the situations differently. He has a goddamn handicap.

But Judah seems to like her new world optimism, brushing off her attempts to make him feel normal with a pat on her butt and a smile. They banter back and forth, and, if I weren't so jealous, it would be one of those cute things you dream of having one day.

"I don't need to do anything, guys, serious. I'm just here to see—to visit with you. You don't have to entertain me."

On my third day here, Erin decides to take us to dinner at the pier in her little Toyota that farts more than it drives and smells weirdly of crayons. Halfway to the restaurant, her brother calls.

"Yes, Joey," she says. "Of course I can … Right now. Okay."

She hangs up and tells us that his ride bailed, and she needs to take him to his therapy session. "If he doesn't go to therapy, he gets super depressed," she tells us.

"You should take him," Judah offers. I suddenly brighten up in the back seat at the idea of getting rid of Erin for the night.

"I'll drop you at the restaurant and pick you up after," she says.

"No need," Judah tells her. "Go be with Joey. We will take a cab home." Erin kisses Judah on the lips, and drives away, leaving us outside The Organic Vixen.

"Wanna go somewhere else?" Judah asks.

"What? You don't like hippies and organics and shit?"

"And shit," says Judah. "Let's get some pizza."

I push his chair along the pier until we find one of those by-the-slice places. I carry our slices to the table on soft paper plates and slide into the bench opposite him.

"Sometimes," he says, "I miss the Bone."

"You do not," I tell him, biting into my slice. The cheese burns the roof of my mouth, and I reach for my Coke.

"Come on, Margo. You don't even miss it sometimes?"

I shake my head. "What is there to miss, Judah? The poverty? The litter? The dead eyes everyone walks around wearing?"

"It's our home. There is something to that."

"Bad things happened there. Things that changed me. I don't see it that way."

"Your mother?" he asks. "Nevaeh? What else?"

He's pushing me. Is that why he brought me here?

I set down my pizza, wipe my fingertips on a napkin, trying to avoid his eyes.

"What are you asking me?"

He looks around to make sure no one is listening, then leans in.

"Lyndee," he says. "Do you know what happened to her?"

"Someone killed her," I say flatly. "It's what she deserved."

Judah draws back as if I've slapped him.

"What she deserved?"

"She killed Nevaeh," I say matter-of-factly.

"How do you know that?"

I hesitate. I don't know how much Judah can handle ... how much he's figured out already. "Because she told me," I say.

He licks his lips. "Margo, did you do something to Lyndee?"

I stand up, mostly because he can't follow me, and back up a few steps. Things flash through my mind: looks, frowns, narrowing eyes. All the times Judah was mentally compiling a case against me. All the times he was right.

"Stop it," I warn him. "This isn't something you want to talk about. Trust me."

"I do want to talk about it," he says. "You've done something..."

This is what it feels like to be found out. I can't decide if I like it or not. There is also the matter of defending myself ... or not. Not, I decide. I start to walk away.

"Margo, wait!"

But I don't. He knows too much. He won't go to the police ... at least I don't think so. I need to keep my distance. Make him think he's crazy. My heart knocks fearfully inside of my chest. My stomach is sour. My brain is working slowly—*shock*, I think. *You didn't think he'd actually find you out.* And if it had been anyone else, I wouldn't have cared: my mother, or Delaney, or Sandy. But it's Judah, the only person in the whole world I admire, and he's looking at me like I'm a carnie freak.

I turn and run. I have my wallet; that's all I need. I leave my bag at the apartment he shares with androgynous-named Erin, and catch a cab to the airport. Gone, gone, gone. It's the end of an era, the finishing of a relationship. That will be the last time I make contact with Judah, or allow him to make contact with me.

I MOVE INTO MY NEW APARTMENT TWO WEEKS LATER. I don't know what Doyle/Brian told his father, and I don't care. I saw the fear in his eyes when I smashed the gun into his nose and heard the crack, and that was good enough for me. He'd do what I said ... for a little while at least. And then he'll start thinking about how he can fuck me over. But that won't be for a while. It will take months for his little pinprick brain to work out a plan.

In the meantime, I'll enjoy my new apartment. Take life one day at a time. Take the stairs instead of the elevator. I take long walks. Always in a new place. Sometimes I drive thirty minutes ... forty ... just to go to a new park, a new pathway. A new walk. I don't know what I'm scared of. People recognizing me? There was an old lady at the park near my apartment. I walked there every day until she started saying hello. So I chose a different park, a new park, until someone there started waving at me. When people look at me, I'm convinced they can see the blood. The blood of all the humans whose lives I've taken. Dripping down my face and running off the tips of my fingers like Carrie when Chris and Billy dump the pig's blood over her head. I am so afraid that someone will see me for who I am.

I think of Judah. Always. Of his hands, and eyes, and voice. If I keep him with me, I don't feel so afraid. I think I've convinced myself that Judah can save me, but wasn't Judah the one who sent me running in the first place? Do we create our own heroes and then kill them with the truth? Judah is just a man, not the god I made him. If I can tell him this, then maybe...

A strange thing happens. There is a man—a not-so-small man, in fact, he's rather large in the shoulders. I see him in the most recent park I'm frequenting. The park with a playground: a giant pirate ship rising from the dirt, a colorful shipwreck where children can flip alphabet blocks and gaze through a looking glass toward Rainier. Their colorfully clad legs scamper over and under, screaming and laughing and darting around each other.

He's standing against a tree, smoking. There is something about his body language that tells me he doesn't belong. He's merely observing. I follow the train of his eyes. He's not watching the children, thank God. I feel the tension leave my shoulders when I realize this. He's watching the group of mothers. Intently. This, too, could be harmless—a husband trying to get his wife's attention, a man who thinks he recognizes someone from his past. I go through each possible scenario in my mind, but nothing I tell myself can save him. He's prickling the hairs on the back of my neck, making my stomach ache. I begin to hear that silent alarm, the same one I heard when I watched Lyndee for all those months. *You're crazy*, I tell myself. *You're looking for things.*

I turn away, start to leave, but I am half way to my car when I stop. The men who bought nights with my mother ... they looked at her that way. The way he was looking at one of those women, with unguarded lust. Like she was an object he got to use. *Use.* I feel my skin crawl. My heart slows. *Ohgodohgodohgod.* What am I thinking? I can't walk away. I take the long way around—through the trees—and the whole time I tell myself how crazy I am. I try to make myself want to stop, go back to the Jeep, hole up in my apartment with movies. I have so many movies I still need to see, I'm working my way through the eighties: Molly Ringwald, Emilio Estevez, Julia Roberts...

I can see his back, the littering of cigarette butts around his tennis shoes. He comes here often. He's chain smoking. I look for the box. I want to know what he smokes, if it's the healthy kind. I'm not exactly sure what I'm doing. I think I just want to watch him, watch her. *Watch who?* I study the playground, the moms. He's staring toward a bench where three women are sitting. Two blondes, one brunette.

Which one is it, you fuck?

I stand there for another ten minutes before he moves. I duck behind a thick blackberry bramble, as he stubs out his last cigarette, casts one more glance over his shoulder, and walks back down the path. He's noisy, cracking branches and stomping around. But he has no reason to be quiet, because he's done nothing wrong. When he's gone, I look toward the bench. The brunette. She's leaving with her kids, grabbing them by the hands as they try to escape and run back toward the playground. I smile because it's funny to watch. Then I glance back the way he went.

"When you don't have anything, you don't have anything to lose, right?" I whisper to myself. Good ol' Samantha Baker and her sage wisdom.

I follow him.

His car—a dark blue Nissan. Nondescript. Then I follow him to the corner store where he buys new cigarettes. He doesn't smoke the healthy ones. Just crappy, old Camels. I'm disappointed. He drives to 405, lazy, like he has all the time in the world. A couple of cars honk at him and speed by. He gives one the finger, the other he waves at. He heads south. *What's south?* Burien … Federal Way … Tacoma … I'm still here—three cars behind, two cars over. I'm ready to cross three lanes of traffic if he decides to exit. He exits in Lacey; he even puts on his blinker to make it easy for me.

"Why thank you," I say. I make sure to keep a couple cars between us. Three rights and a left. I follow him for a few more miles until he turns down a private driveway, overgrown with weeds and sprinkled with trash. I keep driving. It's almost dark. I pull into a gas station a mile down the road. I go in, buy a pack of Camels. I ask the guy working the register if I can leave my car there for a few minutes. I saw a house for sale and wanted to walk back up the street and take a look. He's so stoned he doesn't care. I light the smoke with my pink Zippo as I walk. It tastes wheaty.

I focus on the gravel beneath my boots—my favorite sound. I am calm, because I don't know what I'm doing yet. No raging heart, no erratic breathing. Just me and this awesome gravel. I am stalking this dude for no good reason. That makes me crazy, right? Maybe not. Maybe I'm just curious.

He lives in a house. Number 999. Two stories. His blue Nissan is the only one in the drive. There is a light on upstairs. The bedroom? I watch it for a few minutes before I get bored. His mailbox is on the street. I walk back down the dirt drive and look around before I open the latch. He obviously doesn't care to get his mail, the box is stuffed with mailers, catalogs ... I search for a bill.

"Mr. Leroy Ashley," I say softly.

I take his bank statement ... and a catalog ... and his Netflix movie, tucking them into the back of my jeans.

I crunch gravel back to my car, humming softly to myself. "Now I know where you live, and I have a new movie to watch."

As it turns out, Leroy Ashley has terrible taste in movies. I watch the whole thing anyway—a sci-fi flick about aliens impregnating humans. *Ugh. Gross, Leroy.* I turn away when one of the characters performs an abortion on herself. When the movie is over, I eat the rest of my popcorn while reading through Leroy's credit card statement.

Arby's, Arby's, Arby's. There are a couple large purchases from a chain sporting goods store. One of those large places that sell guns, and tents, and clothes. There are a couple charges from a company called Companionship. The varying increments tell me he's probably calling 900-numbers for a little spicy phone sex.

"Do you ask for a brunette, Leroy?" I say out loud. I put the first page aside and begin scrolling down the second. There is a charge from Mercedes Hospital for four hundred and twenty dollars. Directly below that, a charge from a pharmacy.

"Hmmm," I say. "What's in your medicine cabinet, fool?"

The catalog is Victoria's Secret. Unless Leroy has a wife, or wears D-cups in his spare time, I take it he uses these when he's not utilizing the 900-number.

"I'm not judging you yet," I tell him. "Juuuust checking."

This is how it happens though, isn't it? I become fascinated with someone, and then I stalk them. Stalk is a harsh word. *Follow?* Yes, I follow them for a while. Just to make sure ... I am super precautious like that.

I rub my eyes. I'm in a weird mood. I think of Judah to bring myself back down.

LEROY ASHLEY DOES THE SAME THING EVERY DAY. He smokes
on the porch as soon as he wakes up—a joint not a cigarette.
Cigarettes come after breakfast, once he's dressed in his khakis and
polo shirt. From what I find in his trash, he's fond of frozen
blueberry waffles and canned orange juice—the kind you mix in a
jug with water. He goes through a box of waffles every two days,
folding the empty boxes instead of ripping them up. Once he hauls
his trash to the oversized bins he keeps on the side of the house, he
climbs in his car and drives to work. He is methodical to the point
of obsession. Work for Leroy is the giant fishing and hunting store
off the highway. He works in the camping department, suggesting
tents and gear to fathers trying to bond with their children, hauling
their purchases up to the register, and shaking their hands before
they leave. At lunch he eats at the cafe in the store, ordering soup
and a sandwich with a piece of fudge for dessert. He's not
overweight, but he's a big guy, and he's hung up on carbs. After
work, he drives to the park where I first saw him. He spends about
two hours there, standing against the same tree and chain-smoking
his Camels. He watches the mothers across the way. Sometimes I
go to the park and lean against his tree when he's not there. There

is a scattering of cigarette butts around its roots. I try to understand him, see what he sees.

When he leaves the park, he stops first at a gas station to buy more cigarettes, then a little bar a few miles from his house, called The Joe. He drinks a couple pints while scratching his belly and talking with the other patrons. He's neither overly animated, nor is he overly talkative. Just someone you could forget. I wonder how others see him. *Nice guy. Friendly enough.*

Every two days he stops at the large, chain grocery store. He never gets too much, just enough to get him through another couple of days. *He needs the routine,* I think. He relies on the grocery store, just like he relies on his morning high. It gives him purpose. After that, he settles in at home. I've never seen the inside of his two-story, but his meticulous disposing of his cigarette butts, and the folding of cardboard boxes makes me think he takes pleasure in the order of his home. Outside of his personal sanctuary, he is willing to discard his cigarette butts on the floor. If it's not his, he's willing to destroy it. You can see the flickering of the television through his drapes. What he watches, I do not know. I have never felt inclined to peek through his curtains to take a look. I'm afraid he'll see my reflection in the television, or have a sense that someone is watching him and come charging out of the house. That would ruin everything. He eats microwavable meals for dinner: pot roast, turkey and stuffing with a side of macaroni and cheese. I find the boxes in the trash—all folded into little squares two inches long. I buy the same meals at my own chain grocery store and try to fold them like he does. I can't get them smaller than a notecard. I eat what he eats, I smoke what he smokes, I am him. It's a far cry from the days I spent spying on Lyndee Anthony.

It's not until the weather turns wet, the air gathering the chill of winter, that Leroy changes his routine. He stops going to the park. At first I think something has happened—he's ill, or he's having car problems. I wait for him at the park around the normal time, until I notice that the monkey bars and swings are empty. This was his summer routine, I realize. The mothers have started their winter playtime hibernation. Where does this leave Leroy? The following day I wait for him near his house, behind a copse of trees where I hide my car. He emerges from his driveway at just before two, and drives to a house in the Queen Anne neighborhood—a restored two-story, painted blue. I am curious to know who lives in the house.

I follow him in my nondescript, black Honda I paid cash for the week before. Having an extra car, one that blends in, is important to my cause. I park at a distance, and we watch the house together.

At around four o' clock, the time we usually spend at the park, the brown, wavy-haired woman comes walking out the door. She's toting her two children with her, per usual, all three of them wearing matching North Face raincoats. I am not particularly surprised that he knows where she lives; after all, I've been digging through his trash for months now. She loads them into her car, and Leroy and I dutifully follow. *It's like a mother and her psychotic ducklings,* I think.

She parks in the mall's above-ground garage, and leads her children inside as they struggle and pull to get away from her and run ahead. Leroy and I follow her in. He sits outside of JCPenney, watching the indoor playground area, minus his Camels. Instead, he holds a styrofoam cup of coffee, and a newspaper he pilfered from the trash. I take the escalator to the second floor and look down on both of them. How is it that she has never noticed this lingering man, appearing at the spots she frequents with her children?

I have, on numerous occasions, entertained the idea that Leroy is an estranged relative, or ex-husband of the woman. Perhaps these are his children. Perhaps Leroy is a private detective hired by her paranoid husband, paid to keep track of what she does on a day-to-day basis. Can you really be so lost in your own world that you fail to notice how it's coinciding with that of a sick man? Either way, I'll be her eyes. I won't let him hurt her or her children. I'll hurt him first. There will be no more Nevaeh Anthonys on my watch.

But, she does get hurt, the wavy-haired woman who the news calls Jane Doe. They don't show her face, instead the camera zooms in on her hands, and I recognize the diamond-studded ring she wears on her thumb. The man who sexually assaulted her is still at large. When I turn on the news and see the story, my whole body begins to shake. This is my fault. I had to work. I should have taken off to watch him more carefully. I sit down and press my hands between my knees to keep them still. The reporter is standing in front of a parking garage at a local mall. I recognize it as the one where Leroy was watching her. *The rapist, a man she describes as being in his late thirties, abducted her here in this busy mall parking garage, forcing her into the trunk of her own car, and then driving away. He drove her to a park two hours away, where he brutally assaulted her for hours, and then simply walked away without her ever seeing his face.*

I turn off the television. This is my fault. I knew what he was planning to do, and I could have stopped him. *How?* I ask myself. *By telling the police that I was stalking a man who was stalking a woman?* Maybe they would have listened to me, sent a cruiser to investigate, but without proof, without the crime, nothing could be done.

I think about a movie I watched with Judah, one in which Tom Cruise is part of a specialized crime unit which prevents crime based on foreknowledge. The discussions that resulted between us were heated. I thought that preventing a crime before it happened was ingenious. Judah insisted that tyranny always came wrapped in someone's good intention.

"Any of us *could* do something wrong. Should we be arrested—and possibly executed—based on what we *might* potentially do? Imagine what that would look like in real life. Would you want to live in that society?"

He'd had a point. And I thought about his speech as I followed Leroy around town, waiting for him to do something bad so I'd have a reason to punish him.

I pick up the phone and call the number the reporter gives at the end of the news story. It's a crime hotline; the person handling the call is a man. His voice is high and nervous. It throws me off, and, for the first few minutes of the call, I find myself stumbling over my words, sounding as unsure as he does.

"I have information about the news. I mean, the rape story that was just on the news," I say. Before we can go any further, he asks if I want to give an anonymous tip, or if he can take my information.

"I don't know," I tell him.

I don't want anything tying back to me in the end.

"I suppose they can contact me if they need to."

Once he has everything he needs, I tell him about Leroy. How I saw him following a woman to the mall. And even as I am speaking, I can hear how ludicrous my story sounds. When he asks me why I was following Leroy, I tell him it was because he looked like a rapist. There is a long pause on his end.

"Hello…?" I say.

"Yes, I'm here. I was just getting this all down."

I imagine him rolling his eyes, sharing the story later with his coworkers. *Some girl called in, convinced she's been stalking a rapist.* Another nut calling in and wanting to feel important. Sending the police on a wild goose chase, wasting the taxpayers' money. I hang up before I can finish. This is my fault, and I need to fix it before he starts his ritual again.

I'll take care of Leroy Ashley myself.

I go see the wavy-haired woman. Not see her in the way that normal people do, where you knock on the door and get invited in for coffee. I watch her house for days, parked underneath the wisteria across the street, fresh, black coffee in the cupholder at my side. Cars come and go—family, friends, pizza delivery. I read the book I brought, a bestseller that everyone is talking about. But every few minutes my eyes dart away from the words to check for her.

I don't see her until a week later, when she walks to her mailbox. I remember her from before, carefree and happy, easy smiles for her bouncing children. She liked to wear dresses in bright geometrical patterns, lime green pants, and peasant tops. But when I see her now, she resembles nothing of the before. In a sweatshirt and faded denim, she has her hair piled on top of her head. Her face is pale and fearful. Before she takes the mail out of the box, she looks left and right as if checking for a predator, then she scurries back into the house. Anger floods me. What did I come here to confirm? That Leroy had broken her soundly enough for me to justify punishing him?

I am breathing hard, tears spilling from my eyes. The textbooks say that the sociopath is detached from emotion. I have spent hours comparing myself to the information the DSM and the psychology websites provide. I have grilled my professors until they urge me to further my studies and do my own research.

I have read and reread biographies written about Robert Yates Jr., Ted Bundy, Gary L. Ridgway, and John Allen Muhammad—all one-time residents of Washington. Serial killers born and bred miles away from where I was born and raised. I have examined my own soul, over and over, seeking to understand the ease with which I take life. Wondering if there is murder in the water we drink. And, through it all, I have found in myself these truths: I kill because I can. I kill because no one stops me. I kill because no one is stopping them. I kill to protect the innocent.

WHEN I WAS A CHILD, I did not capture and kill small animals. I take comfort in reminding myself of this as I capture and kill large, soulless animals, assuring myself that I am not like them—the Dahmers, and DeSalvos, and Coles of the world. Who, as children, shot arrows at animals, and impaled their heads on sticks, and stuck firecrackers in their rectums ... just because. Just because. They grew up to kill the innocent. I do not kill just because. I execute the wicked. People who had no place living, sharing the planet with those of us trying to survive—making it harder.

I start planning again, the same way I planned with Lyndee. Lyndee, whose killer is still at large. I look for a conscience, guilt. They are lost.

Unlike Lady Gaga, who asserted her line across radio channels, as millions bopped their heads to the anthem of sociopathy, I was not born this way. I was not born with the capacity to murder. Life brought it out in me. The bad people are slipping through the cracks. They pull over the struggling single mother, who is ten minutes late for a job she desperately needs, because it took longer to wake her kids up that morning, and the drunk driver who kills someone a mile down the road goes unseen. Their focus is off. So

I'm helping. Call it a citizen's watch. Or, maybe, the citizen's death penalty.

And then I do it. Something risky. I crawl through Leroy's kitchen window after he leaves for work, balancing my Docs on the sink, and then sliding my feet to the spotless linoleum. His home has the smell of an animal, but not one with fur and paws. Leroy Ashley's house smells of a predator. There is a metallic dink to the air, like a jar full of pennies. I walk light-footed across the kitchen floor to the avocado-colored refrigerator. Inside is the orange juice Leroy drinks every day. I am hoping he makes it in a jug, one that is not clear. I open the fridge to find a clear, plastic jug with a blue lid. The plastic is frosted, which will do just fine. When I lift the lid and sniff the liquid, I laugh. Leroy spikes his juice with vodka. I take the vial of crushed sleeping pills from my pocket and empty it into his morning liquid, stirring it with a wooden spoon I find in a drawer. When I am finished, I wash the spoon and dry it on my shirt. I go home to get my things.

As I prepare, I wonder if something went wrong. Perhaps, come morning, he will notice the specks of white floating at the bottom of the jug. Or that it tastes different, but no, the vodka would disguise a change in taste. Maybe the whole jug went bad, and he'll throw it down the drain, never drinking it. I'm wound up so tight by all the possibilities that my hands shake. *No*, I tell myself. Everything will go as planned. Tomorrow Leroy will wake up and drink his juice; perhaps then he will get dressed and consider what to do with his day. But, instead of leaving the house, he will become tired and lie back down. Maybe he will call in to work, but it doesn't matter, because no one will come looking for him. Leroy doesn't have people. With his eyes unable to stay open, and his body sluggish and slow moving, he will wonder if he's been drugged. But, by that time, it will be too late.

I'll have made my entrance, coming in through the same window I used this morning, and if that's locked, I'll dig the spare key from the dirt in one of the empty potters in the shed. Leroy Ashley will not be expecting me, because I have been very, very careful. I will punish him for what he's done. I will get what I want: vengeance.

I dress in black pants and a black shirt. I am not slight or skinny. I do not give the appearance of someone able to be blown away by the slightest gust of wind. I have evolved from a pink, doughy girl, who kept her eyes firmly glued to the sidewalk, to a killing woman corded with muscle, who looks everyone in the eye, searching for their sins. I twist my hair into a tight knot on top of my head, securing it with bobby pins. I pull on my steel-toed boots, and then slip my fingers into my gloves. Before I leave, I look at myself in the mirror. Not the girl from the Bone. Not a girl from anywhere. I look dangerous ... like an animal. Or worse. Animals don't kill for sport. They kill to eat.

I carry my weapons in a duffel bag, to the garage where I keep my Jeep. I lay them side by side in the trunk, underneath a blanket—three knives of various sizes, rope, plastic handcuffs that I bought at a fetish shop, a Taser, and a pocket pistol, a Kel-Tec P-3AT that I bought from the fry cook at work. I'd taken it to a shooting range, and was pleased with how light it was. Next to all of my dangerous-looking weapons is a small, pink Zippo, taken from and never returned to Judah Grant. It was this weapon that I intended to use on Leroy. I pocket the Zippo, put the handcuffs, the Taser, and the smallest knife in my knapsack, and cover the rest of the weapons with a thick, felt blanket. Over the blanket I put half a dozen plastic bags of groceries I keep there for show. Bags of canned vegetables, two boxes of Diet Coke, a giant sack of dog food. All deterrents in case the police pull me over.

But, the police do not pull me over. I drive the sixty miles to Leroy's grimy neighborhood, slowing down when I pass his gravel driveway to see if the lights are on in his kitchen. They aren't. Which means he is following his routine and is in bed. Tomorrow morning he will get up, smoke his joint, pop his waffles into the toaster, and pour himself a giant glass of orange juice. Then it will be a waiting game.

A mile from Leroy's, and down a driveway covered in overgrowth, is a dilapidated house that is scheduled to be demolished. I found it weeks earlier, and called the city pretending to inquire about purchasing the property. *It's already sold and set to be demolished*, a woman told me. Then, after a brief pause, she added, *They're building a new house, one with three stories and a pool!* I wondered what anyone in Washington would want with a pool? I thanked her and hung up. I had the house to myself for the next few weeks at least. I pull the Jeep into the garage; the floor is scattered with smashed beer bottles, strewn about like the last tenants had an epic party before they said goodbye. The garage door has to be lifted manually. I pull it down, over the Jeep, over me, and make my way into the house where I wait.

I think about Leroy as I wait, wondering what sort of childhood he had. If he justifies what he does to women, or accepts himself as a monster, like I have about myself. When I think about the big, hulking man as a small, innocent baby like Mo, I feel ill. We are all innocent once—every killer, every rapist, every terrorist. None of us asking for this life, but life as it is, being thrust at us by our parents, who hadn't the slightest clue what they were getting into. And while some parents thrived under the flush of the demands that came from parenting, others grew emotionally slight, withdrawing, silently blaming the small humans who were ruining their lives. Humans who never asked to be brought into their morass in the first place. But still ... not every person who was handed the shitty parent card turned into a murderer or a rapist. People prosper, children are resilient. What is it that turns a soul sour? What is it that turned me sour?

I place the gun on the filthy floor beside me. I am sitting in what was once a dining room; all appearance of what must have once been a beautiful room, is gone. Indigo wallpaper, ripped and rotting, the previously rich, walnut floorboards scratched and sagging from water damage. There isn't a window intact in the entire house, each one boasting a large and jagged hole, the rock that made it lying in a cobwebbed corner. When I found the house, it had one of those heavy bolts on the front door, to keep out the vandalizing teens and the bums. Whoever had installed the lock had forgotten to secure the garage. A silly mistake. I had pulled up the door and walked right into the kitchen from the entrance inside.

I pick up the gun and hold it to my temple. Then I move it to my mouth. If I kill myself, there will be less people dead. But, will that be a good thing? Is what I am doing good or bad? Can you label something like killing a person in the way they killed? What would the American public think of me? If I were caught, I'd be put on death row. My trial would be quick, because I would, of course, plead guilty. There would be no appeals, no drawn out life in prison. When I slammed Vola Fields's unsuspecting head into the side of the dresser, I had not planned on killing again. It was an automatic response based on what she was doing to Little Mo. And even when I stalked, and eventually burned, Lyndee Anthony alive,

I had not taken joy. Yet, here I am: plotting, planning, and looking forward to watching the life drain from Leroy's body.

Margo the Murderess. It has a nice ring to it.

I don't want to hurt people, I don't have an innate need to, but they must be punished. That's what I do, or what I tell myself I do. I punish. I feel responsible for it. An eye for an eye. A beating for a beating. A burn for a burn. I have a conscience. It is different from the conscience of the average person, but at least it's there. It is there, isn't it? Yes, I feel remorse, I feel love, and guilt, and hurt. That counts for something in the study of the broken human brain. And I study my differences, hold them against the rest of the world, and then, very quietly, with my insides quivering like raw egg, against the psychopaths, sociopaths, murderers. I read every piece of information I can get my hands on. I want to know why I feel it's all right to do what I do, and how it became me so easily. But there is no one to speak to, no one who would understand. So I read. I contextualize.

At seven forty-five, I lift myself from the floor, dusting off my pants and allowing the blood to flow back into my stiff limbs. Three cans of Red Bull stand straight up, like sentries, on the windowsill. I take them with me as I make my way back to the garage to prepare.

The window slides open without squeak or protest. My moves are rehearsed. I climb in the way I climbed in last time, taking precaution not to disturb anything. The kitchen light is on, a bag of waffles on the counter, thawed through. Leroy's glass is on the table, drained of the juice, the pitcher empty beside it. I can smell his weed as I walk through the kitchen and enter the living room. The ghost of a smell, clinging to his clothes, I imagine.

I find him upstairs, lying on his back on the floor. I step over his body, pulling the plastic cuffs from my back pocket. His chest is rising and falling in time to his labored breaths. Leroy Ashley is sleeping deeply. I have to heave his body to the side, something I never would have been capable of in my old body. I smile to myself as I lift his wrists, placing one then the other behind his back. Now, my muscles strain and burn as I flip him over. I am barely winded, barely afraid. I hum the tune of "Werewolf Heart" as I work.

WHEN LEROY WAKES UP, he does so with remarkable noise. He's all grunts and moaning as he rises from his drug-induced sleep— ground Ambien and a handful of generic sleeping pills I tossed into his breakfast cocktail. I watch raptly, hungry for his reaction. I feel like a child, eager to see if my experiment with a comb and light bulb has generated a charge. Leroy lies still for the moment, gagged with one of his own sweat-stained T-shirts, and spread eagle on the bed, his limbs secured to the posts with flexicuffs. He looks like a pitiful human sacrifice, one that the gods would find inadequate. The ache in my shoulders and back brag dully, after dragging two hundred and fifty pounds of Leroy Ashley across the room and onto the bed. Even now, as I gaze down at his body, which is trembling in shock, the small half-smile on my lips, I feel euphoric. I succeeded. I have brought another criminal to my version of the electric chair. I sigh contentedly and lift my arms above my head in a stretch, while Leroy begins to fight against his gag.

It looks like he's choking, but I don't care. I let him struggle, his head rocking from side to side. His penis hangs limply between his legs, a shriveled mushroom of a thing. The sight of it revolts me. How can something that looks so harmless ruin the lives of so many women? I bring my hand down and touch his ankle to alert him to my presence. It's vile, touching him. I immediately feel the need to scour my skin with hot water. His eyes, which are two black marbles, search the room for me. When he sees me, he yells something around his gag and yanks at the flexi-cuffs until bright welts appear on his wrists. I laugh.

"Hello," I say. "You took a very long nap."

He can't see my face. He tilts his head this way and that while I hide momentarily in the shadows, buying a few more seconds until my big reveal. Leroy struggles, his solid belly jiggling in the dim light. I walk my fingers up his leg, and he watches me with wide-eyed terror. When I reach the junction of his thick, sweaty thighs, I grab his penis; I grab it hard, squeezing it in my fist, digging in my nails. His eyes flare open, and he screams in pain.

"What?!" I say in mock surprise. "You don't like it when someone roughs up your junk? I thought you were into that sort of thing." With tears of pain pooling down his cheeks, he stills to look at me. Really look at me.

I step out of the shadows, stand where he can see me. Leroy looks genuinely surprised. He doesn't recognize my face—I was too careful for that—but he recognizes my womanhood. He heard my voice, perhaps didn't believe it, but here I am, standing five feet six inches tall. A woman who drugged him, tied him to his own bed, and is now hurting him. He roars.

"What? You think you're the only one who stalks people?"

His nostrils flare in response. I am enjoying this. Though I don't have time to dwell on the worry of why. I am standing in this rapist's house, towering over his trembling body, and all I can feel is ... power. I have the power. I am the power. Margo the Murderess.

"How many women have you raped?" I ask. He narrows his eyes, and I see the full extent of his hatred. *He hates women,* I think. *Women with brown hair.*

"How many?"

When he makes no move to answer me, I pull out my knife and run it along his shin.

"What? Did your mommy do you wrong? Is that what turned you into a filthy pig? Was she a brunette, Leroy?"

Still nothing.

"My mommy did me wrong, too," I say with false cheerfulness. "I guess that's why we're both here!"

I set the knife down and pick up the pink lighter instead, which I had placed on his nightstand after hauling his heavy ass onto the bed. I have been reading the old *Seattle Times*; I've scrolled back ten years, searching the archives for rape stories. What I found was Leroy Ashley. His ability to get away with the crime, but he still left marks, followed patterns. The police couldn't find him because he wasn't in the system. He remained undetected, unseen. A true and accomplished stalker.

I crack my neck. I feel good. I feel so damn good. *This*, I think, *is what cocaine must feel like.* Murder, the upper of uppers.

"I know you know what it feels like to hurt someone. I know you like it. Just so you know, I like it too. So I'm going to take my time."

I flick the wheel of the lighter, and a small flame pops out. I lower the flame to the underside of Leroy's arm and hold it there. He roars so loudly that I'm sure the entire street can hear him. When he opens his eyes, I see tears of either pain or rage trickling down his cheeks.

"Are you afraid of this little, pink Zippo, Leroy?" I say, holding it up. It's about the size of your little, pink dick. I like for weapons to be of equal proportions. Is that all right?"

He looks at me like *I'm* mental. *Me.* I feel sudden rage. I spin the wheel of the lighter and hold it to his rib cage. His skin bubbles under the flame. He thrashes so wildly that he knocks the lighter right out of my hand. It skids across the wooden floor coming to rest in the far corner. I yank the bandana from his mouth, and then pull back my hand and slap him. His head jerks to the side. He slowly straightens it back to look at me, his usually dead eyes lit up with anger.

"You cunt bitch!" he snarls. Spittle flies from his lips, his bared teeth are yellowing and crooked. *If you're going to smoke all of those cigarettes, you should really make an effort to whiten your teeth*, I think impassively. I feel slightly better about his rage; his silence bored me. I pick up the lighter and begin again. Leroy does not cry or beg. I was expecting him to—the sniveling pig that he is. Instead, he takes it, and flings obscenities at me while he thrashes in anger, the corner of his mouth frothy with spit. I urge him in a patient, calm voice to confess.

"You're a rapist, Leroy. Say you're a rapist." He will not. I realize that to beg me to stop would be like Leroy admitting he was wrong, and he doesn't think what he did was wrong. Leroy is narcissistic and delusional. I hold the lighter to his skin until I have burned away my anger. He stopped screaming a long time ago. His eyes look sloppily around the room, one roving left, the other staring up at the ceiling. The room reeks of sweat and human flesh. I am tired. I turn my back to retrieve my knife, just for a minute. A minute too long. It's so quick I don't even feel it. When I wake up, I am the one bound and gagged.

HE KEEPS ME IN THE BASEMENT—a cold and unfair prison since I at least had the decency to tie him up in his own bed. It's damp and barren; there aren't even boxes or junk. I'll die of pneumonia before he can kill me. He's old school. The knots he's used to bind my ankles and wrists look like something you'd learn in Boy Scouts, though I doubt anyone loved Leroy enough to put him in Boy Scouts.

I can't move; he made sure of that before he tossed me onto the cold concrete.

He doesn't rape me, but I didn't think he would. I do not fit the look of his victims, with my white-blonde hair and pale eyes. I am not a mother. I'm just the girl who found him out, and now he's figuring out what to do with me.

I hear his footsteps upstairs, something being dragged across the floorboards, then the solid pop of a hammer. I tortured him until he screamed and wet himself, so I'm sure he has something truly remarkable planned for me. I wait, hog tied, wishing I could gnaw on the rope around my ankles, wishing I hadn't been so arrogant. Arrogance makes your senses dull. I didn't think he'd trump me. I didn't even hear him try because I was so filled with my own small victory.

I roll onto my knees, shivering. My head aches at the base of my skull where he hit me. I close my eyes and let the pain flair and furl. It's a concussion. I know because I've thrown up, and all I want to do is sleep. If I could get out of these ropes, I could reach my thigh—my backup plan. My carefully placed precaution. A Band-Aid—square, and the size of my palm. The type that sticks so hard you need water and a quick rip to tear it off. On top of that is another Band-Aid the same size. And nestled in between the sticky tape, resting on the patch of white in the middle, is a small razor blade. If I could get to it, then I could slit Leroy's throat before he slit mine.

After about an hour, my knees begin to ache. I roll back onto my side. I tell myself that Leroy isn't a murderer. Just a rapist. Maybe he won't kill me. I spend the hours wriggling my wrists back and forth trying to loosen the rope. I was going to be one of those girls who just disappears, no one to even notice I'm gone. Just a smudge on the map of existence. You'd have to lean in real close to even notice I was there.

I float in and out of consciousness. Once I hear the basement door open and the creak of a stair, I bolt upright, forgetting I'm tied to myself, and pull a muscle in my back painfully. I wait, tense, then I hear the door close and Leroy's footsteps across the kitchen floor.

"Why don't you just do something, you fuck!" I yell at the ceiling. I am tired of waiting. I want it over ... whatever he's planning. I can dish it; I can take it. I fall asleep, my left breast in a puddle, my throat burning, realization as thick as mud. I am going to die.

When I wake up, I am being dragged across a floor. My head aches, and my skin feels like it's on fire. My wrists and legs are no longer tied together, and I'm able to flail about as my shoulder hits the bottom stair. He has me by the hair. I imagine he's pulling out chunks, and I picture myself yanking away from his grasp, leaving him with handfuls of it. I realize, at once, that I am very sick. So sick I'm finding it difficult to fight, and each time my head or shoulder slams into one of the concrete stairs, I find it harder and harder to open my eyes. The light in the kitchen is bright. I catch a glimpse out the window and see that it is night. I smell bleach and cooked meat, and I want to vomit, except there's nothing in my stomach. I am a rag doll, popped and propped at his kitchen table.

He reties me as I gaze at him through half-open lids; hands behind my back, he leaves my ankles loose. I need to piss. I tell him so.

When he doesn't respond, I say, "I can do it right here, but then you're going to have to clean it up." This seems to change his mind. He hauls me up by the scruff of my neck and shoves me toward the bathroom. I notice the bandages on his arms and wonder how bad the burns are. I want my pink lighter—a thing of security to me. He frees my wrists and ankles and stands in the doorway with his arms crossed.

God, I think. *I should have just killed him when I had the chance.* He watches me pull my pants down, his eyes on my crotch as I lower myself to the seat. I keep my hands on the top of my pants and lean forward to skew his view. My thumb grazes the band-aid on my thigh. I work at lifting it, swiping my thumbnail back and forth until a piece of the corner raises.

"What are you going to do to me?" I ask. He looks at me with hard hatred, and my toes curl in my boots. It's in that moment that I want my mother. I jar at the thought. How strange that, in this moment, taken and tied in a serial rapist's kitchen, I want the woman who abandoned me. I sniff and look out the window. Leroy looks as if he's deciding whether or not he wants to say something.

"Well?" I say.

He moves quickly, retying the ropes around my wrists and grabbing my arm. He half picks me up as he drags me back toward the basement. I struggle against him. I don't want to go back down there into the cold, but, with my hands tied, I have little to use against his bulk. I don't fall this time. Leroy failed to retie my ankles, and I'm able to catch myself as he throws me down the stairs. I twist my ankle before I can grab onto the railing.

Hours later, shivering in what I've discovered is the warmest corner of the basement, Leroy brings me food. A sandwich, water, and a few potato chips on a styrofoam plate. I wait until he's back up the stairs before I lift the water to my lips. It's a good sign that he's bringing me food. Surely you don't feed the person you are planning to kill. He is thinking, deciding what to do with me.

I stick my tongue in the water to taste it ... no bitterness. I am so thirsty, I chug the glass and am out of breath by the time I set it down. I sniff the sandwich, run my fingernail across the bread. There is no butter—only a slice of bologna. I eat it. That is my first mistake—eating his food. Trusting. Leroy is smart that way. He blends in, wears you down. It is in a sandwich that he hid the pills. I should have known when I tasted butter on the bread.

WHEN I WAKE UP, I am in a white, white room. My arms are restrained. I lift my head to get a look around. There is an IV snaking into my arm, machines gently beeping. My mouth is dry, my throat swollen. A hospital. A hospital. I look for a call button, but can't reach it with my wrists in the restraints.

"Hello?"

The minute I speak, a pain shoots through my head. I flinch back onto the pillow and try again.

"Hello?"

There is the sound of footsteps in the hall. Flat, boring shoes. A nurse is coming. I let my head fall back and stare up at the ceiling. Leroy. His basement. Was it the sandwich or the water? Stupid mistake. The door opens, and a young nurse walks in. She looks unsure of herself. New.

"Where am I?" I croak. She looks over her shoulder before closing the door behind her and walking over to my chart.

"The Evergreen University Hospital," she says in a clipped voice.

"How did I get here?"

She won't look at me. "You should talk to the doctor. He'll be in soon." She walks around the room, humming, and I wish that my arms were free so I could strangle her.

"You have to tell me what's wrong with me at least! Why am I here?"

She walks to the window and closes the blinds. The room is suddenly in twilight.

"You overdosed," she says. "Then slit your wrists."

"Where?" I ask.

She pauses. "In the hospital parking lot." I feel a flicker of admiration. Leroy is a lot smarter than I gave him credit for.

"Why are you restraining me?"

"The doctor will be in shortly," she says.

And then, before I can ask any more questions, she walks briskly from the room. I let my head sink back into the pillow and chew on my lip. *What has he done? What has he done?*

The doctor doesn't come right away. They feed me lunch, releasing me from my restraints long enough to allow me to spoon a brown broth into my mouth. I ask the new nurse if she can leave them off, but she shakes her head sympathetically. No one will answer my questions. The doctor's name is Fellows; he comes to see me a few hours later, walking cautiously into my hospital room like he's lost. He is an older man, balding, with crooked yellow teeth that remind me of Chiclets.

"Hello, Margo," he says, staring down at me. I feel sudden panic. I can't move; they have me here against my will and won't tell me anything. Something bad has happened. I yank on my restraints, and I must look crazy because he takes a step away from the bed.

"Do you have any idea what happened to you?" I shake my head.

"An orderly found you in the parking lot when he came in for his shift. You were behind the wheel of your car—a Jeep?" He looks at me for affirmation, and I nod my head. How had Leroy found my car? How had he known where to look?

I close my eyes so my anger doesn't betray me.

"There was more," he says. "A note…"

My eyes snap open. I want to speak, but I can't.

"Do you remember writing a suicide note, Margo?"

I shake my head. Dr. Fellows folds his lips in, like he doesn't believe me.

"You'll talk more about that with a doctor over at Westwick."

"Westwick?" I say. What is that?

"Sleep," he says, patting my feet. "We'll talk more later."

A nurse comes in and puts something in my IV, and then my head is spinning. I drift.

When I wake up, Judah is sitting in his wheelchair next to my bed. I struggle to sit up.

"Judah?" I say. "What are you doing here?"

It's then that I notice the two people standing in the corner of the room. One is a woman—overweight and pink-faced, holding a file in her hands and staring at me like she expects me to jump up and attack her. The man beside her is black, wearing simple blue scrubs. He glances at his watch twice while I watch him.

Judah looks over his shoulder at them and lowers his voice. "Margo, they're here to take you somewhere safe."

"Somewhere safe?" I repeat. There is something wrong with this moment. Something strangely off about the back and forth glances, the shifting of bodies from one foot to the other. I feel as if we are all perched on the edge of a moment, about to fall off.

"What's happening? Why are you here? Why are they here?"

"You tried to kill yourself," Judah says. "The police found my number in your phone after they found you passed out behind your car, covered in blood." My phone? Had Leroy found that, too? I'd left it in the trunk of my Jeep, parked in the garage of the abandoned house.

I shake my head. I'd never take drugs. It wasn't my style.

"You carved the word 'Icarus' into your arm with a knife, then swallowed a bottle of sedatives. They had to pump your stomach when they brought you in."

I am shaking my head, eyeing the bandage on my arm, but he keeps talking. *Icarus?* Leroy. Suddenly my chest feels tight.

"You had other drugs in your system too…"

Sedatives? Drugs? Something I would never do. I do not wish to die, only to live with purpose. I tell him this as I sit slumped in the scratchy white sheets of the hospital bed, two strangers looking on. Leroy did this. As what? A punishment? A warning? Why wouldn't he just kill me, like I was planning to do to him?

I lower my voice. "Suicide? I don't do that shit, Judah. You know that."

"I don't know anything anymore, Margo. You're not the same..." He won't meet my eyes. I feel something curl and flare inside of me. *Anger? Resentment?*

He steps back, as the two people in the corner step forward.

"Miss Moon, my name is Charlotte Kimperling, John and I are here to escort you to Westwick Hospital."

"Westwick? Isn't that...?"

"Miss Moon, you were found to be a danger to yourself. At Westwick, you will be able to get the help you need. It's one of the best—"

"I'm not crazy!" But, even as my words echo around the room, I know I sound every bit like a woman tethered to denial. How many movies have I watched where a woman at the edge of her acumen screams out *I'M NOT CRAZY* to a group of frightened observers?

I can't believe Judah. That he'd connive with these people to lock me away in a nut house. I look from one face to another, all of them grim, determined. I don't have a choice in this. They are going to take me, and the best chance I have is to be limber ... compliant. I can fight, or I can demonstrate my sanity. For that reason, I press my lips together and study the wall to my right with the intensity of a woman trying to prove something. They wheel me to the ambulance, and when I glance back, I see Judah in his chair. It looks like he's crying, except this time I don't care.

I AM TO BEGIN MY SESSIONS WITH THE DOCTOR in just about a week. I want to speak to someone sooner, explain to them that I do not belong here, but one of the nurses, who has braces and is named Papchi, says that they have to go through the right channels first—get me acclimated to my surroundings, process me in the computer.

I stare at the computer, which sits like a sentry at the nurses' station. It is white and flat, and there is always someone clacking on its keys. I hate it because it's keeping me here longer than I should be. *Listen to yourself. Turning your rage onto a computer. Maybe if it pisses you off too much, you can try to kill it.*

I stay in my room unless they herd me out, which is three times a day for meals and recreation. I have a roommate; her name is Sally. I laugh when she tells me, because who the hell is named Sally anymore? After that she won't speak to me anymore. At night she turns her back to me and sleeps facing the wall.

I spend most of my hours being angry with Judah. *Traitor.* And where is he now? Why hasn't he come to see me? The wound on my arm itches under the bandage. I pull it off to see what Leroy carved into my flesh. Icarus. So neat and precise, like he used a ... razor blade. *My* razor blade. My God. It's badly scabbing; the skin around it looks swollen and red. I've never wanted a tattoo, but I suppose I have one now. I ask Papchi if she knows what Icarus is, and she shakes her head. We are given computer time on Thursdays if we behave. Just thirty minutes to send out e-mails. I write an e-mail to Judah, asking him where he is and end the message signed 'm.' Then I type Icarus into the search bar and find an explanation of Greek mythology.

Daedalus, imprisoned with his son, Icarus, by King Minos built two pairs of wings fashioned from feathers and wax. Before Daedalus and Icarus made their escape, Daedalus warned his son not to fly too close to the sun, nor too close to the sea, but to carefully follow his path of flight across the ocean. Icarus, overcome by the giddiness of flying, soared into the sky, but, in the process, he came too close to the sun, which melted the wax. Icarus fell to his death into the Icarian sea—named for him. A tragic theme of failure, the website called it.

I touch the bandage on my arm, wondering if that is what Leroy meant to convey when he etched the words into my flesh. Failure. Nice try, little girl, but I've been a criminal a lot longer than you. My anger flares, flamboyant in its color. I bite it back. I have to get out of here before I can think about Leroy.

The next time I get computer time I check my e-mail and find that the message I sent to Judah has bounced back. *Return to sender: E-mail address unknown.* I wonder why he would close out the account, but there is no one for me to ask. I think about e-mailing Sandy, but in the end choose not to. No need to drag the Bone into things.

Finally, it is time to see the doctor. I comb my hair, though it is limp and greasy. I try to look normal, arranging my face in a neutral, bored expression. Papchi tells me that I will be seeing Dr. Saphira Elgin. "Everyone likes her," she says. "She's our most popular doctor. Some of the patients call her Doctor Queen!" Her voice is so cheerful.

I am given directions to her office, and I set off, shuffling down the linoleum-streaked halls in my paper slippers. I arrive outside her office, which is in the west corner of the building and the most modern. The nurses here are more cheerful, and I've heard each patient room has a sink. Her name sits regally on a plaque outside her door. I knock.

228

"Come in," a voice calls. I push open the door, expecting someone older, more motherly and plain. Dr. Elgin is not plain. She is exotic in her beauty. Someone you see, and then quickly spin your head around to see again—a portico of otherworldliness. "Hello," she says. She does not extend her hand to me, but rather motions to the seat she wants me to occupy. Her voice is deep and warm; it rattles in her throat before it pours out like a smooth cognac. She's different from the others. I realize this almost at once. She looks at me as if I'm a person she's deeply interested in, rather than a file assigned to her by the state. If she looks at everyone like this, it's no wonder they call her Doctor Queen. Papchi told me that she does not work at the institution full-time, but that she gives fifteen hours a week here and the rest of the time she spends at her private practice.

I wonder what compels Doctor Queen to donate her time with the truly sick people, instead of the depressed housewives and cheating husbands who no doubt visit her office. *It's probably just that*, I think, smiling at her. *She wants to feel like she's actually fixing something broken.*

"Hello, Dr. Elgin."

She is unmoved by my politeness. Perhaps I can move her with my story, and, if she's as good as they say, she can help me get out of here. I put my reservations high up on a shelf and prepare myself to like her.

"Tell me, Margo, all about yourself."

She leans back in her chair, and I am reminded of Destiny when she stretched out, readying herself to watch a movie. I think about where to start. When I arrived here? Why I arrived here? The Bone? Judah?

"My mother was a prostitute…" I begin. I am surprised by my willingness to talk. The ease at which I verbally claim the ugliness of my life. Perhaps this is the first time someone has asked me about myself so openly. Or perhaps I have no choice but to speak, locked in this sterile place, filled with people who don't belong in the regular world.

I tell her about the eating house, and about the men—my father, in particular, with his chunky Rolex. Then our time is up, and we both look disappointed. My confessions have made me breathless. I feel alive; my fingertips are tingling. *It's empowering*, I think. To allow a stranger to know you.

"The state requires you to have four sessions a week, Margo," she says. "I have little room for new patients, but I will move things around for you, yes?"

"Yes," I say. "I would like that very much."

Dr. Elgin sees me on Monday, Wednesday, Thursday, and Friday each week. Tuesdays are her day off, as she even sees patients on the weekend, she tells me. I look forward to our time together. She wants to know about Judah; she is more interested in him than she is in my mother. I ask her about her life, but she is hesitant, always switching back to me, which is expected, and also why we are both here.

But one day she tells me that she used to be married. He died, widowing her before they had the chance to have children. I don't ask her how he died, or how she feels about it. I don't want to think that Dr. Elgin is as messed up and sad as I am. It's better to believe that she became this purring, beautiful person, so beloved by the criminally insane that they announced her Queen of Doctors. I imagine her deceased husband being ridiculously handsome—dark, foreign skin and hazel eyes. He was tall, and he was her first love. It is why she is still single, because no one can compare to the man she had vowed to love for all her moral life. So she wears her beautiful clothes, and eats at fancy restaurants with colleagues who wear black-rimmed glasses and discuss the theories of Gestalt and Freud.

I make up stories like these for the nurses and orderlies at the hospital too. None quite as glamorous as Dr. Elgin's, and, if you piss me off, I'll give you a terribly lonely life with a tray table and Cup o' Noodles.

I did all of this to survive, my soul a beaten and trembling dog. My mind a million compartments filled with holes and questions and drug-induced thoughts that were furry around the edges. Caterpillar thoughts, as Dr. Elgin would later call them. She changes my medication so that I no longer feel so thick and moody, and she brings me a little potted cactus that I keep on the windowsill of my room. I am wholly hers, intent on proving myself, fixing myself. And I should feel manipulated, because that's what she's doing, but I don't care. I kind of like it here.

DR. ELGIN TELLS ME LATER, that in the letter the police found in my car, I outlined the psychotic episodes I'd been having, begging whoever found me—if they found me in time—to put me somewhere I could get help.

"So you see," she says, "you are here of your own accord. This is something you wanted." I nod, though I have no memory of writing the letter. I wonder if Leroy somehow coerced me into it, or if he wrote it himself. Either way, none of it is true. What I was going to do to Leroy was just. Something he deserved.

I grow suddenly depressed while contained in my new prison. One that is clumsier than the eating house and far less experienced at torture. Its white walls and the ever-present smell of bleach make me miss the brown stains and moldy character of my former prison. I speak to Dr. Elgin about my depression, hoping she can help me understand.

"Some people," begins Dr. Elgin, "believe that it's people like you and me who are the problem." She pauses long enough to allow me to wonder after her words. I picture her without the many adornments on her arms and fingers, without her thick, black eyeliner and deep red lipstick, and see her imprisoned in her own eating house. Depression is a deep, black wave—so powerful, building from a swell and rising … rising. Could Dr. Elgin personally know its force?

"What do you mean?" I ask.

"Our society believes that if you suffer from depression of any kind, there is something innately broken inside of you. Especially if there is nothing personal to trigger the depression, like a death in the family or a loss of some sort. If you're just depressed for no reason, they judge you."

"Yes…" I say, fidgeting with the hem of my shirt.

"But I wonder about the people who never suffer from depression," she says, leaning forward. "How calloused their souls are to feel less than us." The *us* rings through my head. "Are they less actualized, less pessimistic, less able to taste the tang of reality on the tips of their tongues? Why are we the broken ones—those who feel things? Who are affected by the changing tides in society?" Her eyes are bright. She's not doing the shrink thing with me, I realize; she's speaking to me from her own heart. I let my guard down a little, and lean into her words.

"We are not the problem, Margo," she says. I nod my head. "It's the people who do not feel as strongly as we do who are…"

Her words surround me. At first they are suffocating. Everything about our society teaches us that what she is saying is wrong. But then I succumb to them. My need to be normal latches on to those words—sucking … sucking.

If what she is saying is true, then the rest of the world is numb, and we who suffer from ailments of the psyche are the ones who are more advanced in nature. We see the decaying of society, the neglect of morals and human decency: the school shootings, the crimes humans commit against one another, the crimes we commit against ourselves; and we react to them in a way that is more intense than everyone else. *Yes,* I think. *Yes, this is the truth.*

I leave her office altered. Perhaps feeling not as alone as I always have. I begin again, not to question who I am, but to embrace it.

It is later that night that I see Dr. Elgin in the hall. Her hair has fallen out of the low ponytail she wears, and is hanging in pieces around her face. She's speaking in earnest to one of the orderlies, a dark man, who turns on his heel and runs toward the nurses' station. When I draw closer, I see that she's out of breath.

"Dr. Elgin?" I say.

She says my name; I can see it form on her red lips, but there is a screaming coming from the room to my left that drowns it out. I jar, my eyes wide. Screaming is as constant in a nut house as medication, but this screaming is different. Perhaps I am too familiar with the screams that emanate from the mouth of a tortured human. They are different from the screams of anger or injustice. The orderly returns with two others. They slip into the room as Dr. Elgin stands slump-shouldered next to me. I try to see into the room, but the only thing visible is their white backs as they struggle to subdue a thrashing body. The first time she says it—the woman in the room—I don't register its meaning. She's chanting it, over and over, the two words running into one another so that you have to break them apart to hear what she's saying.

Pinkzippopinkzippopinkzippo
Pink Zippo
Pink Zippo
Pink
Zippo

I reach up and cover my mouth with my hand. Dr. Elgin, divided between the woman in the room, and the distress on my face, looks for the moment like a cat deciding between the fat mouse in the corner or the skinny mouse in front of her face. She recovers herself quickly and grabs me by the shoulders, ushering me away.

"Let's get you to bed, Margo," she says. "It's verrry late."
Exactly. So why is she here?

I crane my neck, trying to catch one last glimpse into the room…

It's a coincidence, I tell myself. I hurt Leroy as much as he hurt me. He didn't have the time to find someone new. He is methodical. He takes months to search out his prey—watching, stalking, planning. I've been here for a little more than a month. Not long enough. Or did I trigger something by disturbing his pattern? Did he lash out to get back at me? We are back in my room, the bare and dingy walls already wearing down at my hope.

"It's a coincidence," I say out loud.

Dr. Elgin looks at me, her sharp eyes not missing a thing.

"Or is it?" she says softly into my ear.

I am gently left in the center of my room, the door closing behind me. Her soft purr has left me immobilized.

"Or is it?" I say.

The next morning, when the doors open for the day, I dress quickly and scurry out, heading for the nurses' station. Come morning, we are to take our showers in the communal, then we have breakfast, and after that, free time, which I usually spend thinking about Leroy. *The one that got away!*

Her door is on the way to the bathrooms. My bladder is swollen beyond what is comfortable, but I need to see the color of her hair. Her door is not open like the rest of ours. Sometimes this happens when a patient is too ill to come out for the day; they call it 'rest time,' but what it really means is you're having an episode and are too doped up to get out of bed. Nurse Fenn sees me lingering in the hall. We are not allowed to linger, but to move with purpose throughout the day. *Seize! Charge! Believe! Hope!*

"Move along, Margo," she says. "It's your bathroom time."

"Who is in this room?" I ask, pointing.

Fenn looks squirmy, like I've asked her to name ingredients to her grandmother's famous cookies.

"I heard her screaming," I rush. "Last night. I just wanted to see if she was okay."

Fenn seems more comfortable with that, She looks up and down the hall, then lowers her voice. They like me, the nurses. They think I'm kind. "A writer," she says. "Famous."

I blink at her like it makes any difference to me. I need to know the color of her hair, but I realize how crazy I'll sound if I ask.

"What happened to her?" I ask softly.

Fenn folds in her lips, shakes her head like it's too sad to say.

"Assault," she whispers.

I am skilled at containing my emotions. I wasn't always, but killing people will change you a bit. I breathe through my nose—inhale exhale, inhale exhale.

"Nurse Fenn," I say sweetly. "What color is her hair?"

This question does not come as a surprise to her. Crazy people ask crazy questions. What they haven't figured out yet is that I'm not crazy.

Fenn is about to open her mouth to chide or answer me when Dr. Elgin comes striding down the hall. It's a surprise to see her here. The other crazies part for her, giving her room to walk and looking at her with a certain adoration. Everyone likes her, and, by mutual consent, we all wish she were here more often than the stocky, curt Dr. Pengard. She acknowledges me with a nod, because I am her favorite, and slips inside the famous writer's room. The screaming starts five minutes later. I run, not walk, to the bathroom. I might be responsible for her pain.

What color is her hair?

What color is her hair?

What color is her hair?

It's on an endless loop in my brain. A carousel that goes round and round, making me dizzy. She's been locked up in that room for days now, screaming for most of it. On one of those days a man came. Handsome, with a face that wasn't made to smile. He was taken to her room, and then the screaming stopped for a little while.

I ask Dr. Elgin about her, but she presses her red lips together and tells me nothing. I overhear a nurse say her name, and I memorize it for later. It's on the tenth day of her stay that I finally see her. Brown hair. She has a streak of gray at her temple, and I wonder if she had her stylist put it there on purpose. A nurse wheels her into the rec room, and sets her in front of a blank canvas and several tins of paint. She closes her eyes tightly and pushes them away, muttering something under her breath. Then she is gone, her room cleaned out and someone new assigned to it. But I know. Leroy hurt that woman. He took the rage that he felt for me, and he hurt her. And now I have to get out of here and stop him before he does it again. Once and for all. No mercy this time.

ON THE LAST DAY OF APRIL, after I've been at Westwick for just over four months, I tell Dr. Elgin everything. I tell her about Leroy, and what I did to him—the months of planning it took before I climbed through his kitchen window with the intent of killing him. I tell her how he overpowered me, and then deliver my suspicions that he drugged me and wrote the note himself. When I confess that I am the reason the writer screamed 'pink Zippo' from behind the doors of her room, there is nothing on Dr. Elgin's face to give away whether she believes me or not. She simply listens as she always does. When our session is almost over, she promises to look into Leroy Ashley, and I feel a burden lifted from my chest. It's good to tell. To have someone know who you are. But the next time I see her, she does not speak about Leroy or the writer.

"Margo," she says gently, once I am seated. "Why doesn't Judah come here to visit you?"

He has ... or no, he hasn't. Why did I suddenly think he had? I've been here for how long? I've written him letters—five or six— after the returned e-mail-but I hadn't heard back from him. He is in Los Angles with his girlfriend, Eryn ... or is it Erin?

"I ... I ... He's…"

I grasp my head, press my fingertips against my temples. I suddenly feel swarmy. Is that a word? But it's what I feel. Swarmy. Everything melding and melting together. Emotions and thoughts kicking up like a windstorm.

"Look at me," she says. "Tell me about the first time you saw him."

"We were children," I say. "We grew up a few houses away. He just went to a different school."

"No," she says. "The first time you spoke with him. Tell me about that day."

"I was going to get cigarettes from the store. For my mother. I saw him outside of his house so I went to speak to him."

"And that was the first time that you spoke to Judah since you were children?"

"Yes."

"What was different about that day? What made you want to speak to him?"

I close my eyes. I can still feel the rusted gate beneath my fingertips, the moan as I pushed it open and walked down the path to where he was smoking his joint. The sickening sweet smell of pot.

"He looked so confident. He didn't care that he was in a wheelchair. I felt like I needed to know how to do that. Be that."

Dr. Elgin closes her eyes. It looks like she's fallen asleep, except her eyes are roving back and forth behind her lids in a rapid eye awakeness.

"What happened the day before?" she says.

"The day before I spoke to Judah?"

"Yes."

"I don't know. It was a long time ago."

"You do know. Think."

"I don't. It was a long time ago," I repeat. It's the first time since our therapy sessions started that I would rather not be in the room with her. I feel as if she's creeping in on me. She's finished playing nice guy. A heat creeps around the back of my neck like an invisible hand. Even my eyelids feel hot. I pull at the scrubs, which are sticking to my skin.

"Judah has not contacted you since you have been here."

"That's not true," I rush. But, even as I say it, I know it is. "We had a falling out. Before I was admitted to the hospital. We haven't spoken in quite some time." I sound like a formal, well-spoken liar.

"And what was your falling out about?" she asks, her pen poised above her yellow notepad.

I think. It's so hard to remember shit in here, all the drugs pressing against your brain. "His girlfriend," I lie. "There was an argument. She was rude to me."

"How did the argument end?"

"He didn't want anything to do with me. He ... he said he didn't even know who I was anymore."

"But you write to him, yes?"

"Yes," I say, remembering the judicious way I tried to explain myself in them. *Please forgive me. I don't know why I did it. She was hurting Mo. She killed her little girl. I won't do it again. Please speak to me.*

All met with silence. I hunker down in my seat, staring at the floor. I'd write him another letter—five. I'd do whatever it takes. I'd make him realize how sorry I am.

"But he came to the hospital," I say. "Before they brought me here. He was in my room. The two people who transferred me here saw him. You can ask them..."

Dr. Elgin shakes her head. "There weren't any visitors at the hospital, Margo."

"How do you know?"

"You were on suicide watch and in critical condition. The hospital wouldn't have let anyone in there beside family."

"Call his mother," I say. "Go on..."

"I have, Margo," she says. "I went to see her."

My tongue feels sluggish. I can't make it form the words I need to say.

"Do you remember her asking you to buy her shirts, from your job ... where was it...?"

"The Rag O Rama," I answer. "And yes, I do."

"You brought her men's shirts."

"That's what she asked for. Shirts for Judah."

Dr. Elgin reaches into a drawer in her desk and pulls out a stack of white envelopes. I watch as she lays them out—one by one in front of me. A fan of pure white accusation. And then I start to moan.

"No," I say. "No, no, no, no, no."

Scrawled on each of the envelopes, in what looks like red crayon, is Judah's name. Judah on each envelope in a child's handwriting: the jagged J, the crooked h. Judah, who I love. Judah, who loves me. Judah, who I wrote those letters for. I pick one up, pull out the lined paper inside. There is nothing written on the page.

"Margo," Dr. Elgin says. "There is no Judah. He does not exist." Her accent is thick and syrupy.

"You're crazy," I say. "I've known him my whole life. Where are my letters? The ones I wrote? Why didn't the hospital mail them?"

"These are the letters you gave to the nurse," she says. "There was never an address, and the papers are always blank."

"No," I say. "I wrote to him. I remember. He lives in California. He is going to move back to the Bone. Be a teacher."

"There was a boy," she purrs. "Who lived in the house on Wessex Street. I called his mother, Delaney Grant. She said you used to come by a lot ... after he died."

I can't breathe. "What do you mean? What are you saying?"

"Tell me," she says. "About the day before you became friends with Judah."

I have to bend over, put my head between my knees. I feel her presence. She's an absolute, and her absoluteness permeates the air I'm breathing.

"I'm not crazy." I sob these words. They hurt so bad, like someone telling you you have cancer when you've been healthy your whole life.

"Crazy is a simpleton word. You are not crazy," she says. "It's much more complex than that."

I tell her before she asks again. "I watched him his whole life. A boy in a wheelchair while the rest of us had legs."

"But you never spoke to him," Elgin says. "He died when he was nineteen years old. He committed suicide, and you tried to save him."

"No," I say.

She hands me a single sheet of paper, a print out from an internet search. Her nails are lacquered a deep, chocolate brown. I take the paper, not looking at it for several seconds, while I try to control the violent fray between my body and my mind. On it is a picture of a man in his late teens who looks nothing like my Judah.

He is frail looking with deep hollows for cheekbones and hair that lays flat on his head as if plastered down by a heavy rain or days of unwash. Underneath what looks like his school photo is an article.

NINETEEN-YEAR-OLD MAN DIES AFTER ROLLING HIS
WHEELCHAIR INTO THE BOUBATON RIVER

My eyes scan down the length of the article.

On Friday night, Judah Grant, a recent graduate from the
Allen Guard School of Progress, who was scheduled to
start college in the fall, was found drowning in the
Boubaton River by eighteen-year-old Margo Moon. Margo,
who lived down the same street as Judah, and attended
Harbor Bone High School, was walking home from work
when she saw him plunge from an abandoned dock into the
water. Judah lost the use of his legs at eight years old after
he was involved in a car accident where he sustained a
spinal injury. Struggling with depression for over a decade,
his mother, Delaney Grant, said that her son often spoke of
death and lost his will to live shortly after the accident.
Margo, thinking that Judah's chair had accidentally
toppled into the water, dove in in an attempt to save him.

"I pulled him up from the bottom of the lake, but he
struggled to get away from me. At one point, he hit me in
the face, and my vision went completely black."

The ink begins to thin here, like Dr. Elgin failed to load a new cartridge into the printer. I strain my eyes to make out the rest.

Margo, who says she is not a strong swimmer, swam to the
shore to regain her breath, then dove back in for Judah. She
was able to pull his already-unconscious body to the bank
of the Boubaton River, where she reportedly preformed
CPR for five minutes before running to get help.

The article cuts off here. Elgin didn't bother printing out the rest of the story. She wanted to reassure me I was crazy—or complex, as she called it—without giving me too much information. I realize I am very, very hungry and start to think of dinner. Will it be beef stroganoff or enchilada pie?

I look at the blurred lines of the printout, the disjointed, jiggery ink job, and wonder why a fancy doctor like Queen Doctor doesn't have fresh ink. She seems to be waiting for something. I avoid her eyes.

I can feel the cold water on my skin—cold, even though it's summer. The weight of the cripple kid as I try to haul him to the surface ... kicking, kicking ... the burning of my lungs, the numbness of my fingers as they grip his shirt and can't hold on. Desperation. Confusion. Who do I save? Myself? Him? Does he want to be saved? Eventually I had swallowed too much water, and, coughing, I pushed my aching limbs to the shore where I gasped for air, staring back at the spot where he sank ... where he wanted to sink.

The reporter was nice. He gave me a twenty-five dollar gift certificate to Wal-Mart that he pulled out of his wallet and told me that I was a hero. "Not everyone can be saved," he said to my tear-stained face. "Sometimes you just have to let nature take its course."

I thought that was an incredibly selfish and ignorant thing to say to someone who watched a boy die in front of her. A boy she had seen her whole life, but had never spoken to. Suicide wasn't natural. It was the anti-natural. It was natural to want to live. It was unnatural to be bruised in ways that made you want to die.

"Do you remember?" Dr. Elgin asks, her face arranged in way that expressed no judgment. She looks casual, like we are talking about my breakfast.

"I do."

I feel incredibly stupid. Embarrassed. Complex. Crazy. The Judah I have spent years of my life with is a figment of my imagination. How is that possible? And what else have I imagined? You can go crazy just from realizing you're crazy.

"I know his smell," I tell Dr. Elgin. "How can he not be real if I know his smell?"

"I know you do, Margo. The trauma you faced caused you to go into an altered, dissociative state. You made up the Judah you know to give both you and him another chance."

She seems quite pleased with her assessment. I am unimpressed. I can still feel him in the air around me; you can't

242

make up a person in such detail. And if I were going to make up an imaginary friend to help me cope with life, why wouldn't I give him nice, strong legs? I remember the aching in my arms after having pushed his wheelchair through the streets of the Bone. The awkwardness of having to do things like drive him, bathe him, help him onto the sofa the night he slept over.

I leave Elgin's office that day feeling like I am floating instead of walking. I could say that everything feels surreal, but the truth is, *I* feel surreal. Like it's not Judah, but me who doesn't exist. When the doors lock behind us that evening, and I crawl into the stiff, bleached sheets of the mental hospital, I am unsure. I know nothing. I bury my face in my thin pillow until I can't breathe, then force myself to come up for air. I assure myself with a quivering, jelly voice that I am real. I do this all night until the lights flicker on, and the doors open, and the medication is handed to us in little paper cups that smell of old people. *Judah is real, and I am real,* I tell myself over and over. But, by lunch, I am once again unsure. If I made up Judah, I could be making all of this up—the murders, the hospital, Dr. Elgin. I check my door plaque to make sure my name is Margo.

I see Elgin three times a week, then two as she feels I am making progress in our sessions. I stop fighting her after that first time, stop saying that Judah is real. I slip silently into the role of the humble patient, clutching what remains of my sanity between oiled fingers. And then, one day, after I've been in Westwick for a little over five months—and my limbs are growing soft and spongy from the time I spend sitting—everything changes.

THEY RELEASE ME FROM WESTWICK, though I do not feel ready. The revelation about Judah has made me feel strange in my own skin. I am unable to trust even myself. What happens to a person when their own brain becomes the enemy? I don't know. I'm afraid to find out.

My apartment is just as it was, except with a fine layer of dust coating everything. My lease with Doyle isn't up for another year, and unless he decides to be a dick, I don't have to worry about being tossed into the street for not sending a rent check.

The first thing I do is shower. I sing "Tainted Love" at the top of my lungs. At the hospital, the water was always lukewarm, the pressure barely strong enough to rinse the shampoo from your hair. I let the steam grow around me, turning my skin bright red as it licks me with hot pelts. I want to wash away the last few months of my life. Start fresh. And I feel fresh; I have fresh perspective, I have Dr. Elgin, I have a mission ... purpose.

When I finish, I dress and pick up my laptop, which has been sitting on the charger for five months. I have e-mails. I open the first; it is from Judah. I giggle because there is no Judah. Right? Right. There are several from him over the months. In the first one, he apologizes for his anger when I visited, and wants to know how I am. As more time passes, his e-mails take a different tone as he urges me to call him. He fears for my safety; he's afraid of what I am capable of doing. None of this is real, of course. I might have written these e-mails myself, though I have no recollection of it. I delete each one, and then empty my trash so I never have to see them again. I do not need an imaginary friend to show concern for my well being. Dr. Elgin said that if you love yourself, you don't need to create people in your mind who love you. Self-hatred is a form of self-obsession, isn't it? A self-loathing so creatively profound that any concern for others dwindles down to nothing. I don't want to be that person—so infatuated with my flaws that I forget to see the needs of others. My mother loved to hate herself, and, in the process, forgot she had a daughter.

For the next few days, I re-acquaint myself with outside life. I take walks; I buy flowers and fruit from the market. I read an entire book while sitting on a bench near the Sound, the horn from the ferryboats calling out and making me smile contentedly. I am a loony, recently released from the loony bin. How many of the people around me glanced my way and thought I was normal? How many of them did I perceive as normal when in reality they were Volas and Lyndees and Leroys? Life was creepy and people were creepier.

On the fifth day, after I take a brief call from Dr. Elgin, who is checking on me, I climb into my Jeep and drive the sixty-five miles to Leroy's ponky dink town. I don't want to get too close—not this time anyway—but I slow down as I pass his drive and notice his blue Nissan is no longer in the driveway. There is a minivan instead. As I watch, a mother unloads her family, wrangling bags of groceries behind them and through the front door. I lean my head back against the seat and close my eyes. Leroy had me institutionalized for long enough to sell his house and get out of town. Did he know I'd come for him again? Why didn't he just kill me when he had the chance?

I meet Johan Veissler, a South African, who runs his uncle's fishing business while his uncle recovers from a stroke. They are a family of salmon fishermen, my least favorite fish, though lately there is always an abundance of it in my freezer.

He's a solid lover. My first. I didn't tell him that as he explored my body for the first time. I watched his eyes as he looked at parts of me I used to be too ashamed to look at myself. I didn't experience any pain, and it was all very surreal. Johan kissed me when it was over, and went to sleep. You can never tell the extent of what he is feeling on his face or in his body language. He's meticulous in his care of me—always meeting my physical needs—asking, serving, believing. And while it is not necessary in the dealings of love, it is terribly romantic to have a man look at you like you're the last glass of water on Earth. I wonder after my own heart. Why I need to be caressed and assured, fussed over and made to feel edible?

Perhaps because a man has already given me this gift, and I have the taste of it in my past. Perhaps television has worked hard to assure me that this is normal. But I will not be undone by the past. I will adapt. I will see love in the light of truth rather than experience. Only then will I strengthen my own self and speak fluently the language of love. That is my mantra. My saving grace.

It doesn't work. I think only of Judah when Johan kisses me. Only of Judah when Johan touches my body. I think only of Judah when his body goes slack on top of mine, his passion spent. I think only of Judah, my elusive unicorn. Johan doesn't notice my mental absence. He is too busy noticing the way I laugh, which he compliments often, the curvature of my legs, which he compliments often. He thinks I am strong, and thus beautiful because I am strong—like those two things go together simultaneously. A man who values muscle and capability in women, and who laughs at the debutantes who trot across the street in their designer heels. Sometimes I think he sees me more as a companion than a lover. I meet his need for camaraderie, and it leaves me feeling like less of a woman. But, still, we work, and he doesn't ask questions.

We eat enormous amounts of seafood, and spend time on his uncle's fishing boats. I don't care for the water. It frightens me like it did my mother. But. I am too embarrassed to admit my fear—me, a woman who tied up a two hundred and twenty pound man and tortured him for two hours. So I join him on the water as often as my schedule will let me. I find myself making compromises in a relationship that I don't much value. How weak I am. How much I itch to be of use, to not sit idly by on fishing boats with Johan's arm draped across my shoulders, while the world swings by in a blur of color.

We're now five months into our relationship of blackened salmon, grilled salmon, cedar plank salmon, mango salsa salmon, and salmon lemonaise. I think I'm going to go crazy.

Judah comes for a visit. Johan listens to me recount our friendship with a pull of tension between his bleached eyebrows. When I get to the part about Judah being in a wheelchair, he visibly relaxes. A wheelchair does not pose a threat to the tanned, rustic Johan. He insists on inviting Judah onto his boat for a day of fishing and grilling salmon in the Sound. When I text Judah about it, he expresses surprise.

Didn't know you were seeing someone!

It's pretty new, I lie.

I guess I should say that I can't wait to meet him, but I'm not sure I mean it.

That part makes me smile. When I pick up Judah at the airport a few days later, he has a wide smile and a deep tan.

"Look at you! All California and shit."

"And shit," he says as I lean down to give him a hug. He's wearing faded blue jeans and a tight white T-shirt. He doesn't look like a poor boy from the Bone. He looks healthy and well. I help him into the front seat of my Jeep, my eyes scanning for any traces of my hobby, though I know there aren't any. When his chair is folded into my trunk and we are on the road, I turn to him and find him already looking at me.

"You're so different," he says. "I can't believe how much."

"You too," I say. "It's like once you leave the Bone, you are free to develop into the person you were supposed to be."

"Maybe," he says thoughtfully. "Or maybe we just grew up, and it would have happened anyway."

"Yeah right!" I tease. "Like you'd ever have a tan like that in the Bone!"

He laughs in the way that I remember and love, and I feel warm all the way down to my toes.

When we get back to my apartment, Judah insists on wheeling himself up the ramp and into the elevator of my building. I am embarrassed by the slight urine smell in the elevator, and then I am embarrassed by the empty sack of McDonald's someone left outside the door of the elevator on the twelfth floor, sitting proud

248

and stinking of fried oil. Judah doesn't seem to notice any of it. When I open the door to my apartment, he waits for me to walk in first before wheeling himself behind me. He looks around my space like it's the first time he's seeing it. My teal walls, hung with prints of Seattle that I found at Pike Place Market. The striped black and white sofa that I bought from my neighbor when she moved to Baltimore. The flourishing potted plants that I stick on bookshelves and windowsills. His eyes linger longest on my books, piled everywhere in stacks of brightly colored dust jackets. He takes it all in and sighs a deeply satisfied sigh.

"What?" I ask him.

"I like where you live," he says. "I like how you fix your space. It feels like a home."

And I like that he notices. Johan never notices the things that make me a woman: the nesting and painted nails and the trimmed hair. But if I caught a big one on the glimmering fishing rod he bought me as a gift, *oh boy!*

"Do you like salmon?" I ask him. "I'm making it for dinner."

"Sure." He shrugs. "But I kinda wanted to take you out for dinner. Would your boyfriend be okay with that?"

I grin at Judah, suppressing a larger smile. "You are my oldest and dearest friend, Judah Grant. I don't care what Johan thinks about that."

We change our clothes and head to an Indian restaurant a few blocks away. I offer to grab a cab, but Judah shakes his head. "I like to see the city this way."

They seat us outside, next to the hustle and bustle of the city. The air is rich with the scent of the red and green curries they carry out on large servers. I eat my beef curry too quickly, relieved to be having something other than seafood. We laugh and talk, Judah telling me stories of the school where he teaches in LA. When our dessert arrives—two silver goblets of rice pudding filled with raisins—Judah's face becomes serious.

"Margo, I'm moving back to the Bone."

I drop my spoon. It clatters onto the floor, and I bend to retrieve it.

"Judah … no."

I say it with such finality it surprises me.

Judah raises his eyebrows in amusement, licking off his spoon and dipping it back in.

"Well, it's not really your decision." I don't miss the laughter in his voice. He knew this declaration would mortify me. He timed it just right so it wouldn't ruin my dinner.

"Why?" I ask. "We left there for good. We said we'd never go back."

He says one word to me, and it chills my spine.

"Marrow."

I feel the Bone like it is a flesh and blood person, looming behind me, waiting for my answer.

"I have the fancy education," he says. "I can teach anywhere I want, but I'd rather give my gift back to the Bone. They need good teachers there, Margo. You remember."

He says this as if to sway me, but it only makes me resent our former home even more. Judah is right. He can teach anywhere in the country. Why waste his life on the Bone and the worthless excuses who live there?

"Why not come here?" I exclaim. "Like we planned all those years ago."

"So I can watch you and Johan live out your life?"

Why does his voice suddenly sound so bitter?

"Johan and I are not that serious, Judah. Eventually he will go back to South Africa." And then, as if to make myself feel better, I add, "He's on a work visa."

"My mother has high blood pressure; the doctor has her on all kinds on medication. I don't know how long she will be here. I want to spend time with her."

I think of Delaney, and I immediately soften. If I had a mother like her, perhaps I never would have left the Bone.

"When?"

"After the holidays," he says. "I've already let my job know."

"I don't like it."

"I know." He reaches across the table and runs his fingertip along my knuckles.

"Come with me," he says.

I jar. Both at the idea of it, and the fact that he's asking. For a moment I wonder if perhaps his feelings for me have changed.

Before I can answer, my phone chimes from my purse. It's the fifth time someone has called. It's Johan.

"Hello," I say after hitting the call button.

"Hey baby," he says, the richness of his accent pooling through the phone. He doesn't often call me baby. It was more Margie, Margo, and Mar, which I hate. I wonder if Judah's presence is making him feel insecure.

"I was wondering if you wanted to bring your bud to the boat tonight. We can take her out and have some drinks, hey."

I glance across the table at Judah, suddenly annoyed at the way Johan punctuates all of his sentences with *hey*.

Is it, hey?

We have to get some fresh ground pepper, hey.

Remember we have that dinner with my aunt tonight, hey.

"Not tonight, Johan. Judah is feeling a little under the weather."

Johan sounds disappointed, but says he understands. When I hang up, Judah slouches in his seat and pretends to look ill.

"I didn't know I was sick, but now that you mention it…"

"Shut up," I tell him. "I just want you all to myself for one night. Is that so bad?"

"No," he answers. Suddenly the moment feels too serious. Both of our eyes are dewy, and our body language has become stiff and awkward. It's the most peculiar moment Judah and I have ever had. He flags over our server, and we hurry out into the rain.

By the time we reach my building, our clothes are soaked through and my arms are aching from pushing Judah's chair up one of the steeper Seattle streets. We shiver in the elevator, laughing at my streaked makeup and Judah's nipples, which are visible through his white shirt. Our chortles vibrate through the hallway, and then stop short. Johan is standing at my door, sheepishly holding a bottle of wine.

"Hello, gorgeous," he says, pulling me in for a kiss. I feel my body stiffen and try to relax. He's doused himself in cologne, and underneath I can smell the slightly fishy smell of the ocean. I turn my body away from his and look at Judah who is watching us with a strange expression on his face.

JOHAN OVERSTAYS HIS WELCOME. A strange thing to say about my own boyfriend, but it's true. Once I brought wine into the room, both of them relaxed. Johan chatted about fishing boats and his catch for the day, while Judah listened quietly, nodding and smiling at the right times. When the conversation dwindles along with the hour, Judah announces that he is going to bed, and that he'll leave the two of us alone so we can have time together. I shoot him the dirtiest look I can muster, ashamed of my feelings about Johan. *Judah is only here once in a while,* I think.

I watch him wheel himself into my bedroom and close the door. Johan looks toward the bedroom strangely. "It's breezy in here tonight."

"I'm tired," I say. He nods. I walk to the door ahead of him and hold it open, biting down my guilt. I just want him to leave, so why am I with someone I just want to leave?

He kisses me at the door, but I pull away and step into the hallway, closing the door behind me so we have can privacy to talk.

"What is it?" he says.

"Why did you come here tonight?"

He looks embarrassed, glancing over his shoulder and down the hallway like he wants to make a dash for the elevator.

"I wanted to see you," he says. "Is that so wrong?"

"I told you I was busy this weekend."

"You don't look very busy. I thought ... I thought you were seeing someone else."

I'm breathing as hard as a horse. Can't he see that I am? Surely he could pick up on what was between Judah and me. I feel rage— the type of rage that makes me do stupid things. But breaking up with Johan is not stupid; it's necessary. Like throwing out clothes that you've outgrown.

A door opens down the hall and my neighbor steps out, walking toward the garbage shoot with a giant, stinking bag of trash. I wait until he's back in his apartment before I look at Johan.

"I'm in love with someone else."

Johan looks confused. I don't blame him.

"I'm breaking up with you," I say. He opens his mouth to protest, but I shush him. "There's nothing you can say to change my mind. Not, I didn't mean it like that, or you're acting rashly. I'm not. Your visa expires soon. You have to go home. I'm not coming with you, Johan."

He's full of words. I can tell by the look on his face. In the end, he merely nods and walks away. I feel an immediate sense of relief.

When I go back inside and latch the deadbolt, my eyes are on my bedroom door. The light is off, which means Judah is probably already in bed. I take a quick shower and curl up on the couch with my cell phone. Then, without overthinking things, I text Judah.

Are you awake?

I vigorously chew on my lip until my cell phone chimes.

I am now.

I hide my face in my pillow for a second, then start typing again.

Sorry. I think he's jealous. He showed up to check you out.

His reply comes quickly.

I'm sure his jealous streak was sufficiently assuaged after he saw my wheelchair.

What difference does that make? You have bigger arms than he does.

Wheelchairs are heavier than fish!

I giggle and roll onto my back so I can keep texting him.

I broke up with him.

The text dots appear, disappear, reappear like he can't decide what to say.

And then…

That's good. So now I can kiss you.

I choke on my own spit as it pools in my throat. My body feels warm, and all of a sudden I'm breathing like I just ran five miles through a field of feelings. I get up and cross the living room, pausing at the bedroom door, only slightly hesitating before I push it open.

I can see the swell of his body under the covers, the light on his phone as he holds it above his head.

"Judah," I say. He drops his phone on his face and makes a groaning noise. I laugh, then launch myself at the bed. I crawl up his body and straddle him. He's holding his phone again, but as soon as he sees what I'm doing, he tosses it to the nightstand. Light pools in from the kitchen. His face is anxious … intent. I lean my body down until our chests are pressed together and kiss him. The first time Johan kissed me it was awkward, the slow acclimation of lips pressing together until we somehow found a rhythm. With Judah, it's natural, like we do this all the time. My self-doubt races in, and I begin to pull away, but Judah wraps his arms around my back and holds me there. We both smell of toothpaste and shampoo. He kneads my back as he kisses me—his lips fluent and his tongue rhythmic. I feel his hardness between my thighs and know that if I were to touch myself, I'd be wet. When he is assured that I won't leave, he moves his hands to my hips and rotates them down in a circular motion, then back up. He is grinding our bodies together, as if to declare that everything works but his legs. I moan into his mouth, not just to feel the weight of him inside me, but to know what it's like to be that deeply connected to someone I love.

I'm wearing only a T-shirt and panties. I lift my hips so that I can grab at his pajama bottoms and pull them down. He springs free, and as soon as he does, he pushes my panties aside in a single swipe, and slides me down onto him.

"Oh shit," I say. "If you had another one of these things, you could walk on them." He smacks my butt, and it's so dark I can't tell if he's smiling. After that we don't talk. We just move ... the ugly girl and the cripple guy.

The next morning, we lie in bed until my phone begins to incessantly ring. I try to ignore it, but when the caller tries several more times, I gingerly pick it up and look at the screen.

"It's Johan," I tell Judah. "He wants to meet up to talk."

I chew on my nails, feeling the weight of Johan. He must have woken up with renewed perspective after my outburst last night. But I don't want to talk about it. I don't want to spend hours mopping up the mess our feelings have made. It's kaput, as Johan would say. *A dead dog.*

"Maybe you should," he says. I shake my head.

"Right now you're here, and I want to be with you. He can wait."

He searches my face, but I've become better at hiding my expression.

"Do you want to talk about what happened last night?"

I breathe in the smell of his skin. My cheek is pressed to his chest, and I shake my head. "I'd rather do it again actually, and not talk about it at all."

"Okay," Judah says. "But first you have to make me breakfast."

"Perfect. I have frozen waffles and canned orange juice."

DESPITE THE CONSTANT DRIP OF RAIN, thunder in Seattle is as rare as the sun in winter. When it rumbles, shaking the windowpanes in my apartment, I run for the window to see what's happening. Judah, fresh from his bath, is reading a book in the living room. He laughs at me when I trip over a pillow and crawl the rest of the way to the window to look out.

"It's thunder," I say incredulously, still on my knees.

"Yes," he says. I turn and sit with my back against the wall. Because my bathroom is not equipped with the hoist that Judah needs to lift himself in and out of the bath, I helped him instead, surprised at his upper body strength and how little he actually needed me. I think on this now, as I sit staring at the maleness of his beauty—the wet hair, the broad expanse of chest. It was shocking to see his legs. It looked as if two pieces that did not belong to him were hastily placed on his body. Frail and thin, free of hair, I averted my eyes when I helped him out of the bath, and then I felt ashamed. What right did I have to avert my eyes from his body when I was naught but a monster underneath my skin?

"How come you're so good at being in a wheelchair?" I say softly. Judah sets his book aside, folding his hands on his lap.

"I decided very early on that I wanted as little help as possible," he says. "There wasn't always going to be someone around to do things for me, so I taught myself to do them."

"And Delaney?"

"She was tough ... loving, but tough. She didn't do anything for me unless she had to."

I think about the day he called to me from the window, how I crept into his house in the dark and held his hands while he sobbed. It was the only time Judah showed weakness, and I wonder now if it's still there, his feelings of ineptitude buried under the bravado of capability. The tarnished silver.

"But you don't complain. You never look burdened by it."

"I'm not," he says. "Other people are though, when they have to wheel me off the airplane, or bend down at the Starbucks counter to hand me my change. When someone has to hold a door open for me, or pack my wheelchair into their trunk. That's when I become a burden."

I think about what it would be like to have to depend on others for all of the little things, and I instantly know I'd never be like Judah.

"I'd be angry and bitter," I announce.

He laughs. "You're the most hopeful person I've ever met, Margo. That's untrue."

I jump up and run to him, pressing my lips against his, holding his face in my palms. Just because I can.

We stay inside for most of the day, ordering Chinese and watching movies like we used to. This time I have a long list of things I want him to see.

"Well, that was depressing," he says. I eject the movie from the DVD player and slip my finger through the hole in its center while I look for the box. *The Stoning of Sorayah M* is one of those films that leave you in a funk for days.

"How did you go from sappy chicks flicks like *The Wedding Date* to something like that?"

"It's meaningful," I say. "I want to fill myself with images that mean something, not ones that placate my fears."

"How did *The Wedding Date* placate your fears?"

I sit on my heels in front of the TV and stare at him. "I've always been afraid that love isn't real. So I watched movies that assured me that there can be happy endings and shit."

"And shit," he says. And then, "Okay ... okay ... I get it. What else you got for me? Let's see how far we can slump into depression."

I pick up the next movie I have lined up and wave it around. *"The House of Sand and Fog,"* I say.

"Bring it," says Judah. "I'm super in touch with my feelings right now." He rubs a palm over his chest.

The following day I drive Judah back to the Bone. I can barely keep my hands from shaking as they grip the steering wheel in a death vice. I haven't been back—not since I left. Too afraid to go; too afraid to stay. Now I am sick at the thought of seeing the eating house, and Sandy, and Delaney. I curse myself for agreeing to this and wonder if Judah has some ulterior motive in wanting me to go with him. What steadies me is Little Mo. Maybe Mo will let me have him for a little while. He'll be so much bigger by now. Walking. I cheer at the thought and find my foot pressing a little harder on the accelerator. *Yes,* that's what I'll do. I'll concentrate on Mo, and maybe I'll have a little time to pop by Nevaeh's grave. I heard that the city paid for a large angel statue to be placed next to her gravestone. It was a nice thing to do. I glance at Judah, suddenly feeling much better, and find him staring at me.

"What?" I ask.

"You should have seen your face. This entire time I thought I was watching a silent film."

"Oh, shut it," I say. But I can already feel the blush creeping up my neck. *Way to act like a psycho, Margo.*

"You were chewing on your lip and hunched over the steering wheel one minute, the next you were smiling to yourself, and then all of a sudden you're frowning and rocking back and forth like a mad woman."

"Nonsense," I tell him. "But seriously, it's like you just woke up after all this time and realized I'm not normal."

"I guess I've been gone too long. But that'll be different now that I'm coming back."

I glance at him out of the corner of my eye, wondering if he thinks I'll be driving back to the damn Bone every week to see him. Fat chance. I stick a slab of chocolate in my mouth to keep from bursting his bubble.

"My therapist told me you aren't real," I tell him.

He grins at me. "I've always been too good to be true, Margo."

It's the same as it's always been. I keep my eyes fixated ahead, trying not to look at all the things that haven't changed. I don't see the wet paper cups lying in the gutters, or the smoke from the food trucks curling into the sky. I definitely don't see the high school girls wearing mini skirts and hanging all over boys who will get them pregnant and leave shortly thereafter. Judah chats cheerfully next to me, but I don't hear him. I turn down Wessex and pull into Delaney's driveway. It takes all of five minutes for me to drop his bags off at the front door and help him into his chair.

"Come inside with me, Margo," he says. "My mom would love to see you."

I shake my head. "I have to head back," I lie. Before he can say anything else, I'm back in the Jeep and backing out of his driveway. I don't go to the eating house, even though I can feel it calling to me. I pull into Mo's driveway. He must have been standing near the window, because as soon as he sees my car, he comes outside, his eyes narrowed. When he sees it's me, his shoulders lose some of their tension.

"Well, well … look who's back," he says. He's not smiling. My stomach does a little turn as I slam the door and walk up the drive.

"Hey Mo."

"What you want, girl? You never been the drug type."

I grin. "I came to see Little Mo, actually."

He looks surprised. "Yeah, he's in his cage. You can go in. Want to watch him for a bit. I have some business to take care of."

"Sure," I say. He doesn't even go back inside the house. I watch from the open doorway as he drives off in his Lincoln. Mo has never invited me into his house. I suppose he's desperate enough to let his former neighbor play babysitter to his motherless son. Little Mo is playing with a set of plastic keys as he sits in a stained pack-and-play in the living room. His face is smeared with chocolate, but other than that, he looks fine. When he sees me, he smiles. I can't control the utter happiness I feel. We spend the afternoon together, and when he naps, I walk around the house and look in Mo's drawers. I find tiny baggies of cocaine under the bed he shared with that child-beating whore, Vola. I empty them out one by one into the toilet, then I re-fill each bag with flour and replace them. When I drive out of the Bone, long after the sun has gone down, for once I feel refreshed. I haven't thought about Leroy in hours. My mind is a clear sky.

A WEEK LATER, I drive to the Bone to pick up Judah and deliver him back to SeaTac airport.

"How was it?" I ask as we cruise onto the highway. The air is warm, and my hair is whipping around my face.

"Good. I'm ready to come back."

"Great," I say. But it's not great. Judah going back to the Bone feels like a bad omen. If the Bone can call him back, what can it do to me?

"You don't mean that," he says. "You hate that I'm going back."

"Yeah."

We don't say much after that, but when we cross the water into Seattle, he asks me something that makes the hairs stand up on the back of my neck.

"Did you do something bad? Is that why you don't want to go back?"

"Why would you say that?" I narrowly miss hitting a car and swerve back into my lane. I press my foot against the accelerator.

"When I asked you about it in California, you ran. Didn't even say goodbye."

"There's more than one reason I did that," I say, thinking about Erin/Eryn/Eren.

"Margo, tell me what you did ... also, you're going really fast."

I change lanes, then change again. I can see the tension in his upper body. I cut off a semi and the driver blares his horn.

"I killed Vola Fields and Lyndee Anthony. I killed a man in an alley who was trying to rape a girl." I hesitate for a moment before I add, "And then I tried to kill Leroy Ashley."

He's quiet for a long time. Traffic gathers along my exit. I slow down, but I want to keep driving, keep going fast.

"Who is Leroy Ashley?"

"A rapist," I say.

"But, you haven't killed him yet?"

I glance at him, and he's looking at me.

"No."

I see the relief.

"How do you know?"

"How do I know what, Judah?" I flick the hair out of my eyes, annoyed at his questions.

"That he's a rapist!"

"It's a long story," I say. "But, I know."

He's rubbing his jawline, looking out the window then back to me. If he had working legs, I wonder if he'd already have asked to be let out of the car.

"Why, Margo? Why didn't you go to the police?"

I laugh. "Are you kidding? After what happened with Lyndee? Judah, why are you even saying this to me?"

"Why did you have to kill them? You could've..." He's focusing on the women, not Leroy. Maybe because I haven't killed him yet.

"What? Sat them down and had a nice little chat with them about what they did?"

"Maybe ... it seems more reasonable than taking someone's life."

I think about this. Possibly for the first time. *Why* did *I have to kill them?*

"I had no proof," I say. "The police wouldn't have done anything. I believe in swift justice."

He slams his fist on the dash, and then keeps it clenched as he speaks to me through his teeth. "You are not the law. You do not get to administer your own brand of justice on humankind. How could you be so stupid?"

"Stupid?" I sound distant when I say it. My tongue is fat with the confessions I've just made. I never considered what I did to be stupid. I never considered what I did. I just ... did what my body told me to do. I moved like a person who has cut ties with her mind and was relying on the guidance of some deeper force. A possession of sorts.

"Maybe..." I say. And even to me, my voice sounds noncommittal. Judah stirs at my words. Becomes angrier. His irises boil around his pupils, making him look like a cartoon version of himself. Eyes never lie. Not the emotions we convince ourselves to experience, or we convince others we are experiencing—the real ones. You can listen to words, or you can listen to a person's eyes.

"Why are you so angry with me? You left me."

But he's not listening anymore. He's putting things together.

"That's why you were in the hospital," he says. "You almost got yourself killed."

"Go on," I say. "Rail me with how stupid I am. How I should have told the police, left the punishment of criminals to the infallible law. But you and I both know how it really is. We lived in a world where children were not protected from their parents. Where you can hurt someone because someone once hurt you."

It's all true to my own ears. They lived in a form of ignorant hubris—Vola and Lyndee. At least Leroy knew what he was doing. He was looking to be caught. Even if he didn't know it.

I want to execute my plan, and this time I am not acting on impulse. I will not make mistakes. I am, I think with little mortification, an evolving killer. We are at the airport. I help him out of the Jeep and into his chair. When I bend down to say goodbye, he's teary-eyed.

"Why does it have to be like this, Margo?" he asks.

I kiss him on the forehead. "Baby, I'm crazy."

I watch as the attendant pushes him away. He doesn't look back at me, and I think this is a good thing. Maybe it's over for good between us. I feel proud. Like maybe I am in control of my life, and I can walk away from Judah when I need to. Dr. Elgin thought he was bad for me. Someone I needed in order to cope with the bad things in my life. But, it isn't true anymore. I am in control of my own life. I don't need Judah. I just like that he is there. I dial her number as soon as I get home.

"I saw Judah," I say. "He didn't understand." She asks me if I've been taking my medicine, then tells me to come in to see her right away.

Leroy thinks he's won. Most men think they are born with a gold medal growing in their nut sack. *Winner winner chicken dinner!* That's what Howard thought when he stole that little coffin from the eating house. I'm not done with Howard yet, and I'm not done with Leroy. Leroy Ashley doesn't know I survived my little ordeal, and with stronger resolution. He's run from me, but I will find him. If he knew my anger, he'd be preparing. Perhaps he'd buy a gun, or lay off the vodka cocktails he drank every morning for breakfast. He'd take a close look at the burn marks on his body and remember that his skin popped and crackled like bacon when I held my lighter to his flesh. I don't need to watch him this time. I don't need to spend hours planning. I know exactly what I'm going to do to him. An eye for an eye. And not for myself. I won't take revenge for a thing that was done to me, but for each of the girls whose lives he ruined. Because you can't just do that—knowingly ruin people's lives. Something will eventually come for you.

THE FOLLOWING SPRING I get my CDL, enroll in a three-week training course, and take a job with a trucking company called Dahl Transport. It's a desperate measure, one to keep myself out of the eyes of the law and spread myself so thinly across America that I wont be able to hunt humans. I am one of three women who drive rigs for Larry Dahl, and, by anyone's standards, the most attractive. The men outnumber us twenty-to-one. Linda Eubanks, Dodo Philbrooks, and, of course me.

Linda and Dodo are what the company calls old-schoolers. They wear their rigs just as well as they do their 'Fuck you, you fucking fuck' T-shirts. Linda still has a mullet—gray at the roots and bright red the rest of the way down. She lumbers into a room on barrel-sized thighs, her hacking laughter always preceding her. Her counterpart, and sometimes nemesis, Dodo, is the opposite. All bones and wrinkles, her face looks like an old piece of leather with too much hot pink lipstick and blue eye shadow. Dodo always smells like she's been rolling around in an ashtray. When she's angry, she throws things around and calls everyone a pansy bitch. I am the youngest hire in the company in twenty years, and the only reason I got the job was because I served Mr. Dahl coffee at the diner and asked him to make me a big, bad trucker. At first he laughed, but when I stayed glued to the spot, staring at him with the half empty coffee pot in my hand, he'd handed me his personal card and told me to come into his office.

I'd made an appointment to see him, and the following week I'd walked to his office on Madison, dressed in ripped blue jeans, my steel-toed boots, and a T-shirt that said: "Born to be a trucker." Before I'd left my apartment, I'd tied a blue bandana around my head. It gave me the air of toughness. Mr. Dahl's receptionist had looked me over like I had maggots dripping from my nose. But I knew a little bit about the shrewd Larry Dahl. He was an avid lover of the theater, a Star Wars groupie, and every spring he attended Comic Con, where if you scrolled back far enough on his personal Twitter page, you could see pictures of him dressed up as Obi Wan Kenobi. His fleet of trailers was painted bright colors, works of art according to their owner. Mr. Dahl was a flamboyant artist and nerd, and I was going to give him a show if it would get me the job.

When I walked into his office, he stood to greet me, laughing loudly at my ensemble and pausing to take a picture of me with his iPhone.

"Why do you want to drive a truck?" he asked, after he settled down behind his desk. "Why no college? Fashion school? Career waitressing?"

I pulled a face at all three of his suggestions.

"Because I like to do things that women shouldn't be doing."

"It's a lifestyle, Margo. One that affects your family and friends. Don't you have anyone to stick around for?"

I think of Judah, then shake my head. "No, no one."

Mr. Dahl sat back, stroking his chin. It was a baby's ass chin— not even the slightest bit of stubble there. "I see," he said.

I took that as my cue to convince him. "Mr. Dahl. I am not like other girls. I don't desire for silly, frivolous things. I like to drive. I like to see things. I like to be alone. I'm tough. You won't have to worry about me. I handle high stress like I was born for it."

He didn't look convinced.

"My dad was a trucker," I lied. "He died before I was born. It's a profession I respect and believe in."

The gavel of decision was struck. Mr. Dahl offered me a job, saying they'd train me themselves. I left his office with my new hire package clutched under my arm, marveling at my good fortune. I'd have to keep convincing him, of course. He'd be watching me carefully, making sure I had what it took to keep in time with the boys. But I didn't care. I'd found that I was perfectly adaptable and good at most things I tried.

I got my first rig nine weeks after my training began. It was a Detroit Diesel DD15—beautiful and powerful. The smell of newness lingered around the cab when I climbed in for the first time. I was not as large or commanding as Dodo Philbrooks or Linda Eubanks, but I wasn't a small, frail girl either. I fit in with these people the same way an ostrich fit in with the rest of the birds: classified as, but slightly off. And so began my new life as a trucker.

I've found Leroy Ashley. Tracked him down to a small beach house in the Florida Keys. I had to call his favorite lingerie catalog, a small company based out of Raleigh, North Carolina that specialized in crotch-less panties. At first I called pretending to be his wife, calling to confirm that they had the catalog shipped to my new address.

"Can you tell me what the new address is?" the girl said. "And I'll let you know if it's what we have on file."

"No," I snapped. "I already made this call, and you people messed up. You tell me what you have so I can see how incompetent your people are."

"Ma'am…" she said.

"Look, I say. I lied. My boyfriend broke up with me and took our dog. I'm not sure where he is, but I need to find her. This was the only thing I could think to do." I wasn't sure why she believed my lie, or chose to have pity on me, but I hung up the phone with Leroy's address scribbled on the back of an old power bill. A larger company would never have released that type of information. I lucked out.

I haven't spoken to Judah since the day I left him at the airport. He's tried to call, but I'm not ready. His e-mails say that he's moved back to the Bone and has taken a teaching job at my old middle school. I think about Mo having him as a teacher one day, and I smile.

Mr. Dahl calls me into his office one day and asks if I want to take a job driving a truck of spearmint oil to North Miami Beach.

"It's not your usual route," he says. "But Sack is having that Lasik surgery on his eyes and can't do this trip."

I pretend to be put out, and then reluctantly agree when he offers me time and a half. *Score-score!* As I pass through the long stretch of Everglades called Alligator Alley, I wonder what is going through Leroy's mind. Did he really think I wouldn't find him? That I'd let it go? I laugh out loud and turn up my music. Taylor Swift, man; gotta love her.

Leroy is much the same. His hair, his diet, his job. His smug fucking face. I admire his moving across the country to get away from whatever trouble I could bring. It took dedication.

He must have Pine-Sol'd the shit out of his new house, the OCD beast. The morning after I drop off my load, I enter Leroy's house much the same way as I did the last time. Everything is set up similarly, except he finally bought a new kitchen table. I like it; it's black. I find his porn stash under the bed and page through the magazines while I wait. He has a gun in his bedroom, hidden behind the air conditioning grate. This is for me. I'm honored. I play with it for a while before I get bored and go look for a snack.

He gets home at six o' clock. I hear him whistling as he walks through the door and drops his keys on the table. I know what he'll do next; I smile when he opens the fridge and the bottle clanks. It'll be a PBR for Leroy. Some things never change. I situate myself in the far corner, next to the window, and point my gun at the door. When he sees me standing in the shadows, Leroy Ashley drops his beer.

"Well, hello there," I say.

The Pabst pools on the tile while Leroy stares at me.

"Oh come on," I say. "You thought they'd keep my crazy ass locked up forever?" I toss him a pair of handcuffs. "To the bed," I say. "And it would be my pleasure to blow a hole in that smug little mug of yours, so no tricky business."

He lumbers forward. I watch him, my finger hooked around the trigger. I want him to do something stupid, just so I can shoot him. No. I can't get emotional. An eye for an eye. I have to do this the just way.

"Anything you'd like to say?"

"I'll fucking kill you, you cunt."

I backhand him. "You're all talk, you fuck. You should have done it when you had the chance."

Oh my God, he's so angry. I sit on the edge of the bed closest to his head.

"Tell me something," I say. "Were you born this way? If you had better parents, would you still be a rapist?"

He blinks at me and yanks on his handcuffs. I tap him on the forehead with my pistol.

"Stop. That."

"Fuck you," he says.

"Leroy." I laugh. "I have blonde hair!" I pat my ponytail to make my point.

"I don't think you would. Seriously, that's the saddest part. If your mom hadn't been a selfish cunt, you'd be a semi-normal person."

"Don't talk about my mother," he roars. I'm happy; it's the first time he hasn't cussed at me.

"You think we're different? You're better than me? I see the sick in your eyes," he says. "I'm going to kill you."

"This was a good conversation," I say, patting his head.

He's hollering loud as he can, eyes burning with hate, when I inject him with a sedative. Right in the neck. He flinches and tries to bite me. I smack his cheek and tell him, "No."

I wait in my corner while he falls asleep, humming the new Taylor Swift song that I heard on the ride over. When Leroy is asleep, I cut off his penis. I put it into the little pink cooler that I brought with me and cauterize his wound with a new pink Zippo I bought at the 7-11.

I pack ice around his member, and then I take his eyes. Super messy work. But I think it's fair. Without eyes, he will no longer be able to see women or carry out a plan to hurt them. I take off his handcuffs before I leave and pat his belly. "Rot in hell, you sick fuck."

I carry the cooler with me, on the Greyhound back to Miami. It sits in the cab of my rig until I throw it into the desert somewhere in New Mexico. I didn't know I was going to allow him to live until he let me live; an eye for an eye. But he will not live the same life as he did before. Perhaps this one will be worse than death. Leroy Ashley has been brought to justice.

epilogue

I WAS BORN SICK. As was my mother, and her mother before her.
It's in our marrow. The eating house calls to me one day, and, just
like that, I pack up my things and go back to the Bone. I don't even
have to think about it. It's just time to face who I am. I paint it red,
for all the blood I've shed. Then trim the windows in the purest
white. I hire a man to lay new wood floors, and replace the cabinets
and countertops in the kitchen. By spring of my first year back, the
eating house has new smells, a new glow. There is even a shower in
the bathroom where the old, chipped blue tub once sat. It has
shiny glass doors and sprays water from two directions. It's still the
same, scary house, but I fixed it up to serve a new purpose. Dr.
Elgin calls me once a week for the first year I'm back, but then I
stop hearing from her. I think she knows I'm okay now. Mo
knocks on my door almost every afternoon during the winter. We
drink hot chocolate in front of the fireplace, and he tells me about
the girls he likes at school. In summer, the most I see him is when I
drive by a field and watch him passing a football back and forth
with his buddies. He lifts a hand to wave at me and goes back to
what he's doing. He still hardly ever smiles, but I've come to like
that about him. If I'm lucky, he stops by with a basket of
blackberries that he's thought to pick for me. I grin and bear those
summers, because Mo always comes back to me in winter. My
father comes to see me once, when he hears that I've moved back
to the Bone. He's old; his skin hangs from his bones like it's
melting away. I sit him at my new kitchen table—black, in honor of
Leroy—and make him tea. He wants to tell me he's sorry. I take his
apology because I know he's just a fucked up human like the rest
of us. Before he leaves he tells me where he buried the tiny coffin I
found that day in the oven. I'm glad. I want to take my sibling

flowers. He tells me it wasn't his baby, but I don't believe him. He might have apologized, but he's still a lying scumbag. He dies two months later. I won't be taking him flowers, but I'm glad he made his peace.

Delaney passes one August; she simply falls into the grass while she's gardening and takes her last breath under the sun. It's Mother Mary who finds her. Mother Mary, who is ninety-seven years old, and will probably outlive us all. She says she knew to go to Delaney's that day because the week before she predicted her death. When his mother passes, Judah moves out of his apartment and into her house. He tries to convince me to sell the eating house and move in with him, but I'll never let the eating house go, or maybe it won't let me go. It doesn't matter anymore. So we take turns visiting each other's spaces—a night here, a night there. He uses Delaney's life insurance money to outfit the kitchen, lowering all of the countertops and buying custom made appliances. He leaves one counter high enough for me to stand and cut things when we cook together. The sentiment makes me cry. I never do buy a TV. Judah makes me watch his.

We are sitting side by side on the couch one evening, a bucket of popcorn between us, when he turns on the news and leaves to use the bathroom. The news makes me anxious; whenever Judah puts it on, I leave the room, but this time I turn up the volume and lean toward the picture of a man with extraordinarily kind mazarine eyes.

"A man is at large tonight in Washington," the reporter says. I glance at the bathroom door, and scoot forward 'til my rear is barely on the couch. "Cult leader Muslim Black escaped his Minnesota compound last week when police arrived to arrest him. He is said to have fled to Spokane, where police are searching for him now. During Black's twelve-year reign as leader of the Paradise Gate Group, he reportedly raped and kept more than three dozen women prisoner…"

I hear the knob on the bathroom door rattle, and quickly change the channel. Judah smiles at me when he settles back down, and for a moment his face is enough to cleanse me of the sinister rage that I am feeling. All of his open beauty, his effortless love, the boldness with which he embraces his wheelchair. I smile, too, but for different reasons. Underneath my skin and underneath the sinewy tendons of muscle, my bones are rattling.

Rrrrrra ta ta ta

My marrow cries out, reminding me of who I am. I am Margo Moon. I am a murderess. I believe in poetic vengeance. Muslim Black is at large. It's time, it's time, it's time ... to hunt.

I ONCE SAW A YOUTUBE VIDEO of a woman beating her baby. I was shocked by how calm she was. She wasn't being forced; she wasn't visibly angry or flustered. She sat with her back to the camera, punching, slapping and pinching—over and over while he screamed.

Why did I spend six minutes of my life watching as a child, who could not yet sit up by himself, was brutally beaten by his mother? Because he suffered, and I didn't want to turn my face away from his suffering. Some might say that you don't need to see it to know it exists. And while that is true, I felt that if he was hurting, the least I could do was hurt along with him. Somehow, by watching his pain, I was also acknowledging it. I have to tell you, the images of her hand coming down on his skin are ingrained in my memory, probably for as long as I live. He was too little to know that he was not supposed to be beaten. His mother's harsh cruelty was his norm.

I will not forget him. I will not forget that people hurt each other, or that children suffer for the sins of their parents, and their parents before them. I will not forget that there are millions of people crying out for help at this very moment. It makes me feel hopeless … like I'm not enough.

To cope with this very aggressive reality, I started typing. Because if I could not take vengeance on behalf of that small child, I would have Margo do it for me. Margo and her poetic vengeance. I killed them all in this book: the rapists who took from my friends, the rotting sadists who hurt children, the takers of life, the killers of hope. I killed them and I enjoyed it. And while that makes me equally as corrupt—a murderess in my own right—we are what we think, after all.

I want to make it clear that I believe in justice both in this life and the next. I believe we ought fight for the hurting, open our eyes to suffering. Not just our own, but the suffering around us. Sometimes, by saving someone else, you save yourself a little as well. By loving someone else and expecting nothing in return, we learn to love ourselves and expect nothing in return. Perhaps it is the simple act of doing for others that makes us feel more valuable in our own skin.

I want to implore you not to hurt yourselves. Not to cut your skin, or swallow pills, or drink to drown pain. Not to hand yourselves over so easily to men for validation. Stop feeling useless and worthless. Stop drowning in regret. Stop listening to the persistent voice of your past failures. You were that child once, who Margo would have killed for. Fight for yourselves. You have a right to live, and to live well. You'll inherit flaws; you'll develop new ones. And that's okay. Wear them, own them, use them to survive. Don't kill others; don't kill yourselves. Be bold about your right to be loved. And most importantly, don't be ashamed of where you've come from, or the mistakes you've made. In blindness, love will exhume you.

Love,
Tarryn

EATING DISORDERS HELP LINE: 1-800-382-2832

CHILD HELP USA—CHILD ABUSE REPORTING:
1-800-4-A-CHILD

SUICIDE HELP LINE: 1-800-SUICIDE

RAINN—RAPE SUPPORT LINE: 1-800-656-HOPE

RUNAWAY HELP LINE: 1-800-621-4000

NATIONAL TEEN GAY & LESBIAN HOTLINE: 1-800-347-TEEN

acknowledgments and shit

I'LL START WITH THE PERSON I DEDICATED THE BOOK TO—my mom. Who is nothing like Margo's mother, I might add. I would have been a sociopath if Cynthia Fisher had not raised me. Thank you for teaching me kindness and what it means to love without the presence of self. If everyone had a mother like you, there would be less hurting in the world. My dad, who has very strange things in his marrow and passed them on to me.
My team of supporters—otherwise known as Tarryn's Passionate Little Nutcases. Fierce and brave and frightening. I hope you've all seen the movie *300* because that's what you remind me of. I wish I could thank you all individually and give you a hug. You girls truly brought me back to life.

Lori Sabin—my person. Simone Schneider, Tracy Finlay, Madison Green—people I love and wish I could see more. Nina Gomez and all of her alter egos. Some of my best times are spent with you. James Reynolds, for always encouraging, gifting, and giving that extra help when I need it. Rhonda Reynolds, for always being my mother.

Jenn Sterling, Rebecca Donovan, Tali Alexander, and Claire Contreras—Your encouragement and texts are always much appreciated. Alessandra Torre, for rescuing *Mud Vein* from *Marrow*! So grateful for that insight!

The bloggers who take the time to so eloquently review and support my books. Indie Solutions by Murphy Rae for the beautiful cover that encompasses everything *Marrow* is. Jovana Shirley at Unforeseen Editing—You always drop everything for me. Much appreciated.

Michelle Wang and Kolbee Rey—Thank you for sharing your stories with me. Human nature may have bullied your childhood, but you are tough and kind and full of light. I hope you never let other people's mistakes dictate your worth. You are so loved.

Jonathan Rodriguez—You were aged in oak. Thanks for always being everything I need right when I need it and for making Knick Knack your favorite character. You get me.

Amy Holloway, my friend and muse, who inspired some of the deeper thoughts in this novel. You give me such peace. We are the color of BANG!

Madison Seidler, my editor, my business partner, but most importantly, my friend—I choose you! And then, Judah comes for a visit...and shit gets real scary.

Serena Knautz, my assistant and possibly the best human on the planet. Leader of the fierce gang. Rebel and out drinker. Loyalist. I would be lost and confused without you. Your love and unfaltering support carried my heart across dark places. I learn more about love every day from you. Olive you! Please don't ever leave me (not even to go to France).

Colleen Hoover, who always gives me advice in the form of song lyrics. I've tried ten times to express my love and adoration for you, but I keep seeing you chase pigeons down Bourbon Street, and I get distracted. Baby, you crazy! I would kill for you. Seriously, I would. Just tell me who, and I'll do it.

My little people, Scarlet and Ryder—Mommy is crazy, but everything I do is for you. (Yikes!)

OTHER BOOKS BY TARRYN

Mud Vein

LOVE ME WITH LIES SERIES
The Opportunist
Dirty Red
Thief

Never Never

TARRYN WELCOMES STALKING

HTTP://TWITTER.COM/TARRYN_FISHER

WWW.FACEBOOK.COM/AUTHORTARRYNFISHER

HTTP://INSTAGRAM.COM/TARRYNFISHER/

BANG

book one in the Black Lotus series

A PSYCHOSEXUAL THRILLER WRITTEN BY

E.K. BLAIR

Preface

THEY SAY WHEN YOU TAKE REVENGE against another you lose your innocence. But I'm not innocent. I haven't been for a very long time. My innocence was stolen from me. Taken was the life I was supposed to have. The soul I was born with. The ruby heart embedded in a life full of hopes and dreams. Gone. Vanished. I never even had a choice. I mourn that life. Mourn the what-ifs. But I'm done. I'm ready to take back what was always meant to be mine. Vengeance is what I seek to reclaim what was viciously ripped from me. So now? Now I plot. Now I take control. Now I don my crown of hatred.

Chapter One

(Present)

"HONEY, ARE YOU ALMOST READY?" my husband's voice calls from the other room.

I look at my reflection in the mirror as I slide in my pearl earring, whispering to myself, "Yes."

Straightening my posture and smoothing the slick fabric of my dress, I run my fingers through my long, red hair. A blanket of carmine. Loose waves falling over my bare shoulders. The coolness of the midnight blue silk that clings to the slight curves of my small frame. The stoic good wife. My husband, the beacon of my admiration, or so it seems.

"Stunning."

My eyes shift in the mirror to Bennett as he strolls into my closet and towards the island dresser where I stand. He drags my hair to the side, exposing my neck for his lips to land.

"Mmm," I hum at his touch before turning in his arms to adjust his black bowtie.

His eyes are pinned on me as I focus on his neck, and when I flick my attention up, he gives me a soft smile. I return it. He's striking with his strong bone structure, square jaw, and chestnut hair with the faint flecks of silver. A sign of his thirty-four years and his influential status. A mogul. Owner of the world's largest steel company. He is power. And I the recipient.

"Baldwin is ready with the car," he says before kissing my forehead.

I grab my purse and Bennett helps me with my coat before we take the elevator down. As we walk through the lobby of The

Legacy, my home for the past three years, Bennett keeps his hand on the crest of my back, guiding me out into the night's bite of winter.

"Mr. Vanderwal," Baldwin, our driver and good friend to my husband for years, greets with a nod before turning his attention to me, "Mrs."

"Good evening," I say as I slip my hand in his, and he helps me into the back seat of the Land Rover.

Bennett slides in after me and takes my hand in his lap when Baldwin shuts the door and then hops in the front seat. 'Metamorphosis' by Glass, Bennett's favorite, swallows the silence and fills the car. Lifting my free hand up, I place it on the ice-cold window, feeling the dampness and chill as it seeps into my skin.

"I love the snow," I murmur, more to myself than to my husband, but he responds anyway.

"You say that every winter."

Turning to look at him and then down at our linked hands, I release a soft hum before he shifts and says, "So Richard said he stopped by this hotel the other day and mentioned that it would be a good location to hold our New Year's Eve party this year."

"What's the name?"

"Lotus."

"Interesting," I note before asking, "This is McKinnon's new hotel, right?"

"His son's, actually. I've yet to meet him."

"Hmm."

Giving my hand a light squeeze, he questions, "What's that look for?"

"McKinnon can be, well . . ."

"An ass?"

I smile and agree, "Yes. I just never knew he had any children, that's all."

Driving through the Saturday evening traffic in the loop of Chicago, we finally pull up to the newly built boutique hotel that will cater to the city's elite. We tend to find ourselves at a monotonous number of events such as this. With Bennett's status, not only in this city, but worldwide, his presence is of an accord that is sought after for publicity and other reasons. But Bennett has found himself in several business dealings with Calum McKinnon over the years, so tonight's event wasn't one that we could skip out on.

When Baldwin opens the door and helps me down, I right myself and adjust my long dress before being led through the glass doors and inside the lobby of Lotus. While Bennett leaves my side to check our coats, I take in the decorum of guests and bite the inside of my cheek. I know I'm with the wealthiest man here, but my nerves tend to stain my gut, wondering if these people can see right through me.

I'm greeted with a glass of champagne and the eyes of a few women that serve on some of the charity boards that I sit on.

"You ready, honey?"

My husband wraps his arm around my hip and guides us over to the first of many interactions we will have. I gloss on my smile, raise my chin, and play the part. The part I have played since I met Bennett.

He's a loving husband, always has been. Firm in his business, but so very gentle with me, as if I'm breakable. Maybe I used to be, but not anymore. I'm as strong as they come. Weakness derives from the soul. Most everyone has one, which gives a woman like me leverage. Leverage to play people to my liking, and so I do.

"Nina!" I hear my name being drawn out by one of my *friends*.

"Jacqueline, don't you look lovely," I say as she leans in to kiss my cheek.

"Well, I can't even compete with you. Gorgeous as always," she says before turning her attention to Bennett and blushing as she says hello. I'm sure she just soaked her panties as well. She's a desperate flirt. Her husband is a sorry excuse for a man. But that husband is a business partner with Bennett, so I put up with his misogynistic bullshit and feel sorry for the twit that he married. She's been trying to get into my husband's pants since I first met her. I've never said a word because desperation is not something that Bennett is attracted to.

While Jacqueline flirts with my husband, I scan the room. Everyone dressed in their finest, drinking and socializing. I turn away from the mindless people and take in the sleek, modern design of the hotel. A minimalistic fitting but clearly bathed in money. As I float my gaze around the room, I land on a pair of eyes staring at me. Eyes that catch my interest. Standing in a small group, not paying attention to a single person around him, a man—

a startlingly attractive man—is watching me. Even as I look at him from across the room, he doesn't divert his lock on me; he merely cocks a small grin before taking a sip out of his highball. When a slender blonde strokes his arm, the contact is lost. Impeccably dressed in a bespoke suit, he has a slightly uncaring look about him. His hair is styled loosely, as if he just ran his hands through the thick locks and said *fuck it*, and his defined jaw is covered in day-old stubble. But that suit . . . yeah, that suit is clearly covering a body that is well maintained. The lines and cuts hug his form, accentuating broad shoulders that V down to slender hips.

"Honey?"

Pulled away from my lingering eye, I turn to my husband's curious look and notice that Jacqueline is no longer by his side.

"What's got your attention?" he asks.

"Oh. I'm just taking everything in. This place is amazing, huh?"

"I was asking about the party, but I guess you were zoned out. So what do you think?"

"Yes, I agree. This would be a great venue and a nice change of scenery," I tell him, and when I do, I see *fuck it* guy approaching. He has an ease with his stride, and the other women in the room see it too.

"You must be Bennett," he says in a silky, rough Scottish brogue that's reminiscent of his father's accent as he reaches out his hand to my husband. "I'm Declan McKinnon. My father speaks very highly of you."

"Good to finally meet you, Declan. I haven't seen Cal here tonight," Bennett says as he shakes *fuck it* guy's hand, who now has a name.

"He's isn't here. He had to fly to Miami to take care of some business."

"That old bastard never stops moving, does he?" Bennett laughs and Declan joins, shaking his head, saying, "Sixty years old and still barking orders to anyone who will listen. Hell, even to those who won't."

When Declan looks over to me, my husband apologizes and says, "Declan, this is my wife, Nina."

Taking my hand, he leans in and kisses my cheek before pulling back and complimenting, "It's a pleasure. I couldn't help but take notice across the room earlier." Looking at Bennett, he adds, "You're a lucky man."

"I tell her that every day."

I wear my smile as a good wife should. I've been doing this for years, numb to the ridiculous accolades these men tend to throw around in their lame attempts at gentlemanly ways. I can see that Declan makes no attempts though. His shoulders are loose. He's relaxed.

"This place is quite an accomplishment. Congratulations," Bennett tells him.

"Thank you. It only took a few years off my life, but," he says as he takes in the surroundings, "she's exactly how I envisioned her," before bringing his eyes back to me.

This guy is outright flirting, and I'm surprised when it slides past Bennett as he continues in conversation.

"I was just telling Nina that your hotel would provide a perfect backdrop for our year-end party that we throw for our friends."

I butt in with a smirk, saying, "It's a once-a-year event where my husband releases the reins, allowing me to create an event to accentuate his financial power, simply to remind everyone who's on top. A penis extender, if you will, and he's due for his annual visit." I tease with a tender femininity that has the boys laughing in amusement at my tart words. I laugh along with them as I shoot my husband a flirty wink.

"She's got a sweet mouth on her," Declan says.

"You have no clue," Bennett responds as he looks down at me with his grin. "But despite what she says, she loves planning this yearly engagement, and I get a thrill out of watching her spend all of my hard-earned money. But we're in a bind because the venue we selected a few months back is now under renovation and the space won't be ready in time."

"When does this event take place?"

"It's a New Year's Eve ball," he answers.

"Sounds like that is doable," Declan says as he takes out a business card from inside his suit jacket, and instead of handing it to Bennett, he hands it to me, saying, "Since it seems you're the woman I'll be answering to, here are my contact numbers."

Taking the card from between his fingers, I watch as he turns and tells my husband, "I'll be sure to oversee the planning to ensure that Nina gets everything she requests."

"Looks like I'll be writing a big check this year," my husband jokes. "Well, Declan, it was great to finally put a face to the name, but if you'll excuse us, I'd like to show off my wife on the dance floor."

When Bennett leads us to the full dance floor and wraps me in his arms, I take the opportunity to peek over his shoulder to find Declan watching me intently. This guy makes no qualms about his interest, and a pang of elation thrums inside me as my husband slowly moves me with ease.

We continue to spend the evening mingling and visiting with friends and business associates before we retire for the evening and head back to The Legacy. Stepping off the elevator and into the penthouse that Bennett owned when I first met him four years ago, we walk through the darkened living room. The only light is from the moon that's casting its glow behind the snow-filled clouds outside the floor to ceiling windows that span across the two walls. I enter the master suite behind Bennett, and as I slip off my heels, I look up to see that he has already undone his bowtie and it hangs around the collar of his white tuxedo shirt, which he is now unbuttoning.

His eyes are rapt as they move down my body. I stand there as he slowly approaches and then slides his hands along the length of my sides until he finds himself on his knees in front of me. He runs his hands up my legs through the opening of the slit in my dress, and as soon as his fingers hit my panties, I turn it off.

The steel cage wraps around my heart and before my stomach can turn, I shut down.

Numb.

Vacant.

He drags my panties down my legs and I step out of them before I feel the warmth of his tongue when he slides it along the seam of my pussy, but I am able to keep myself from entertaining the slightest impulse of intimacy. I've been sleeping with my husband for years, but I refuse to allow the pleasure I lead him to believe I'm experiencing.

Why?

I'll tell you why.

Because I hate him.

He thinks, in this moment, that we're making love. His cock fills me slowly as I lie beneath him. Arms laced around his neck.

Legs spread open wide, inviting him in deeper as he makes a meal out of my tits. He believes everything I want him to. He always has. But this is merely a game for me. A game he foolishly has fallen into. He never questions my love for him, and now my body writhes underneath his and moans in mock pleasure as he comes hard, jerking his hips into me, telling me how much he loves me, and I give his words right back.

"God, Bennett, I love you so much," I pant.

His head is nestled in the yoke of my neck as he tries to calm his breathing, and when he lifts up, I run my fingers through his hair and over his damp scalp as he looks into my eyes.

"You're so stunning like this."

"Like what?" I question softly.

"Sated."

Idiot.

BOOKS IN THE BLACK LOTUS SERIES

Bang
Echo
Hush

STALK E.K. BLAIR

HTTP://WWW.EKBLAIR.COM

WWW.FACEBOOK.COM/EKBLAIRAUTHOR

HTTP://TWITTER.COM/EK_BLAIR_AUTHOR

HTTP://INSTAGRAM.COM/AUTHOREKBLAIR/

WWW.GOODREADS.COM/AUTHOR/SHOW/
6905829.E_K_BLAIR

26301407R00162

Printed in Great Britain
by Amazon